Praise for Kathryn Fox

'Comparisons with Patricia Cornwell and Kathy Reichs are inevitable' . . . *Malicious Intent* is the most exciting crime fiction from Australia for a long time.'

The Times

'Patricia Cornwell's forensic fantasies may have cooled, but Fox's morgue-talk promises to plug the gap with a crime debut that nicely marries the personal life of the sleuth with that of the murder victim.'

Independent

'*Malicious Intent* will keep you gripped from start to finish. Author Fox displays the deft hand of a natural writer, whether she's weaving her break-neck plots, imparting fascinating medical and police procedural details or breathing life into her characters – both good and bad. What a compelling new talent!'

Jeffery Deaver

'Kathryn Fox has created a forensic physician who readers of Patricia Cornwell will adore.'

James Patterson

'Fox is stomach-churningly good.'

Mail on Sunday

'Kathryn Fox'. . . doesn't hold back.'

Sunday Telegraph

'Brilliant and breathtaking, *Without Consent* is a tour de force for rising star Kathryn Fox'. . . Lock your doors and read this book.'

Linda Fairstein, *New York Times* bestselling author

'A police procedural that twists and turns in unexpected ways . . . Overall it's a quality piece of work.'

Observer

'Unputdownable'. . . Fox is a talented and bold writer. This is a novel which will have the hairs standing up on the back of your neck.'

West Australian

'Australia's answer to Patricia Cornwell and Kathy Reichs'. . . Fox is hot and skyrocketing to the top of the crowded fictional forensic world.'

Sun Herald

'Clever'. . . a good mystery with a thrilling denouement.'

Australian Women's Weekly

'A confronting blend of investigati[on] . . . must-read.'

'Fox amply confirms the promise of her first book.'

The Times

'If you like a tale written like a violent film, this fast-paced novel will do the job.'

Washington Post

'Meticulously researched and seamlessly plotted, *Malicious Intent* marks out Kathryn Fox as a name to watch.'

Crime Time

'Fox forgoes conventional plot twists for far darker ones that are genuinely surprising.'

Baltimore Sun

'It is a wonderful moment when you track down something that's really worth reading. And Kathryn Fox's first novel, *Malicious Intent*, is just that. A forensic thriller, it has just the right balance of pathological detail and tight plotting. Think *ER* meets *CSI: Crime Scene Investigation*'. . . Gripping from its very first page, it carries you breathlessly through its deftly plotted twists and turns.'

Vogue (Australia)

'Forensically speaking, *Malicious Intent* is top-notch in its genre.'

Sunday Telegraph (Sydney)

'A finely crafted novel.'

Sydney Morning Herald

'Watch out Patricia Cornwell. Kathryn Fox's experience in forensic medicine gives authenticity to *Malicious Intent* without making it too drily scientific'. . . an assured literary debut.'

Gold Coast Bulletin

'The plot is original and engaging'. . . (and) has obviously been well researched. Fox has created an appealing character, whose personal life and family background set a good basis for any future novels in a series'. . . I look forward to reading the next one.'

Goodreading

'*Malicious Intent* is'. . . much better than anything Cornwell has written lately, and much superior to anything Reichs has ever written. Fox may be a medical practitioner, but she knows how to write decent prose, create sympathetic characters and pace a thriller, and she keeps the reader turning the pages. It's all very unsettling and deeply satisfying.'

Australian Book Review

'Highly recommended reading.'

Daily Telegraph (Australia)

BLOOD BORN

KATHRYN FOX

HODDER

First published in 2009 by Pan Macmillan Australia Pty Ltd.

First published in Great Britain in 2009 by Hodder & Stoughton
An Hachette Livre UK company

1

A CIP catalogue record for this title is available from the British Library

ISBN 978 0 340 93309 1 (B format)
ISBN 978 0 340 99407 8 (A format)

Typeset in Plantin by Hewer Text UK Ltd, Edinburgh
Printed and bound by Clays Ltd, St Ives plc

Hodder & Stoughton policy is to use papers that are natural, renewable
and recyclable products and made from wood grown in sustainable forests.
The logging and manufacturing processes are expected to conform to
the environmental regulations of the country of origin.

Hodder & Stoughton Ltd
338 Euston Road
London NW1 3BH

www.hodder.co.uk

*For Mum. Your selflessness, kindness
and love will always be an inspiration.*

Doctor Anya Crichton prepared to face the violent offenders. Hundreds of thousands of taxpayer dollars had gone into first the trial and now the retrial of the four whose heinous crimes had horrified even the most jaded police and lawyers. Their young female victims continued to suffer thanks to the drawn-out legal process which seemed to favour the rights of the accused over the rights of the victim.

The Harbourn Four and their legal team were expert at playing the system to their advantage, but today would put a stop to all their legal games and manipulations.

Anya removed the digital thermometer from her ear. Forty-one degrees Celsius. She downed a couple of para-cetamol tablets and anti-inflammatories to accompany the first dose of antibiotics, then wiped her forehead with a wet facecloth, lingering on the temples to alleviate the splitting headache. Anything stronger might blur her mind, and she knew how alert she had to be on the stand.

There was time for one final check in the hallway mirror. Hair pulled back, but not too severely. Pale blue blouse and navy skirt declared professional expert. The jury had to care about her testimony, not be distracted by her appearance.

A small amount of eye make-up and lipstick, her version of war paint, complemented the outfit. This had been a damned long battle and one the prosecution had to win. She had never felt so strongly about a case before and a high temperature would not interfere with her job.

While wiping perspiration from the back of her neck with a tissue, she hurriedly checked the locks on the downstairs windows.

Last night had been spent in fitful sleep, violent nightmares brought on by her body's attempt to fight the chest infection. The bugs might not survive high temperatures, but the fevers made her entire system miserable as well. She coughed and felt the inside of her chest burn. Too late to pull out now.

Besides, it was the price she paid for travelling. Airconditioned planes and hotel rooms, fatty food and fatigue never failed to beat down the immune system. Once her sleep pattern improved, the infection would clear quickly. It had to.

Anya slipped her stockinged feet into the black court shoes she kept by the door and grabbed her briefcase as the doorbell rang.

'Won't be a minute,' she called, before checking the downstairs windows just once more.

Mary Singer had a broad smile when Anya opened the door.

'Welcome back.' She embraced her colleague with both arms. 'We've all missed you.'

Anya kept one arm by her side. 'We should probably make a move.'

The sexual assault counsellor agreed. 'Traffic's pretty hideous this morning. You'd think that work on major roads could be done at night, but no, that would be far too simple.'

Anya punched the alarm code into the unit inside the doorway. A few seconds of slow beeping and the pair were away.

'Bad flight?' Mary opened the car door she had double-parked and climbed into the driver's seat. 'You look exhausted.'

'I picked something up on the leg home,' Anya said, trying to focus on the day ahead. Private case work across the US and Europe had been physically and emotionally gruelling. But the fact that she'd had little sleep for forty-eight hours meant nothing to a judge or jury. This was not about her. The trial was the reason she had rushed back home to Sydney from overseas, leaving her son and ex-husband to enjoy Disneyland without her.

The painkillers had eased the headache but her arms began to shiver. Fighting the effects of the self-prescribed medication,

2

her body was doing everything it could to push her temperature back up. She clutched her ribs and tried, unsuccessfully, to suppress a cough.

Mary Singer shot her a look but resisted commenting.

Anya took a breath and felt the stab in her ribs; pleurisy as well as bronchitis. She fiddled with the car heater, craving warm air. 'How is Giverny coping?'

'This last month has been rough. Since the mistrial was declared she's been more agitated.' Mary was clearly concerned about the young woman due to testify in the Supreme Court at Darlinghurst.

Anya felt for the seventeen-year-old girl who had been abducted while walking home from the bus stop less than a year ago. If it had not been for her beloved weekly ballet lesson, the petite teenager wouldn't have been out alone. The four Harbourns had forced her into their car and raped her multiple times. Not content with assaulting the girl, as a final degrading act her attackers had stripped her naked and hosed her with icy water near an abandoned warehouse. The last thing Giverny remembered about them was their laughter as they drove off.

Anya vividly recalled that night, performing the medical and forensic examinations on the traumatised, injured girl. As a forensic physician, Anya's role was critical in beginning the long and tortuous healing process for victims. The physical evidence she had collected, along with Giverny's detailed police statement, had eventually led to the arrests.

'It won't be easy, facing those four again in court, but I think she's strong enough,' Mary offered unconvincingly. The counsellor had met with Giverny following the attack, then more regularly during the lengthy trial process.

Not having managed to scare Giverny into silence, the four accused Harbourn brothers had tried every legal manipulation to delay the trial and intimidate the only witness. Meanwhile other family members had made veiled threats against the 'lying slut', as they called Giverny. She was the only one who could identify the brothers as her attackers, and her testimony was what threatened them most. Even so, it was difficult for the terrified seventeen-year-old to see it that way.

The attack and ensuing year of legal tribulations had taken their toll. A bright student, Giverny had dropped out of school months before, unable to cope with the stress of exams as well as being the key witness in the retrial. Her friends had long since abandoned her, choosing to get on with their social lives while Giverny stayed home, afraid to go out or trust anyone.

The pair sat in silence as Mary took back streets to avoid congested main roads.

Anya checked her watch. 'Let's hope Giverny's ready and not having second thoughts. We don't have a lot of spare time.'

Mary honked her horn at the car ahead for cutting in on her. He responded by raising a finger in his rear-vision mirror and hitting his brakes – hard.

Mary stopped just short of his bumper bar.

Anya's head jerked forward and she saw the driver open his car door. 'Go around him. He's getting out.'

She leant forward and punched the central locking button on the dash. Just in case. The last thing they needed now was to be involved in a road rage incident.

'What is it with men? They make a mistake and then abuse you for it.' Mary manoeuvred the car into the next lane and darted across lanes. Anya watched in the vanity mirror, but the man got back in his car, turned off and disappeared from sight. She breathed out.

A few minutes later they arrived to pick up Giverny, as arranged. She had requested moral support on the way, aware that Anya would not be able to be seen with her once they were in court. As an expert witness, Anya had to be seen by the jury as independent or her evidence would be discounted as biased.

Even so, Anya understood that Giverny would find being cross-examined lonely enough without feeling abandoned by the very people who had encouraged her to testify.

Mary pulled into the driveway and kept the engine running. 'You can listen for traffic reports,' she said, turning up the radio.

Mary walked up to the front door, sunglasses over her unruly mop of grey hair. The counsellor waited, hands on her hips. Anya knew they were all edgy about today's court appearance. She watched Mary knock again. When there was no response the counsellor raised her arms to the sky and came back to the car.

'Maybe she's in the bathroom and can't hear.' Anya pulled out her mobile and dialled Giverny's number. 'It's diverting to MessageBank.'

Mary moved around to the back of the house; when she returned to the front she cupped her hand around her eyes and peered in through the windows.

'Curtains are all drawn and I can't see a thing,' she called.

Anya stepped out of the car, the chills returning to her body. She noticed the garage door slightly ajar. Security obsessed since the attack, it was unlike the young woman to leave anything undone or unlocked. The hairs on the back of Anya's neck prickled.

Bending down, she yanked on the garage door handle, which clunked in resistance before giving way. The door moved upward and light flooded the area.

Across the doors and rooftop of Giverny's blue Morris Minor were scrawled *DIE SLUT* in large red letters. The back wall was covered with *LYING BITCH*.

The words were like a punch to Anya's stomach. After seeing what the Harbourn brothers were capable of, she feared the worst.

'Giverny!' she yelled, her hands trembling as she dialled emergency on her mobile. 'It's Anya and Mary. Can you hear us?'

Mary entered the garage and covered her mouth in shock. 'God, no—'

Anya hoped her instincts were wrong but she remained careful. 'This could be a crime scene. Wait here for the police and don't touch anything. I'm going inside.'

Mary stood in silence, staring at the car. Anya stepped

around the vehicle, careful not to brush against it. With a cloth from a shelf at the back, she turned the handle of the inside access door and returned the cloth to its original position.

Moving the door open with her foot, she whispered, 'Please be okay.'

In the tiled living area there was enough daylight to see the rolled, unopened newspaper on the table, along with a neat pile of papers. She took a breath. The place hadn't been trashed so maybe the Harbourns hadn't made it inside.

Just maybe.

'Giverny. Can you hear me?' she shouted. Beads of perspiration covered her neck and forehead. The kitchen was clean and there weren't any plates left out from breakfast.

A door banged behind Anya and she jumped.

'What the hell's going on? Where's our daughter?'

Bevan Hart pushed past Anya into the corridor, presumably towards the bedroom. His wife Val followed.

'I told you we should have stayed with her.'

Turning the corner, Anya stopped, just as someone let out a guttural sound behind her. Val Hart had seen the same thing.

Giverny Hart knelt on the floor with her head slumped forward in a praying position. Attached to the front door handle was a cord. The other end disappeared around the girl's neck.

Anya rushed forward and felt for a peripheral pulse. The right wrist was limp and cold, but she felt a beat. It bounded – too hard for such a cold limb. Anya timed it with her own carotid. The pulses beat in perfect time. They were both her own. Damn!

'Do something!' the father begged.

With two hands, she lifted the girl's face. It still had some heat. Encouraged, she felt for any sign of a neck pulse.

Giverny's left index finger was trapped beneath the cord, as if trying to release the pressure.

'This can't be happening,' Bevan Hart muttered and stepped back. Mary was quickly at the parents' side. She must have heard the wife's howl.

'Mr Hart, we need you to call an ambulance,' Anya instructed. 'Your daughter needs your help right now.'

He responded and disappeared. The counsellor moved over to Anya. 'What do we do?'

Anya grappled with the cord but it dug too deep into the girl's flesh.

'She's still warm. I can't get the cord off her neck. It's pulled too tight. Get a knife or scissors as fast as you can.' She tried to sound calm. She needed their help and quickly.

Mary ran off with Val.

Anya tried slipping her hands under the girl to lift her and relieve the pressure caused by the pull from the door handle, but she knew it was useless. The cord had tightened when the head slumped forward. No height needed for this hanging.

'It's okay, Giverny, we're here now,' she offered. 'You're going to be all right.'

Something crashed in the kitchen, then Mary appeared with two different sized knives. One could have carved a chicken, the other was a boning knife with a pointed end.

'Cut her from the door first.'

Mary chose the larger knife and handed the other to Anya.

Trying to hold the head upright, Anya used the smaller one to cut where Giverny's finger held the noose slightly away from her neck.

On the first attempt she nicked the neck and blood trickled out, making the cord slippery.

She felt the body drop. Mary had cut the cord above her head. She laid the girl flat on her back and this time the cord gave way. The left hand did not move. The young woman's lips were blue and her face a dusky shade.

Anya felt again for the carotid pulse. Nothing.

She lifted the girl's head up and back, pinched the nose and breathed twice into the mouth.

Come on! This isn't over.

Moving to the chest, she clenched her fingers, one hand on top of the other and began cardiac massage. Thirty short, sharp pressures then two more breaths. She heard a rib crack but kept going. She had to, for Giverny's sake. After a few rounds her fingers cramped but she kept going.

She heard a siren in the distance and Mary left to flag it down. She barely noticed Bevan behind her when the paramedics appeared.

'I'm Matt,' one of them announced. 'What have we got?' He placed his pack on the floor.

Breathless and exhausted, Anya continued to pump the heart as the second paramedic, a female, pulled out a face mask and oxygen tank.

'Giverny Hart. Seventeen years old. We found her on her knees, with a cord attached from the door knob to her neck.'

Matt shot a look at his partner.

'How long have you been going?'

It felt like hours had passed, but Anya had no idea how many minutes she had been attempting to resuscitate.

'I started the exact time you were phoned.' Anya knew that all calls were logged.

The paramedic checked his watch. 'We'll follow our protocol. Let's intubate and see if we've got a rhythm.'

Anya stopped pumping long enough for him to cut open Giverny's shirt and place three leads on the girl's chest, which he then connected to a portable ECG machine.

'Asystole.'

'I'm in,' the partner said, letting them know she had intubated her patient. 'If there's no other access, I'll try adrenalin from here.'

Anya moved back as the paramedic squirted a syringe filled with adrenalin into the endotracheal tube.

The small cardiac monitor remained unchanged. The line was flat.

'Anyone know the medical and drug history?' Matt asked, trying to get a cannula into Giverny's arm.

Anya turned around but Mary must have removed the parents from the horrific scene.

8

'She was otherwise well, apart from an assault last year. She's supposed to testify in court this morning.'

The paramedics paused briefly as Matt checked his watch again.

'Are you a relative, ma'am?' he asked.

'No. I'm a forensic physician. I saw her the night she was assaulted.'

Anya knew the girl had experienced horrors beyond belief. The physical healing had taken months, but the emotional scars were permanent. Even so, none of this made sense.

Matt removed the paddles from the defibrillator and turned the charger up. His partner placed two gel pads on Giverny's chest.

The machine let out a piercing sound.

'One hundred joules. Clear.'

His partner slid away from the head and Anya moved further back.

Giverny's body bucked but her heart did not respond.

'One hundred and fifty joules. Clear.'

'Could she have drugs on board?' Matt remained calm as his partner continued squeezing oxygen into Giverny's lungs in between electric shocks. They were a well-rehearsed team, and for them this was simply part of a day's work.

Even so, the question threw Anya. It hadn't occurred to her that the teenager might have used illicit drugs.

'She had been on antidepressants, but nothing else as far as I know.'

Anya suddenly realised how little she really knew about Giverny. She had studied every aspect of the young girl's wounds and the mechanisms of her injuries; she had asked detailed questions about the night of the attack; but they had never discussed her personal life, apart from how the trial had affected her studies and her parents.

'Doctor, could you check the bedroom and bathroom, see if there's anything, prescription or otherwise? It would be a big help.'

Anya stepped away as the paramedics continued their emergency protocol.

She returned minutes later with a full bottle of paracetamol and a newly opened pack of prescribed antidepressants from the bathroom cupboard. 'Nothing to suggest an overdose.'

The reality of the scene hit Anya like a blow to the chest.

'I'm sorry, Doctor,' Matt said, sitting back and checking that damn watch again.

'We have to call it.'

She heard his next words but they were meaningless.

'Time of death, 9.15 am.'

He turned to Anya. 'I'm sorry, Doc. There's nothing more any of us could have done.'

2

Detective Inspector Hayden Richards arrived just after Anya broke the news of Giverny's death to her father. Mary sat next to Bevan Hart at the kitchen table, as stunned as Anya by what had just occurred. In shock, Val had been taken outside by Matt's colleague.

Anya knelt down next to the bereaved father; he was clutching Mary's hand and his eyes were glassy with disbelief.

'I just went out to pick up Val. We promised to be a family again for the trial. For Giv's sake.'

'It's been a difficult time for all of you,' Mary acknowledged.

Since the attack, Bevan Hart had demanded justice for his only daughter, regularly phoning the police, Anya and the Sexual Assault (SA) unit for updates. This had put him in direct conflict with his wife, who didn't want her daughter dealing with the trauma of a trial. When Giverny dropped out of school, the couple had separated and Val Hart had moved out – alone.

'Those bastards didn't give her a chance when they attacked her, now they've killed her, after everything she had to live for.' He stared at the table and sniffed back a tear. 'She's a fighter, our girl, always has been. It's why she wanted to go to court and testify against those evil bastards. She wanted them to pay for what they did to her. She just had to get through today. That was all she had to do, but those mongrels came back and killed her before . . .' His voice trailed off and he hunched forward against the table, shoulders heaving with each agonising sob.

Hayden tapped Anya on the shoulder. The pair stepped into the hallway as Mary tried to offer comfort.

'I'm sorry you had to be the one to find her.'

Head of the sexual assault task force, Hayden had met Giverny's father the night of the attack, and kept the family informed at every step in the investigation. He, too, looked as though he had just lost a friend.

The pair returned to the doorway, where Giverny lay. The paramedics had disconnected the ECG cords but left the leads and pads on her chest and the tube in her mouth – protocol for what was now a coronial case.

Crime Scene Officer Detective Sergeant John Zimmer arrived dressed in his police overalls and accompanied forensic pathologist, Doctor Jeff Sales. Both seemed more sombre than usual. For once, the CSO didn't have a wisecrack.

'I know this is hard for all of us,' Hayden Richards announced, 'but we've got to treat this like any other investigation. For the sake of Giverny and her family.'

Anya nodded.

'Can you tell us exactly what you found when you arrived? Walk us through it. Anything you can remember at all.' Hayden took out his notebook and pen.

Anya clasped her hands, as though that would help her focus as she replayed the scene.

'She was on her knees, head bent forward, the ligature around her neck attached to the doorknob. Her hands were untied, the right one by her side and one finger – the left index – was between her neck and the cable.'

Zimmer took some photos from different angles then homed in on the young woman's left hand. He clicked away.

'What did the body look like?' Jeff asked.

'Cyanosed, she was obviously without oxygen, and pulseless.'

'Signs of lividity?'

Anya knew it could take an hour for blood to pool due to gravity. Although Giverny's legs were tucked under her, there was nothing to suggest lividity.

'No, her head was still warm.'

'Did you notice any petechial haemorrhages on her

face or conjunctiva before attempting to resuscitate?' Jeff enquired.

Hayden interrupted. 'Doesn't anyone who has been hanged or strangled have those?'

'Not necessarily. If both the carotid artery and jugular vein are occluded and pressure isn't released until after death, the face doesn't become engorged. It's because blood isn't able to surge back up the neck.'

'So if you see them?' Hayden leant closer to observe Giverny's face.

Anya breathed out. 'If you see them in cases like this, they're suspicious. It suggests someone strangled the victim and staged the hanging to cover it up. It's tough to strangle anyone, so killers usually release pressure, then apply it again.'

The implication of her words was clear to everyone present. Giverny may have been murdered and the scene made to look like a suicide. Anya suddenly remembered the threat painted on the car in the garage.

Jeff Sales continued his external examination. 'Don't forget to get a photo of the knot in the cord.'

Zimmer donned rubber gloves and bent down. 'Not this one. It's been cut right through and unravelled.'

'Damn!' Hayden muttered, hitching up his trousers at the waist.

In the emergency, Anya hadn't thought about the knot. All she'd cared about was saving the girl's life. There was no way that Mary would have known how important it was to preserve the knot as evidence when she followed Anya's instruction and cut the dying girl down. Anya's hands began to tremble again.

'Mate, you did the right thing.' Zimmer moved to her side. 'We're all trained to prioritise. Save survivors first and make the scene safe. That's exactly what you did here. It's what any of us would – and should – have done.'

Anya suddenly wasn't so sure. It had never occurred to her that Giverny could have already been dead when they arrived.

She saw the girl and automatically reacted, more with emotion than clinical acumen.

She hadn't looked beneath Giverny's closed lids to check for haemorrhages on the conjunctiva, and she couldn't remember whether there were any on the girl's face. She assumed there weren't but could never swear to it. She may have simply failed to notice. God, how could she have missed something so important?

'I didn't notice any haemorrhages. I'm sorry. It all happened so fast.'

Hayden offered, 'None of us would have swapped places with you. We all knew Giverny and her gentleness got to all of us. But if those bastards did this to her to stop her testifying, we need to know every possible detail, no matter how insignificant it might seem.'

Jeff Sales clicked on a hand-held dictaphone.

'One hundred and twelve Levy Road, inside the front door is the body of a female adolescent, weight approximately fifty-five kilograms, height one sixty centimetres. ET tube is in situ, as is cannula in right forearm. A cream computer cable appears to have been removed from her neck.

'The face is engorged and petechial haemorrhages dot the area around the eyes and conjunctiva. A ligature mark consistent with the width of the computer cord extends from below the earlobes, under the chin. There is a small area on the left side of the neck, two centimetres inferior to the left ear, where the skin has been pierced. Blood has flowed vertically and then appears to travel towards the nape of the neck.'

Anya listened, still unable to accept that the body in front of them was the young woman she had known and treated. She looked down at the dried blood on her fingers. Giverny's blood.

'I cut the cable with that knife on the floor,' she said, pointing to the smaller knife by the door, 'while I was holding her upright, then when Mary freed her from the door tie I laid her flat on the ground to begin resuscitation. That's why the blood dripped down then behind.' Her hands shook again as her temperature climbed. 'Mary used the larger knife.'

She held her ribs and coughed again.

'You okay? You look flushed.' Hayden had a worried expression.

'I'm fine.'

'We can take a break if you want.'

'No. Let's keep going.' Anya's words were more curt than she had intended. It was best they finish going over the details while everything was still fresh in her mind.

'Were the knives near the body when you arrived?'

'No, I told Mary to quickly find something to cut the tie to the door. I assume she got them both from the kitchen.'

Zimmer photographed the knives then placed them in paper evidence bags. The bloodstained cord went in another bag. 'We'll need to fingerprint Mary, as well as the doorknob.'

Jeff Sales lifted the skirt of Giverny's dress then replaced it.

'Underwear intact. No external evidence of sexual assault.'

All Anya could do was stand and watch, feeling as though Giverny's body was being violated yet again.

3

After giving formal police statements, Mary dropped Anya a few blocks from her home. Anya wanted to clear her head and walk the rest of the way. By trying to save Giverny, she and Mary had contaminated what was considered a crime scene. As a result, if anyone had murdered Giverny Hart, evidence could be too blurred to lay charges.

She pictured the threats painted on the car and garage wall. *DIE SLUT* and *LYING BITCH*. Had she seen that and panicked? Replaying the scene in her mind, she couldn't be sure her emotions hadn't got in the way of common sense. On top of that, the fever could have affected her reactions and clouded her thinking.

Damn! Why couldn't she remember what Giverny's face had looked like before she had freed the cord from her neck? The small face was bent forward, barely visible until the ligature had been severed and released. It was the priority under the circumstances.

She knew better than anyone that in order to cause petechial haemorrhages, a killer would have to have cut off the blood supply to the neck, then relaxed the grip long enough for blood to surge back into the head region, before tightening the grip again. Even the strongest of men had trouble maintaining a hold long enough to kill in one episode of pressure.

If that happened, Giverny could have been in and out of consciousness, knowing she was going to die.

Anya coughed and a pain shot through the middle of her back. She slowed her pace and paused by a tree to let an elderly couple pass on the footpath.

The only ones who would benefit from the girl's death were the Harbourns. The thought of her failed attempts at resuscitation helping them get away with murder brought bile to her throat.

She walked slowly, pain shooting through her back. Leaning over the body, doing cardiac massage had been exhausting. Now her muscles were in spasm.

Her thoughts wandered to her mother, a family doctor in Tasmania. Doctor Jocelyn, as her patients called her, had often come home dejected about losing one of her patients. Too often, as one of the few doctors in the area, she was the one to pull victims from mangled cars on the highway, or deliver stillborns of women she in turn had delivered all those years before.

Up until today, Anya hadn't truly appreciated the impact that must have had. Her mother knew – and cared for – almost everyone in their area.

Giverny was a kind, sensitive girl who had touched all who had met her after the assault. The one hope was that she had not suffered any more in death than she had in life. If she'd hanged herself, unconsciousness would have come within about fifteen seconds of the cord tightening.

But if she were murdered . . .

Despite being terrified of facing her attackers in court, Giverny had talked about finding strength knowing that without her evidence the brothers would get away with their crimes. In spite of that, the multiple delays in the trial had worn her down. Having dropped out of school, her spirits were low. Her parents' separation was undeniably stressful. But was she depressed enough to commit suicide?

Anya thought about how much the Harts had lost. Bevan's only daughter had been brutally raped. His determination to see a conviction had driven his wife to leave; she had wanted Giverny to move on with her life, not remain a victim. In contrast, the trial had become the focus of her husband's life.

Looking at a passing couple in her street, hand in hand, doting on their baby, Anya felt a terrible pang for the Harts. No parent should ever outlive a child. Bevan and Val would never experience the joys of watching their daughter fall in love and have her own children, their grandchildren. That had all been taken from them.

As Anya walked slowly on, rain began to spit from a charcoal sky. The day could barely be any more miserable. A minute from home, the drizzle became a downpour.

Anya didn't increase her pace; she was numbed by the morning's events. It was only weather, and rain wasn't capable of hurting her or causing her pain.

People were the experts at that.

Once inside her terrace house, she dropped her soaked leather shoes in the corridor and was greeted by Elaine, her secretary.

'You'll catch your death of cold,' the middle-aged woman scolded.

Anya didn't bother arguing that bacteria and viruses caused infections, not the weather.

'I'll put the kettle on while you get out of those wet things.'

Anya knew from experience that Elaine would not take no for an answer, so she automatically complied. Elaine's fussing was her way of showing affection, and at the moment, Anya appreciated that.

The soggy stockings were removed next and deposited in the laundry at the back of the house. On the way through the lounge, she flicked on the television for any bulletins on the case.

She wondered how Natasha Ryder, the prosecutor in the trial, had taken the news. Years spent trying to make the Harbourns answerable for their crimes were suddenly wasted. The senior prosecutor had endured two other trials with the brothers, each ending in acquittals when key witnesses refused to testify.

Without Giverny's testimony, the current case came down to whether or not the teenager had consented to group sex. With DNA evidence to show sex with a number of men had taken place, the Harbourn brothers all claimed that Giverny had begged them for a 'gang bang'. The thought made Anya shudder as she headed upstairs to change. Pulling on an oversized jumper and pair of yoga pants, she quickly towel-dried her hair and headed back down.

Elaine had a mug of hot chocolate waiting. Just like her mother used to do.

'Rough day?'

Anya took the offering and warmed her hands with it. 'You could say that.'

'Detective Richards rang to see how you were doing. He explained why court was postponed.'

A news bulletin flashed on the screen, catching Anya's attention. She moved to the lounge and hit the volume button on the remote.

Holding a press conference outside the family home was Noelene Harbourn, matriarch of the twisted criminal family. She was dressed in her trademark blue apron, to make herself look like a benign suburban mother, Anya supposed; some of her younger children were offering biscuits to the waiting media.

'I have just heard that the trumped-up police case against four of my sons has fallen apart. The only witness they could find to testify passed away unexpectedly this morning. I expect Mr Argent, our lawyer, will be making a statement later on about when my sons will be released. Boys, we can't wait to have you home and I've been baking all day to celebrate.'

A flurry of microphones moved forward and reporters shouted questions.

'Have you heard how the witness died?'

'What happened?'

'What's going to happen with the trial?'

'Well, I don't think anyone knows for sure, but when a young person dies suddenly, isn't it normally due to a car accident or suicide?'

Or murder, Anya thought, tightening her grip on the mug.

'And I must say, I don't think I was alone in worrying about the stability of that poor young woman. I mean, to make up so many lies like she did. My boys could never hurt anyone. I guess she knew she had made a terrible mistake and couldn't live with the guilt and shame of what she'd done.'

This was unbelievable. Noelene Harbourn was standing there celebrating Giverny's death. How had she found out so quickly? If the trial were to continue, she had virtually declared that the police's only witness was not only mentally unstable but had committed suicide rather than face the men she had falsely accused.

The charges would surely be dropped.

4

After a few hours of restless dozing, Anya weaved her way past the tight groups of suit-clad men and women spilling out from the Star Bar. She coughed as a well made-up executive in patent leather heels exhaled smoke in her direction. The woman barely acknowledged the offence before drawing her next puff and continuing her conversation.

The combination of perfumes, aftershaves and second-hand smoke irritated Anya's inflamed, bronchitic lungs.

Inside, hip-hop music pulsed over alcohol-fuelled conversations while big-screen televisions highlighted the latest sports results. Even up-market pubs like this one had never appealed to Anya. Then again, she wasn't into networking or climbing the corporate ladder.

And she definitely wasn't interested in a relationship that began over drinks and then soured when all effects of alcohol wore off.

Upstairs in the restaurant, the pub noises became muffled. In the corner Anya could see Natasha Ryder at a table, sipping from a large wine glass. Anya had been surprised by her request to meet over dinner. It was the last thing she wanted, but the prosecutor for the Harbourn trial deserved to hear what had happened from someone who had been there.

Anya headed straight over, took off her jacket and hung it on the back of a chair. 'Sorry I'm late. I tried to call but your phone's off.'

The prosecutor glanced up. 'Didn't fancy talking to anyone. Hope you don't mind, I started without you.'

She pointed to a variety of breads with olive oil and balsamic vinegar. 'I was starving.'

The waiter appeared and asked Anya what she would like to drink.

'Mineral water, thanks.'

As tempting as it was to use alcohol to obliterate the day, the combination of antibiotics, fever and painkillers was a far more potent cocktail.

'And I'll have another pinot gris,' the prosecutor announced, dipping a bread stick into the oil.

'I appreciate your coming, I know it's been a tough day all round.'

The image of the young woman hanging from the doorknob was still vivid, as if the whole scene had been burnt on Anya's retina.

'I can't help thinking what might have happened if we'd found her sooner, if the CPR had been effective, if the paramedics had been faster with the defibrillator . . .'

Natasha toyed with the bread stick on the plate.

'My father used to say that there are two phrases that should be outlawed from the English language. "What if" and "if only". Those words have ruined countless careers, marriages and lives.'

She drained her glass. 'What's happened is done, and you can't torture yourself with what might have been. We have to move on. My problem now is what to do with the trial.'

The waiter arrived with the drinks and placed them on the table. 'Are you ready to order?'

Anya didn't feel hungry but she knew she should eat something. The restaurant was known for hearty rustic cooking. 'I'll just have the soup of the day.'

'To start with,' Natasha began, 'the smoked salmon salad with the vinaigrette on the side, followed by the rump steak – cooked medium-rare, oven-roasted potatoes, string beans and aioli on the side, thanks.'

Despite her key witness dying, the lawyer had lost none of her appetite or fussiness. Anya baulked at the almost callous attitude.

'I assumed that you'd have to drop the charges, given that Giverny can no longer testify.'

'That's what the Harbourns and their legal team will assume. But this time they're not getting away with rape and grievous bodily harm. The way I see it, we still have your evidence, what you found when you examined Giverny. The damage to her skin from the hose pressure is impressive and supports her version of events. A jury won't be able to ignore your evidence.'

'I can only objectively describe what I saw.'

Anya recalled the night she had met the then sixteen-year-old girl, dragged into a car by the four men while she walked home from a ballet lesson. Giverny remained quiet but stoic after telling how she had ended up at a disused warehouse where the degradation and violence continued. During the physical examination it was apparent that Giverny had been comparatively fortunate to suffer only severe bruising to her body and grazing to her arms, back and legs; but the psychological injuries suffered that night were far more severe.

'Ah, this is where we use the law to our advantage for a change.'

The waiter returned with the pumpkin soup and salmon salad.

'I'm going to argue that Giverny's video testimony from her police statement and interview is admissible. Of course, the defence will complain that she can't be cross-examined, but we can also offer the testimony from the aborted trial. Giverny was cross-examined then, by the same legal team. They're hardly going to complain that they disadvantaged their own clients by being incompetent.'

Natasha made a good point. The defence team took turns grilling Giverny for a day and a half on the stand. To her credit, the teenager answered every question, no matter how demeaning or traumatic to recall.

It was only after the cross-examination that a female juror commented that she had believed from the start the boys on trial were good-looking and could have slept with any girl they wanted so would never need to commit rape. Another juror informed the presiding judge, who immediately called a mistrial.

The result devastated Giverny and her family. The worst part was having to go through the trauma all over again.

The prosecutor softened, 'We can't let bastards like these get away with what they did to Giverny, and the other women who were too scared to come forward and testify against them. We owe Giverny that much.'

Anya sipped her soup and studied the woman across the table. Natasha's second glass of wine arrived and disappeared quickly.

'You're not responsible for what happened to Giverny,' Anya offered, concerned that Natasha might blame herself for the girl's suicide – if that's what it was. She herself felt more responsible than anyone, especially after failing to resuscitate Giverny. No amount of consoling could take that feeling away.

'Don't be too sure about that. Last week she said she was scared that she couldn't face the stand again, and I threatened to charge her with contempt.'

Anya couldn't believe what she was hearing. The last thing Giverny needed was legal threats from the woman responsible for bringing her case to justice.

'Listen, I know what you're thinking, but this wasn't just about Giverny Hart. Rightly or wrongly, I represent society, not individuals, and those bastards are a real danger to every woman out there, including you and me.' She stuck her fork into some salad as another glass of wine arrived.

Although Natasha was claiming the moral high ground, her aggressive manner and heavy drinking suggested she did feel guilty about Giverny. Anya assumed she had heard about the paint slur in the garage and the possibility of a staged suicide, but a day spent in legal arguments might mean she hadn't been fully informed.

'I assume you've been told the police are treating this as a suspicious death?'

The prosecutor took a gulp of wine. 'I was in court and received the message about her being found but unable to be revived. I couldn't face going back to the office so I didn't get many more details, apart from the paint scrawls in the garage.'

'There's not much more I can tell you until after the post-mortem. Her left index finger was trapped underneath the cord when we found her. There were no signs of a struggle, though.'

'So Giverny tried to stop it strangling her.' She pushed the bread plate to the side and wiped some crumbs off the table. 'What else? Anything.'

'She wasn't dressed up, no make-up. Come to think of it, she didn't really look like she had dressed for court.'

'Not wearing make-up is no surprise. We talked about it because I thought it was better if she appeared her age in court. She said it wasn't a problem because she didn't like it anyway. Who's working the homicide angle?'

Anya had seen only Hayden Richards at the scene. 'Not sure yet.'

The prosecutor began dialling her mobile phone. 'Homicide, thanks . . . Natasha Ryder. Who's working the Hart case from today? Good. I'll need the forensics ASAP and I want to know exactly where each and every other member of that family and their closest friends were last night and this morning.'

Anya was relieved by this positive turn-around in the case, even though she still felt inadequate about what had happened at the house.

Natasha hung up. 'Kate Farrer's in charge. Do you know her?'

Anya knew the detective well. They had become friends through a number of cases, each sharing a mutual respect for the other's work. Having been back from overseas for less than two days, there hadn't been the opportunity to catch up. That was something she would do tomorrow or the next day when the jetlag and fever had abated.

'Kate's very professional. Thorough and right down the line,' Anya said.

'Good. That's what I've heard.' Natasha grabbed her bag and stood just as the waiter arrived with her steak. Her phone buzzed and she checked the message.

'I've got work to do. Can I have a doggy bag for my meal?' The waiter nodded and collected her plate. 'Dinner's on me. I'll take care of it at the bar.' She took a few steps before turning back.

'And thanks for what you did to try to save her today. She was a nice kid. What really gets me is that it wasn't enough for those bastards to abduct and rape her. Even though the four who did it were in jail, somehow they made damn sure she wouldn't testify against them again.'

5

Anya Crichton shuffled downstairs in her ugg boots and thick cotton gown. The house was still in darkness, but once she was awake there was no point staying in bed. All she could think about were the facial haemorrhages she may or may not have missed.

The events of the last few months now felt like a blur. Working on cases in New York and Mediterranean Europe had been exhilarating and exhausting. Flight delays had meant there had been no time to catch her breath before preparing for the Harbourn trial. At least she'd managed one day in Disneyland with Ben and Martin, seeing her son delight in meeting Mickey Mouse and begging to do the Pirates of the Caribbean ride again. In truth, it was a toss-up as to who enjoyed it more, Ben or his regressed, childlike parents. And Martin had been so affable, she'd almost remembered what had attracted her to him so many years ago – until the need for them to be organised brought his aversion to responsibility to the fore once again.

She checked for messages and updates from the various people she had worked with while away. A couple wished her safe travels, but nothing else.

Thankfully, Elaine had cleared the diary for the trial appearances and so Anya was free to rest and try to shake off the fever and chest infection. If she were being honest, it was what her body craved. Working overseas had challenged her in many ways, and now she needed a day to recuperate, stock up on some fresh fruit and vegetables and get back into a routine.

She filled the kettle, switched it on at the powerpoint, and wondered whether to catch up on paperwork or try to put together the bookcase for Benjamin's room. He would be back next week and she hoped to have it completed by then as a surprise for his access visit. Besides, the wooden planks supported by bricks were bowing under the weight of his Mr Men collection and beginner readers. The thought of assembling prefab furniture was a little daunting, though. It might be better for her health to go for a gentle walk to the greengrocer instead.

Pulling the milk from the fridge, she noticed some fresh vegetables in the chilling drawer and a home-cooked lasagne on the shelf, courtesy of Elaine.

Her secretary was always quick to criticise her eating habits – going weeks without having 'proper food', the stuff that was unprocessed and free of every preservative and artificial colouring known to man.

A dedicated foodie, Elaine didn't appreciate that eating wasn't high on Anya's agenda. It provided sustenance and energy, but didn't have to be consumed with clockwork regularity or even much attention.

That didn't matter now, the lasagne was a mouth-watering treat and Anya was touched by Elaine's thoughtfulness.

The kettle steamed the window and she felt a shiver. As she pulled her gown tighter, the phone pierced the quiet.

Anya let it ring a few times. Calls this early were never good news. Ben was not allowed to ring until eight o'clock at the earliest, no matter where he was.

It had to be work.

Anya lifted the receiver and instantly recognised the voice of Hayden Richards, from the sexual assault task force.

'We need you right now for a victim.'

'Good morning to you, too.' No apology for the hour, Anya noted. For Hayden that was unusual.

'I know it's early, but we need you to come in.'

Anya lifted a peppermint tea bag from a plastic container on the bench into her *World's Best Mum* mug and poured boiling water over it.

'Good news is, I'm not on call. It's my day off to shake this chest cold. If you hang on, I'll check who's on instead.' She leant over to the noticeboard in the kitchen. A new doctor on the sexual assault roster was listed for this week.

'Listen, Doc, I understand that, but we want you to do this one.'

Hayden sounded anxious.

'I wouldn't ask if the victim was in better shape. Trust me, it needs someone with your experience.' He paused. 'I've honestly never seen anything as bad as this.'

Anya had worked with the senior detective on a number of cases. His experience, knowledge and unflappable demeanour made him perfect for the SA squad. She thought by now he would have seen everything a deranged human being could do to another. Something had to be very wrong. In the background, she could hear muffled voices.

'I don't have a good feeling about this. Where are you?'

'Western District emergency department.'

The relief in his voice was evident.

'Liz Gould is with me now and Kate Farrer's at the scene.'

Anya swallowed. If Homicide were already involved, someone had been killed, or this victim wasn't expected to live. It was unfair to expect a novice doctor to cope with the examination.

'All right.' Sleep, the bookshelf and groceries could wait. 'I'm on my way.'

'Thanks, Doc, I've already sent someone from the squad to pick you up.'

The line went dead.

Anya forgot the tea. No time for a shower; upstairs she slipped into fresh underwear, dark jeans and a navy shirt, then scraped her hair into a ponytail with her fingers, securing it with an elastic band.

She heard a knock on the front door. A detective constable introduced himself as Shaun Wheeler and already had the car's passenger door open and the engine running. She slung a leather satchel over her shoulder, collected her doctor's bag and slipped her feet into the damp court shoes still positioned by the door.

'I need to check the windows,' she called, but the constable was back in the driver's seat.

She went back to the lounge room and clicked on the television. It would sound as though someone was home, in case anyone had noticed that the house had recently been empty.

In the car, the detective said little apart from telling her he had driven Bevan Hart home after he had given his statement at the station yesterday. Anya could picture the broken man and his estranged wife and wished things could have been different.

'What can you tell me about the victim we're seeing?' she asked, keen to change the subject and prepare for the task ahead.

'Sorry, all I know is that I have to get you to the emergency department – p-p-pronto.'

The constable's stuttering might have explained why he was loath to engage in conversation. Besides, a junior constable may not have been privy to any details about the case, or have been warned not to divulge confidential details by his superiors.

Traffic slowed when a delivery truck parked in one of two lanes on Victoria Road. Wheeler opened his window and put the blue flashing light on the car's roof. With the siren blaring, they crossed the median strip and bypassed the obstruction.

In record time, Shaun Wheeler delivered Anya to the casualty entrance; the same double doors through which she had begun and ended innumerable shifts during her internship and residency.

Homicide detective Liz Gould paced inside, talking on her mobile. Last Anya heard, she had been on maternity leave. Her presence was reassuring. A kind, warm manner complemented Kate Farrer's more brash approach. Hayden Richards stood nearby.

In the reception area a uniformed officer sat with a middle-aged man on plastic chairs that, like everything that could possibly be stolen, were bolted to the floor. The man glanced up at Anya with partially raised eyebrows, almost pleading for something. She had seen that look many times before in people desperate for the smallest bit of hope.

The waiting room was almost empty. Staff would be handing over soon. A cleaner whirred a polisher across the floor, preparing for the daily onslaught that made every day in this place feel like Groundhog Day.

The place looked exactly the same. Only the familiar blue vinyl chairs lining the walls now had holes in the padded armrests with yellow foam poking through. So much for prioritisation of health care, she thought.

Liz hung up and led Anya to a small examination room, often used for breaking bad news to relatives. Neither woman sat.

'Victim's name is Sophie Goodwin. Fourteen years old. She was found about an hour ago on the roadside, with serious stab wounds to her neck, chest and stomach. The paramedics brought her in a few minutes ago.'

Anya knew that was longer to deliver an acute trauma patient than the protocols permitted. 'What took them so long?'

Liz shrugged her shoulders. 'They had to protect her neck, they said.'

The detective spoke without emotion, simply stating the facts. But her eyes concentrated on the door, as though she were expecting someone to come in at any time.

Lowering her voice, she explained, 'From the blood trail, Sophie crawled about forty metres to the road from the house she was in. A neighbour out looking for his dog found her and called the paramedics. They worked on her all that time, but apparently the doctors here don't give her much chance.'

Anya knew the injuries had to be extensive and blood loss substantial if the girl had left a trail of blood that far. Protecting the neck meant either her airway was compromised, cervical vertebrae were broken or a wound was life-threatening.

'Are you sure she was sexually assaulted? Was she conscious?'

'No, but she was found naked below the waist and bleeding vaginally.'

Anya thought of the poor man in the waiting room. The young woman sounded as though she had already defied all odds by surviving this long. 'Is that the father outside?'

Liz nodded.

'He isn't ready to be interviewed yet. He's in shock. Whoever did this raped and murdered her older sister during the night. We found her body back in the house by following Sophie's trail.'

One daughter dead and the other in a critical condition. Anya did not want to think about how their father might be feeling.

'The girl is the priority,' she said. 'The surgeons have to do what they can to save her. You have to understand that collecting evidence comes second.'

'I know that, but I want you in there. You understand about preserving anything that can help us. Photograph the wounds, get the clothes, do a rape kit. If you have to, follow them to the operating room.' Liz grabbed Anya's arm. 'Whoever did this needs to be found. What happened at that house was beyond horror. The sister was tied down and stabbed over a dozen times.' She let go and stepped back. 'We have to find whoever did this before they attack again.'

Hayden Richards opened the door.

'The head doctor told the triage nurse you could go in now.'

Anya stepped out of the room and tried not to look at Sophie Goodwin's father.

The triage nurse handed her a white gown, which she pulled on and tied at the back of her neck. 'Gloves are on the wall inside.'

'Thanks.' Anya took a deep breath to steel herself before pushing through double plastic doors. A male nurse carrying two bags of blood rushed behind the curtain to the first resuscitation bay.

'Blood warmer's coming. Group specific is still a couple of minutes away. They're still working on the full cross-match.'

'Hurry them up,' a male voice boomed. 'She's leaking like a sieve.'

Two paramedics hovered near the central desk area, sipping from paper cups. Judging by their proximity to the cubicle, they were the ones who had brought Sophie in.

Anya peered through the gap in the curtains but could see only the lower part of the girl. Heads and hands moved quickly, each with a specific role.

Inside the cubicle she recognised Mike Monsoor, a surgeon she had trained with, and emergency specialist, Greg McGilvray. The hospital had quickly mobilised the acute trauma team.

A small figure lay on the bed, naked, her flesh covered with mixes of dried and fresh blood. One gloved nurse put pressure on a blood-soaked bandage over the girl's abdomen.

A woman in blue surgical scrubs was at the head end, with a nurse, squashed between the bed and the wall.

'Doctor Crichton, I heard you'd been called.' Dressed in a sterile procedure gown, Greg McGilvray held a plastic bone-gun in a gloved hand. The gun was used in the army for administering fluids to injured troops in the field. Instead of wasting critical time trying to find venous access, the plastic gun drilled directly into bone. Advocates claimed it could save large numbers of lives.

Anya hoped Sophie Goodwin's was one of them.

'We've just lost the antecubital cannula. It's tissued,' a younger doctor said, feeling for a groin pulse. 'My concern with a femoral line is that any fluid could just fill the abdomen. We need to go in to know what damage is in the belly.'

He had to be a surgical registrar.

'I'm in the humeral head,' Greg announced from the girl's right shoulder. He flushed the line with saline and attached the blood for immediate transfusion. A nurse stood, arms above her head, squeezing the blood to get it into the body faster.

The monitor beeped seventy-five, a dangerously low blood pressure. Even if the girl survived, there was a chance she could suffer organ damage because of the prolonged poor blood supply.

The number on the monitor slowly increased with each squeeze of the bag. The blood was doing some good.

'Everyone, this is Doctor Crichton, a pathologist and forensic physician,' Greg introduced.

'Aren't you a bit early? Business must be slow in the morgue,' the surgical registrar muttered and stepped outside the curtain.

Some things in hospitals never changed.

'Don't suppose you want to put in a subclavian line?' Greg looked up. 'Your anatomy is better than all of ours put together.'

'Not today, thanks. But I will bag her shirt if anyone knows where it is.'

'Ah, I listened to your last lecture and split it along the buttons so knife cuts stayed intact.'

'Much appreciated.' For the first time, Anya had a clear view of Sophie's head and neck. The wound gaped from one ear to the other, exposing veins and vital structures.

'I've never seen a wound that deep on anyone alive,' Anya thought out loud.

The breathing tube was placed straight into the trachea, bypassing the mouth and upper neck, kept stable by a towel clip attached to the sheet. In this instance, everyone was improvising as best they could. Textbooks couldn't cover situations this complicated.

No wonder the woman at the top was keeping the head stable. Even a slight movement could tear large veins and prove fatal.

Greg glanced at Anya then paused to look at his patient. 'God knows how she crawled all that way without severing a vessel completely. The ambo officers did a top job getting her here alive.' Gloves on, he wiped his forehead with his forearm. 'You know, I've got a daughter the same age.'

Moving a piece of hair from the neck area, he paused. 'It's hard to believe someone did this deliberately.'

Blood pressure hovered at eighty to eighty-five.

The surgical registrar returned. 'Vascular surgeon's upstairs prepping. No time for a CT scan. As soon as that other line's in, we'll take her straight to theatre.'

'What about gynaecology?' As the forensic physician, Anya

was concerned about Liz's mention of a bleeding vaginal injury.

Greg explained, 'Registrar's upstairs standing by. You might as well photograph what you can. It's the best chance for the neck and stab wounds you're likely to get.'

Anya already had the digital camera in her hand. Any opportunity to examine the wounds would be gone once surgeons started operating. With no time to grab a tape measure, she pulled the lid off a pen and placed it on the skin near the girl's left shoulder. The lid would be the consistent measure of scale for each wound.

She recorded a number of stab wounds on the chest without interfering with the resuscitation. The woman at the head mentioned marks on the forearms and Anya gently collected images of them as well as of the hands and fingernails with the assistance of another nurse. Classic defence injuries, she thought. Sophie had tried to fend off her attacker, or attackers. She had probably seen whoever stabbed her.

'Thanks, Greg.'

'They should know to expect you in theatre as well. Any problems, get them to ring me.'

'Give us a few minutes,' said the woman still quietly holding Sophie's head. 'You can meet me in the anaesthetic bay. I'm Jenny Rafferty.'

Anya recognised the name of the Director of Anaesthetics and Intensive Care. Sophie was in the best possible hands.

Moving out to let them take the bed away, Anya turned around. The two paramedics were still by the nurse's station. One was in his thirties, the other in his fifties.

'Excuse me, Doc,' the older man said. 'But if you're going to stay with Sophie, could you give her this?'

In his hand the man held a silver and gold medallion on a thick chain.

'Does it belong to her?'

'No . . . but it's got me this far safely and now I figure Sophie needs it more than I do.'

Anya took the medallion. On it was the image of Saint Jude, the Catholic patron saint of hopeless cases.

'I don't know if she's a believer or not, but it might protect her. Can you make sure she gets it?'

Anya nodded. 'I'll do my best.'

An alarm sounded as the bed wheeled past them, Jenny Rafferty clinging to the young girl's head.

'Blood pressure's dropping. She's bleeding again. We need to get to theatre now!'

The older paramedic's face tightened as he closed Anya's hand around the medallion. 'Don't let it out of her reach. It may be the only thing that can save that poor kid's life.'

6

Anya left the operating theatre an hour and a half later, with three surgical teams still fighting to save Sophie Goodwin's life. In the change room she took a few minutes to wash her face in cold water and absorb exactly what she had witnessed.

Never before had she seen injuries so severe on a survivor. It was the degree of trauma that might be found following a fatal road trauma or plane crash.

Despite all the years of pathology and examining wounds, it was difficult to accept that a human being had done this to a young girl. She could only imagine the pain the sister had gone through before dying.

She was grateful for the way the gynaecologist had not hesitated to take the vaginal swabs while examining Sophie, who remained unaware of the bodily trauma thanks to the anaesthetic. Anya had managed to collect important samples while the vascular team tried to repair the massive neck wound. She included clippings and scraping from fingernails along with a short dark strand of hair from Sophie's sparsely blonde pubic region. Each item was meticulously labelled.

Anya did not want to make any mistakes with these specimens.

Unusually, none of the surgeons present objected to a forensic physician's presence in the theatre. Egos appeared to have been temporarily shelved. Each member of the team wanted Sophie to live, but the mood made it clear that everyone present also wanted the perpetrator to be caught.

Silence fell over the group when the gynaecologist announced she would have to perform a hysterectomy to stem the haemorrhaging. The knife used to stab her had penetrated Sophie's young womb. Removal was the only option. If she lived, she would be unable to have children and would have to face a gamut of medical complications related to premature menopause.

Armed with the bags and vials of forensic evidence, Anya headed downstairs. Outside emergency, she dialled Liz, who had been with Sophie's father in a private room.

Within moments of hanging up, Liz appeared from inside, black sunglasses masking her eyes.

'Guess you want a lift to the lab with that lot.'

'Considering you had me chauffeured here this morning . . .' Anya clutched the bags, relieved that her job was over for the moment.

'Sure, but we need to make a detour first. I want to check out the scene. It might be helpful for you too.'

Anya took an extra breath; visiting the scene would be draining for both of them.

Liz unlocked the unmarked Commodore and Anya placed the bags on the floor in the back before getting into the passenger seat. She buckled her seatbelt as the car left the parking bay and waited until they were in traffic to speak.

'How's the father?'

'As you'd expect. He's just lost one kid and the other's not expected to make it. So what do we do? Treat him like a suspect and interview him as he stares at the doors of ICU for anyone with news of his daughter.' She checked the rear-view mirror. 'Not the most satisfying part of the job.'

Liz Gould was unusual in Homicide. A new mother and back full-time within weeks of the birth, she had to be under considerable stress. Her usual warmth was understandably lacking today. She seemed shut-down. Sitting with the father would have taken its emotional toll.

'Should he be a suspect?'

Liz stared at the road ahead. 'Gut feeling tells me no but the stats aren't in his favour. His grief seems pretty genuine to me, but that doesn't always mean much.'

Anya knew the police would need to exclude the father and close family members before they even considered any other suspects. Experience taught them to look at those closest to the victims then work outwards. Unfortunately, that caused even more distress for those already suffering the worst imaginable loss.

'Is the girls' mother around?'

'Divorced years ago. She died last year from breast cancer and the girls decided to stay on in her house. There's something I don't understand. If the slash to the neck was so dangerous, how did Sophie manage to crawl without killing herself?'

'No one knows. The ambulance officers did a hell of a job just transferring her safely.'

Liz Gould's phone rang a number of times. On speaker-phone, a male voice proudly announced that their little boy had just sat up for the first time. He was about to send a photo.

'Honey, that's great but I'm with someone and can't talk.'

Liz's husband sounded deflated when she said she would be home late.

The female detective let out a sigh and glanced over at Anya.

'Sorry about that. He thinks his child came out a genius.'

Anya remembered what those early few months were like. As she was struggling with exhaustion after a marathon labour and delivery, Martin would brag to anyone who would listen about how great their child was, how well behaved and what a perfect sleeper. Her recollections of Ben as a newborn were very different from her former husband's. Instead of time mellowing those images, they had been permanently etched onto her memory.

'What is your son – six months?'

'Four and a half. He probably pulled himself up and waited a second before tipping over. To his father, that counts.'

It triggered memories of Anya's experience. Just when she thought she could not cope any longer with sleep deprivation and motherhood, Ben looked at her with huge blue eyes and beamed a smile. One relaxation of a few facial muscles and she thought her heart would burst. From that moment on, she was tied to motherhood and adored her only child.

Liz paused at the lights. 'How old is your little one?'

'Ben just turned five and started school.'

With one hand, the new mother fiddled with her bra strap beneath the collar of her shirt. 'Please tell me it gets better.'

Anya grinned. 'Every day. Once the overnight feeds stop, everything becomes easier. Can I make a suggestion?'

The lights turned green and the car accelerated forward.

'Sure.'

'Check out YouTube. Search for laughing baby. There's a clip on there of a baby laughing at some noise. Just hearing it makes you want to keep going.'

'I'll do that.'

The car pulled up at a bend along Rosemount Place, a quiet suburban street. The crime scene had been cordoned off with tape. Up a long, sloped driveway was the house. A uniformed constable stood guard to direct any traffic around the scene. The detective removed a nail file from the middle console and slipped off both shoes.

'New leather soles,' she said, scraping the bottoms of her shoes with the file into a backwards 'G'. 'Now if I stick my hoof in the wrong place, everyone will know it's my print, no one else's.'

Anya preferred the disposable shoe covers pathologists wore in the morgue and at scenes.

The pair climbed out and the car beeped when the doors locked. The evidence bags would be safe with a policeman standing guard nearby.

Liz pointed to an area of dirt at the bottom of the drive.

'This is where she was found.'

Anya surveyed the ground. Numerous footprints and the wheel tracks of what had to be the ambulance gurney had made impressions in the soil.

'Has your photographer been through?'

Liz nodded and the pair squatted to look more closely at a blackened area on the sloped driveway.

'Sophie must have lain here for a while. Allowing for absorption, it's a significant amount of blood loss. If she crawled along, her head was pointing downhill the whole time, which might have just saved her life.'

'The trail goes back up to the house.'

The women slowly stepped along the drive, careful not to disturb the bloodstains soaked into the white gravel.

'She must have been on her stomach for most of the way.'

Anya thought of the blackened fingernails and the samples she had taken from beneath the fingernails.

'I'd say she stopped at least three times for a rest, judging by the pools concentrated at various intervals.'

The neck and abdominal wounds would have oozed and been further traumatised by the driveway. 'What was the temperature overnight?'

Liz Gould pulled out her notebook. 'Your colleague asked the same thing, apparently. Got down to four degrees Celsius. Sophie's lucky she didn't die of exposure.'

'Or the cold slowed the blood loss and her metabolic rate long enough for her to be found alive.'

'Barely – she's not out of the woods yet.'

Anya knew that even if the young girl survived theatre, there was the possibility of kidney, lung and brain damage. For the moment, she kept those thoughts to herself.

As she and Liz approached the house, the photogrammetry team appeared with their array of digital equipment. One crime scene officer held a vertical stand supporting two cameras mounted on either end of a crossbar. The other held a computer bag and recorded findings. By combining the two images taken of the one object or area, the police would establish a 3-D image and from that calculate distances and depths of objects without touching and disturbing them any more than was necessary for the pictures.

The one with the computer offered Anya disposable gloves and shoe covers. She took them gratefully.

Despite the warmth of the midmorning sun, Anya felt a shiver as she crossed the threshold into the house.

Two crime scene officers swabbed separate patches of living room floor in silence. They looked up at the sound of footsteps on the polished wooden boards.

'Anyone from Homicide here?' Liz asked.

'Try the bedroom. Third door on the left.'

With a narrow frontage, the cottage was surprisingly large, extending down the block. Exposed wooden beams gave the place a country feel. Dried flower arrangements and wallpaper friezes at hip height were dated but homely. Anya suspected the mother had been crafty and, since her death, the daughters had kept things as she'd left them.

Until last night.

Broken mugs lay alongside the coffee table along with a pool of water and fresh flowers. The petals had been crushed, presumably by shoes. Anyone in bare feet or socks would have been cut by the shards of vase.

'Sophie was out here, we think. Her sister was in the bedroom.'

Either someone had smashed the items to scare the girls, or Sophie had fought her attacker. Judging by the strength the girl had shown by crawling for help, there might have been a significant struggle.

'We've bagged a small pair of underwear from under the coffee table,' offered one of the officers, 'and a pair of jeans from just near the door. There are some smears of blood on the outside, so we assume her attacker removed them then assaulted her. If the blood came from the older sister, then the younger girl was stabbed second.'

'We won't know until we interview Sophie.' Liz moved further inside.

If she survives surgery and regains consciousness and remembers, Anya thought. The odds were still against her surviving, let alone recovering with full function.

The two women followed the corridor to the second bedroom. Inside, Doctor Jeff Sales leant over the bed and Kate Farrer stood by his side.

'Didn't expect to see you here,' Kate said. 'Natasha Ryder said you were off colour.'

The pathologist looked up from his task, clutching a pair of plastic tweezers.

Anya suspected her friend was being kind, giving her the option of leaving the scene. But having seen Sophie, she wanted to follow this through in spite of how she felt, physically and emotionally, after the trauma of yesterday.

'Just needed a good night's rest,' Anya lied as she entered the room. 'Cattle class from NY is a shocker.'

Violent deaths had their own distinct stench.

Immediately she was struck by the smell of body odour. Male sweat. Whoever had been here had left part of himself behind and it reminded her of fear and adrenalin combined. Then there was the almost metallic essence of blood.

'Hayden roped Anya in to examine Sophie Goodwin, our survivor. We've just come from the hospital.'

All eyes in the room turned to Liz Gould. 'She's alive but hasn't woken up. What can you tell us so far? Do we still think the deceased is definitely Rachel Goodwin, Sophie's older sister?'

'Going by the photos on the noticeboard, but we'll have to get dental records to confirm it. The body is consistent with a woman in her early twenties. She suffered multiple stab wounds to her torso and abdomen whilst restrained. Judging by the amount of blood on the sheets, at least one of the stab wounds was severe enough to be fatal, but I won't know which until the post-mortem. There are signs of pre-mortem sexual assault as well.'

If Sophie had lived through hell, her sister had died from it, Anya thought.

The body was naked and hands fixed to the rails of the bedhead with scarves. One side of the young face was bruised and swollen. Long black hair was tangled and knotted on one side. This woman had struggled on the bed, even with her hands bound.

A quilted cover lay beneath her, soaked in blood.

'Someone put a lot of love and time into that,' Liz Gould nodded towards the bed covering. 'It looks handmade.'

Soft toys – a tattered rabbit and a rag doll – lay on the floor near the window.

Anya recognised the young male detective, Shaun Wheeler, standing nearby, pale and quiet.

'Remember Doctor Crichton?' Kate asked him. 'She's a pathologist and forensic wound expert.'

The constable nodded in acknowledgement and rocked backwards and forwards on the spot, hands behind his back. Anya suspected he had been told not to touch anything so, like a child, he was doing as he was told. Judging by the way he rocked and the paleness of his face, he was struggling to keep from fainting.

Kate's eyes relaxed into a half-smile and Anya knew they were sharing the same thought.

'It's pretty stuffy in here, how about you take a break. See what you make of the living room. We'll be with you in a minute.'

Shaun Wheeler didn't need convincing. He sidestepped the bed and was quickly out the door. The odour lingered; chances were the killer had left more tangible evidence behind if he was nervous and high on adrenalin.

Jeff Sales was ready to turn the body. He removed a pair of clippers from his kit and snipped through the scarves, careful to leave the knots binding the wrists intact.

'Where are her clothes?' Liz Gould looked around the room.

'I think you'll find the bra under here.' With a gentle movement of the body, Jeff removed a blood-soaked item from under the girl's back.

Anya held the undergarment, hooks and eyes still clasped. The front had been cut through. She placed it inside double layers of paper.

The pathologist concentrated on the wrist marks while the detectives looked under the bed, then around it. Liz stopped at a teddy bear propped up in the corner on top of a set of drawers.

'There's blood on the bear's face,' she said, touching its ear.

If only it could talk, Anya thought. She pictured her own son having conversations with his soft Dalmatian puppy when he was supposed to be asleep. That dog had been with him for every milestone of his five years, whether it was tucked inside a kindergarten bag or snuggled in his bed.

This bear's fur was well worn in patches. One arm and hand were particularly threadbare. It, too, looked as though it had been through a lot and for a while had been inseparable from its owner. The blood spatters across its fur made the scene suddenly even more vile.

Anya moved towards the wall. Above chest height, small stains marked the wall nearest the foot of the bed. Each series of fine droplets was splayed in vertical lines.

Kate's gloved hands flicked through some magazines on the night stand and routinely tipped them up for notes or missing pages – any possible clue. 'Has anyone located the panties?'

Jeff shook his head. 'Not that I'm aware. Maybe they were taken as a souvenir.'

'Did someone mention missing knickers?'

Anya turned and looked up to see the grinning face of John Zimmer from the crime scene team. With his usual blue overalls and baseball cap, he held a digital camera around his neck.

'Guys, I'm serious. If they're here, I'll find them.'

Anya caught Liz rolling her eyes. Kate tensed her shoulders and jaw.

Doctor Sales looked up. 'Anya, what's caught your attention?'

The pair moved closer to the wall.

'It's cast-off from the weapon. Can't be arterial spurts, there's not enough blood and the force isn't strong enough. The droplets are too fine.'

She turned and faced the body. 'My guess is that the killer

was on the bed, probably straddled on top when he stabbed her.' She lifted her fist above her shoulder with a slightly bent elbow. 'He used a lot of force because he's pulled the knife out and up. The blood's come from the knife and travelled backwards through the air. And he's done it more than once.' She looked over at the bear.

Zimmer smiled again. 'Top of the class. Why can't my officers be more like you?'

'Then they wouldn't sleep with you,' Kate quipped. She turned to Anya. 'Your lot don't usually bother with blood spatter patterns.'

Jeff Sales joined in. 'Can you blame us – if it's not in the report to the coroner and directly relevant to cause and manner of death, there's no point. And some lawyer will tear us apart in court anyway for going beyond our level of expertise.'

Anya knew he was right, but she had been around enough crime scenes to learn a lot more than study and exams had taught her.

'Ah, might have just found the missing item of clothing.' With latex-covered hands, Zimmer reached down behind the set of drawers. Wedged between the wall and the back was a pink piece of material.

Zimmer carefully unfolded the item. It turned out to be a small cropped top.

'Jackpot! Look at the size of this little beauty.'

Liz whacked Zimmer's back with her hand. 'For Pete's sake, show some respect –'

'I was.' Zimmer held up the top indignantly. 'I was merely worshipping at the altar of good fortune. What we have here is akin to perfection. A bloodstained fingerprint.'

Liz blushed. 'With your track record, what was I supposed to think?'

'Don't sweat it. If I didn't deserve it this time, you probably owed me one anyway.'

Anya knew Zimmer had a point. He frequently pushed the boundaries of decency with female officers and techs. She

46

also knew how seriously he took his work, which was how he redeemed himself.

He proudly clutched his find.

'If the bastard's on file, we've just nailed Rachel's killer.'

7

Anya signed over the forensic specimens to Shaun Wheeler who dropped her home on his way to the crime lab.

She appreciated not having to make conversation in the car when every muscle in her ached with fatigue and her mind still raced with the details of Giverny's death. Inside, she locked the door and switched off the alarm. Everything was as she had left it. The unworn leggings and sloppy joe protruded from the opened suitcase on the floor. She grabbed them and headed upstairs to the bathroom.

After a hot shower she felt even more exhausted, but had at least washed the smells and horror of the Goodwin house from her skin and hair. Back in her ugg boots, she scuffed downstairs. A message on the machine from her ex-husband explained that the plane had been delayed another day due to electrical storms at LAX airport. Ben excitedly shouted something about loud thunder before the message cut out.

She had to smile. Even a delayed flight was an adventure for her child. Martin probably didn't see it as quite as much fun. Travelling with a child was challenging enough without flight complications.

The instructions for the bookshelf kit were where she had left them on the kitchen bench. So much for a day off to rest and recuperate. After tipping the morning's tea into the sink, she boiled the kettle again, this time opting for a strong black coffee and scrambled eggs whipped up in the microwave.

Smelling the toast and eggs made her realise that she hadn't eaten all day. She devoured the eggs while standing at the kitchen bench, then washed down another antibiotic dose with the coffee. Thankfully her cough was less frequent already – the only positive thing in the last two days. Feeling miserable and sore would improve with more sleep.

Back in the lounge room, the television blared with news updates of a vicious knife attack on two sisters that had left one dead and the other in a critical condition. Anya moved onto the couch and blew breath across her coffee with relief. At least Sophie was still alive at the time the show went to air. Maybe the Saint Jude medal was lucky for her. God knew nothing else had been that day.

She pressed record on the DVD remote just as photos of the girls smiling and embracing filled the screen. What struck Anya was how pretty the girls were, and how much alike they looked. Nothing like what she had seen today.

Elderly neighbours were reportedly 'shocked' by what had occurred in their 'quiet' street and spoke about the family keeping to themselves. Reporters implied there was something odd about that, but Anya believed privacy should be respected. Having grown up with incessant media interest in her family, she fully understood the desire to mind only your own business. She wished more people shared that view.

She wasn't sure whether it was the effects of the chest infection, seeing Sophie or being overtired and missing Ben that made her think about Miriam. Little Mimi, the one who loved to run around outside. Two years older, Anya was asked to watch her little sister at a local football match while their mother tended to an injury on the field. One minute they were playing chasings, then Mimi was gone. She was only three years old. Vanished.

No one ever saw her again or found clues as to who had taken her. Each year meant less chance of finding out.

Media accused their father of killing Mimi, stories of sex slaves and paedophile rings abounded in the state and national press. So much so, that Anya changed her surname to avoid the scrutiny – Crichton was her grandmother's name. Even thirty years later, the speculation and media interest persisted.

The next news story brought her back to the present. Noelene Harbourn, with a frilly blue apron this time, embraced four solid men, her sons, while announcing that she would sue the police.

The brothers were remarkably alike in build, colouring and facial features. They all had short necks, which made them stockier and more thuggish – almost Neanderthal. One had a mole on his chin that distinguished him from the others.

The reporter declared that the popular local identity, Mrs Harbourn, had held a well-attended street party last night to celebrate her sons' release from custody after the department of public prosecutions decided not to pursue the case.

Anya sat forward in disbelief. The department of public prosecutions had dropped the charges against the brothers. What the hell was Natasha thinking, after promising to go on with the trial?

Anya tried to study the brothers' faces, as if they could reveal what they had done to Giverny, but they just smiled and laughed while they talked to reporters; they were dressed in suits, as if that made them respectable and therefore innocent. Earlier footage showed one with a beard, another with a moustache, but all four were clean-shaven this night as they picked up younger children to present a loving family image.

Anya almost gagged on her coffee. An 'exclusive interview' with the devoted mother would be aired on the tabloid news show that followed. 'Police persecution and false allegations,' the heavily made-up anchor declared.

Anya's thoughts turned to Bevan and Val Hart. Hopefully, they wouldn't see the show and have to endure more grief, if it was possible.

The chime of the doorbell startled her. Whoever it was could come back another time. The chime continued. Anya pulled herself off the lounge and checked the peephole. Kate Farrer. She opened the door to her friend who proffered a plastic bag. The fragrant aromas had to be Indian food.

'Can I come in? Thought we could have a chat away from

all the madness. Besides, if the spices in this lot don't send your germs packing, there's no hope.'

'Smells wonderful.' In honesty, Anya appreciated the gesture, and the opportunity to catch up. 'I was just about to throw something through the TV anyway.'

Kate walked straight through to the kitchen. 'Guess you already know the media's all over it.'

Anya watched the detective pull plates from the cupboard and forks from the drawer. For the first time, she noticed the shorter hair and coppery tinge. 'When did you change your hair?'

'While I was on leave. You're lucky you didn't see it before it grew back.' She tugged on strands at the base of her neck.

'No, I mean it looks great. It really shows off your face.'

Kate responded by shoving a forkful of tandoori chicken into her mouth. 'Heard you did well in New York.'

The topic of hair was now closed. Kate gestured with her fork at the egg remnants on the plate near the sink.

'If you've already eaten, don't feel obliged. So, tell me all about it.'

The combination of flavours made Anya's stomach grumble. She responded by piling her plate with pilaf rice, green curry chicken and pappadams. 'The eggs were breakfast.'

The pair moved to the kitchen table, just large enough for two plates. 'The trip went well. I met some interesting people, made some great work connections too.'

'Uh-huh?' Kate said with a mouthful. 'What about *other* kinds of connections?'

Anya felt her face heat up. 'One of the investigators and I did get along really well, but I haven't heard from him since. I probably misinterpreted the signs.'

'Yeah, you're pretty thick about things like that.' Kate swallowed, grinned and shovelled more chicken into her mouth.

'So, how was the new partner and where did he go? Not like you to mention something as trivial as a work partner in an email.'

Kate stopped chewing. 'Oh, him. Yeah, well, new partners can be difficult. He was good to work with but Homicide wasn't a long-term option. I'm teaming with Liz Gould for the moment. We take turns babysitting Wheeler. Liz's reliable and smart and doesn't go on about her baby, not like some of the others in the office.'

That was one of the things the friends had in common. A lack of interest in small talk.

'What happened to him?'

'He works for the Feds. We keep in touch.' Kate crunched on a samosa. She had brought enough food for four people but had already consumed a plate's worth.

'So he's married?'

It was the detective's turn to blush.

'With kids, worse luck. Good thing I knew from the first day.'

Anya knew by now that for Kate this meant he was off limits, even if he didn't think so. No matter how much she may or may not have liked him, he had the two biggest strikes against him. He was a work colleague and a family man. Case closed.

'Speaking of kids, Ben is coming home in the next few days and will be around on the weekend. If you want to catch up, he's just discovered baseball.'

Anya stood and grabbed a wine glass from the cupboard.

'My favourite little guy. We can toss a baseball, no problems.' Kate wiped sauce off her chin with a paper serviette. 'Oh, no wine for me thanks, I'm still working. I'll get a coffee in a minute.'

Anya clicked the kettle on and sat back to her meal.

'So what made you want to destroy the TV?'

Anya put down her fork and swallowed. 'Why did Natasha Ryder drop the charges against the Harbourns? After everything that girl went through.'

'We're all cheesed off. Word is, she got pressured by her boss. He doesn't want her to go to trial yet, after what happened to Giverny, so reckons it's better to drop the charges for now and then have another go at them later. Of course, we're supposed to come up with magic new evidence, or even new witnesses.'

The argument made some sense. Without the only eye-witness, the prosecution faced an even greater onus of proof. Any reasonable doubt would see the perpetrators acquitted and immune from further prosecution for Giverny's rape ordeal, thanks to double jeopardy.

Anya's appetite suddenly waned. 'How did the Harts take it?'

'The mother's sedated so I talked to the father.' Kate chased the last of the rice on her plate and headed for second helpings. 'He's still in shock but kept saying he just wants to bury his daughter with dignity.'

Anya appreciated how difficult the emotional parts of Kate's job could be, particularly breaking bad news to victims and families. It was a side of police work and medicine that the public and media understood little about. It was also something that was impossible to do well, which was why it could be even more traumatic for all concerned. Judging by the amount Kate was eating, seeing the Harts had taken its emotional toll, not that she'd ever admit to it.

'That may not be so easy. The current affairs shows are all over Noelene Harbourn, claiming police harassment and mentally ill accusers. You know the drill. Exclusive interview, and all that goes with it.'

'I can just see it.' Kate downed another pappadam back at the table. 'At least the exclusive means the opposition will run an anti-Harbourn story.'

'If you've got time, I recorded it. Might give you something if the mother slips up on camera.'

Kate returned her plate to the bench and the pair watched the news report, followed by the interview. Noelene Harbourn was dressed in lime chiffon for her moment in the spotlight. She described how the family troubles had started when her drunk, abusive husband attacked her with a knife while his step-kids were asleep. In his stupor, as she described it, he tripped on the coffee table and the knife fatally pierced his chest. In the background, tacky re-enactment style, a blurry female figure screamed at the sight and children ran out of bedrooms.

'What she doesn't tell you is how like bloody Caesar's assassins every kid was. They all put their hands on the knife while it was in the old bloke's chest. The mother swore it was in grief and shock at what had happened to their father. It was more likely to stop police from finding out what really happened. That family sticks together, no matter what.'

'Was he violent?'

'Not according to his former wife. She claimed Noelene Harbourn enjoyed more than the occasional drink and would beat him with whatever she could get her hands on.'

The same footage of the brothers before and after release appeared on the screen, along with collages of them in earlier times.

'Can you pause that?' Kate disappeared out the front door and returned with a box of files. 'The one with the mole on his chin is Gary, the eldest and the gang leader.'

'How many others are there?'

'In total, six boys and three girls. They range from eight to thirty. That mother's womb is in and out more often than an accordion.' She rifled through the box and removed a manilla folder. 'Among them they have over twenty-five convictions for armed robbery, aggravated assault, extortion, drug and firearm offences. Prison's got a revolving door on it just for them, thanks to bleeding heart judges.'

'At the time of Giverny's rape,' Anya said, 'Gary must have had a beard.'

'She didn't remember seeing a mole and we assumed it was because it was dark and she didn't get a chance. We thought Peter, the middle one, was the only one who had a beard. Why didn't anyone think to check?'

More photos were pulled out and laid on the floor. Some of them were taken outside court and were accompanied by lengthy charge sheets. Facial hair made both of these men appear more menacing outside court. Anya wondered what legal advice they had been given. Usually, defendants were clean-shaven, to give the impression of respectability for judges and juries. It was the same reason they wore suits.

'This is Peter clean-shaven for trial,' Kate said.

Anya didn't follow the logic. Why would one grow a beard when facing trial?

'Surely some jurors wouldn't find that face sympathetic.' She pointed to the screen image of the eldest brother.

Kate crouched down and grabbed another photo. 'I don't know why I didn't see it before. See in this other one. It's their tactic. I'm guessing their lawyer put them up to it.'

Anya shrugged. 'Why would you want to look guilty if the witness describes one with a beard, why would he shave it off but his brother grow one?'

Then she realised why. A clever defence lawyer could confuse a witness by asking her to identify in the courtroom the bearded man she claimed had attacked her. Given the strong family resemblance, chances were she would point to the brother who had the beard, rather than the actual attacker, who by now would be clean-shaven. The jury would see she'd made a mistake and suddenly there might be enough doubt for acquittal.

'We thought the problem with identifying which brother did what was because of how similar they look. These bastards committed crimes knowing they'd take on another brother's appearance if caught. That's how they've got away with so much before, like the two other trials Natasha was involved with.'

If there were twenty-five convictions among them for violent crimes, the mind boggled to think what else the career criminal family had got away with.

More importantly, if the appearance ploy was so successful, then what did they have to fear in Giverny's testimony?

Jeff Sales was performing Rachel Goodwin's post-mortem and invited Anya to attend. It wasn't necessary, but she felt as though she should be there. She could comment if there were any similarities to the sister's injuries.

Beforehand, there was just enough time to check on Sophie in intensive care. Anya stood outside the double plastic doors and buzzed. Through the doors, she made out the figure of a uniformed officer, guarding the victim in case her attacker returned. A nurse appeared in corporate uniform with a white plastic apron on top.

'How can I help you?'

'I'm Doctor Crichton, forensic physician. I examined Sophie Goodwin yesterday.'

'Detective Farrer said you might pop in and put you on the visitors' list.'

Kate knew Anya well enough to understand why she would want to check in on Sophie now and again.

'How's the patient doing?'

'Not too well. Still on a ventilator. Urine output's poor, she's on dopamine and noradrenalin infusions and just maintaining blood pressure. Our intensivist thinks she's oozing from one of the abdominal wounds so she may have to go back to theatre.' The nurse lowered her eyes. 'Still critical condition, I'm afraid.'

Anya thought of the parent she had seen outside casualty and the hell he must be going through.

'How is her father coping?'

'As you'd expect. Poor, poor man. He's devastated and just sits holding his daughter's hand. We can't get him to rest or take a break.' She touched Anya's arm. 'Maybe if you're here he will take a few minutes. I'll go tell him.'

'No. Please don't. I can't stay.' The truth was, even if she had time, Anya had no idea how to deal with a grieving father whose life had been ripped apart by senseless killing. 'We didn't actually meet.'

The nurse nodded. 'Can I at least tell him you stopped by?'

'No need to bother him. I'll check back later.'

Medical school taught facts and formulae, but not how to handle grieving relatives, many of whom were angry and had every right to be. Pathology had the advantage of being clinical and removed from the emotional fallout of death, while helping family to get answers and achieve closure.

But even that hadn't been completely satisfying. Frustrated by the lack of expertise in sexual assault injuries, Anya had decided to train physicians in examinations and specific wound interpretation. In the process she had become more expert than anyone else in the state and therefore in high demand by police and prosecutors. It had given her an avenue into specialised private practice, and enough income to pay maintenance to her ex-husband and support their son.

The worst aspect about dealing with sexual assault was that she was thrown back into dealing with victims, relatives and their emotional distress. Anya never felt more inadequate than when dealing with people's emotions. No amount of experience could make her feel adept in the role of comforter. She would be of no possible help to Mr Goodwin.

Maybe that was because she'd seen her parents in a similar position after losing Miriam. Nothing anyone said helped, and often comments proved upsetting and insensitive, despite being well intentioned.

She followed the path to the lifts and headed to the lowest level. The secretary buzzed her in and informed her that Jeff Sales was already in the autopsy suite.

Down the corridor, with a plastic apron and shoe covers to protect her clothes, she entered the familiar suite. The smell of formalin filled her nostrils. Four of the eight stainless steel tables were in use, which meant a slow morning in this part of the city.

Liz Gould had 'babysitting duty'. She and Shaun Wheeler stood just past arm's reach from the remains of Rachel Goodwin.

'Didn't expect to see you here,' Liz blurted, seemingly grateful for the distraction.

Anya had never known a member of the police to enjoy attending post-mortems. Kate was habitually late for the event, timing her arrival for the summary at the end.

'Remember Shaun?'

Anya nodded.

The young detective uncrossed his arms and raised a hand but failed to speak. His cheeks had even less colour than at the crime scene. She gave him a sympathetic glance. Squeamishness was something only experience would help him overcome. Or he'd soon be out of Homicide.

'Here's something interesting.' Jeff looked up through round rimless lenses.

Blood no longer obscured the multiple, varied stab wounds and they were prominent on the clean skin.

The pathologist had a probe in the throat and moved the overhead light for a better view. 'The larynx is oedematous, or swollen, as is the epiglottis.' He reached for a pair of tweezers. 'There's something on the back of the left tonsil.'

He reached in and retrieved two small fibres – pink.

'From the pink top?' Anya offered.

'Something was used to gag her and may have even caused some degree of asphyxiation. Taking an educated guess, it could well have been the shirt from the scene.'

'Hang on,' Liz Gould interrupted. 'What do you mean, asphyxiation? She was stabbed – multiple times.'

'Yes, but it's not uncommon for attackers to use gags to silence victims, even if they don't intend for them to die. The nose can become congested and, after a short while, impossible to breathe through. If the gag makes its way towards the back of the throat, it can obstruct the posterior larynx, causing asphyxiation. I grew up thinking gags were harmless, can't think how many times they were used on *The A-Team* without anyone getting hurt.' He smiled to himself. 'Reality is far different.'

Liz scratched her head. 'Did she suffocate on the gag or not?'

'Once the lab compares the fibre with that of the shirt we'll know if it was the one used inside the mouth. Without any markings on the skin around the neck, I'd suggest that something internal caused the swelling in the throat, but not enough to cause death. Given the degree of blood loss from the other wounds, she was still alive when she was stabbed.'

Anya thought back to the scene. Someone gagged Rachel and maybe removed it while she was still alive, or as she lay dying. She had seen crimes in which a gag had been removed, but only to heighten the thrill of the attack. If that were the case, Rachel's killer either wanted to hear her scream or beg for mercy. If screaming wasn't the reason for the gag, its intent must have been to torture the victim even more.

Anya felt a wave of cold. Sophie may have heard what was happening to her sister in the bedroom. She might have even witnessed it. In a way, the longer the young girl stayed sedated and ventilated, the more time she had to recover before reliving the nightmare.

Jeff turned his attention to the skin on the dead girl's chest and abdomen. The shapes of the six wounds varied but the distribution was evenly divided between the chest and abdomen.

Liz Gould cleared her throat. 'Can you tell us anything about the weapon, or are we looking for more than one knife?'

'Different sized and shaped wounds don't imply more than one weapon, although I can't exclude that yet. The shape of the wound isn't only dependent on the shape of the blade, but also on the properties of the skin and location of the wound. It's quite possible that all of these were made with the one instrument.'

Shaun Wheeler had begun taking notes, but paused, looking at two of the skin incisions – one narrow, the other wider.

59

'How can there be that much variation if the blade is just one size – one length and one width?'

'The force needed for the knife to perforate the skin depends on a number of other things, like the sharpness of the blade's tip. The sharper that point, the easier it is to penetrate skin.'

To demonstrate, the pathologist poked his metal probe in one of the wounds. 'Once the skin has been cut, the blade slides easily into the body, readily passing through organs.' Most of the metal probe disappeared beneath the skin. 'Even a blade driven its entire length can have been inserted without a great degree of force.' He withdrew the probe. 'However, if the blade hits bone, the distance it tracks can be much shorter than the length of the blade.'

'So how can you tell the size of the blade?' Wheeler seemed to have forgotten his queasiness.

'By examining all of the wounds,' Anya replied. 'The blade length can be either less than, equal to or greater than the depth of the wound.'

'Hold on, how can it be deeper than the blade length?'

Liz clenched her fist and faced Wheeler. 'Say this is a knife. If you are moving towards me and I use a fair amount of force . . .' She slowly pressed her fist into his upper abdomen until he flexed at the waist.

Anya continued, 'Because your skin is being pushed backwards. Once it recoils to its normal position, the end depth of the wound is going to be longer than the blade. It depends on the degree of force used.'

Wheeler's face brightened. 'That makes sense.'

'I always say you have to see these things to understand them.' Jeff Sales seemed to enjoy the demonstration. He preferred interaction with staff, or classical music if no one else was around, and revelled in any chance to educate police.

'Similarly, the length of the skin wound can be equal, less than or greater than the width of the knife.'

'I must be thick. You've got me again,' the younger detective mumbled.

'Always admit when you're unsure or don't understand. There's no such thing as a stupid question.' Liz patted Wheeler on the back. 'Mistakes come from not asking. And don't care what anyone thinks of you. Chances are, if you want to ask it, so do others.'

Wheeler put the notebook in his back pocket and folded his arms. 'Okay. How can the entrance wound be longer than the blade is wide?'

'Another good question.' Jeff was in his element. 'If the blade has one cutting edge, it can slice through the skin, lengthening the incision. Skin is also elastic and that can make the wound shorter than the blade's width.'

Liz frowned. 'There's something I don't quite get. The pink top had a bloodied fingerprint in it. You think it might have been used to gag her, but before she was stabbed, given the amount of blood she lost.'

'Correct.'

'Then why does it have bloodstains on it?'

'Maybe she screamed at the first stab wound and that's why it was put in,' Jeff suggested.

'Her hands were tied to the bed, she wasn't going anywhere. So he stabs her then stops, with bloodstains on his hands, to stuff her shirt down her throat. We know she's still alive because of the swelling you mentioned. Then he goes back to stabbing her.'

'Or moves on to the sister. He could have immobilised Rachel then attacked Sophie and cut her throat. Thinking she's dead, he goes back to finish off his first victim,' Wheeler suggested.

Liz shook her head. 'The sadistic bastard would have had blood all over him at that stage.'

Anya recalled that the house didn't show signs of someone traipsing through back and forth, with blood on them.

'Maybe he's organised,' Wheeler suggested.

'Or there was more than one killer,' Anya said.

The prospect of two people combining to commit that degree of violence was even more disturbing. She needed to know more about the pattern of genital injuries.

'Jeff, what do you notice about the vaginal area?'

'There's marked purpuric bruising inside the thighs, as you can see.' He moved one knee to face outwards and a series of large purplish bruises was apparent.

Anya moved closer. 'There's tearing of the fourchette and a large haematoma.'

The lab assistant arrived with a digital camera and without speaking began to photograph the injuries Jeff described.

'We'll need close-ups, thanks. I've taken some swabs,' the senior pathologist added, 'but we'll have to wait and see. There were a couple of darker pubic hairs, none with roots, I'm afraid.'

Jeff concluded the gross examination with photos of the probe through each incision. Then began the long process of internal examination.

Anya's mind wandered to the scene. 'Were any of the locks damaged?'

Liz shook her head. 'Whoever it was walked in the front door, or pushed their way in once it was open. The girls could have known their attacker or attackers.'

'Do you have any suspects yet?'

The female detective frowned and waited for the stryker saw to stop.

'Still canvassing the neighbours, who don't seem to have seen or heard anything. We've had only a few calls after a media appeal for witnesses to come forward, but nothing helpful as far as we know.'

Anya had once assumed that people would feel so disgusted by what had happened to victims like the Goodwin girls that they would willingly volunteer information. She had learnt over the years that many people were too scared to get involved with the police, or too busy to be aware of what appeared on the news or in papers.

Jeff Sales looked up from his task. 'What about an angry ex-boyfriend? Nothing like a disturbed lover who's been spurned. The worst examples of violence against women are by men who claim to love them more than anyone else.'

One of Anya's first pathology cases was the massacre of an ex-girlfriend and seven of her family members. The former boyfriend had gone to the home and blown off the mother and little brother's faces with a shotgun, then casually driven to the family business and killed the remaining members, leaving his ex-girlfriend until last. Even in prison he still claimed that he loved her more than anyone else ever had.

'I can do without that sort of affection,' Kate Farrer said as she entered the suite. 'Did I miss anything?'

'Just tracking the chest wounds internally,' Jeff replied. 'One of them just missed the aorta by millimetres.' He probed more. 'Aha. She's had a tamponade. This wound nicked the pericardium.'

'Meaning?' Liz moved forward for a better look.

'The tip of the blade pierced the outside portion of the heart, where there is a potential space between the cardiac muscle and a lining we call the pericardial sac. It's like the lungs being surrounded by the pleura. I doubt our victim would have felt any pain for long after this.'

Anya could see that with the volume of blood in the sac, death would have been within seconds to a minute after the knife entered her chest that time.

'When blood rushes into the sac around the heart, it can't escape. It constricts the heart and stops it from beating effectively. Pretty quickly the heart can't supply blood to the body.'

'So that was the official cause of death – stab wound to the heart.' Wheeler was scribbling notes as they spoke.

'Whoever did this wasn't messing around,' Kate said. 'Anya, can I have a quick word?'

Jeff Sales had removed the heart and was placing it on the scales as Anya and the detective excused themselves.

In the corridor Kate spoke quietly. 'I've just come from Giverny's PM. It's why I'm late.'

'Please tell me they found evidence of homicide.'

Kate stood, hands in her trouser pockets, and scuffed one

shoe on the lino floor. 'Unless you can confirm whether those facial haemorrhages were there *before* you started cardiac massage, there's no way of proving she was murdered . . . Sorry, but I didn't want you hearing this from anyone else.'

Anya swallowed, her mouth suddenly dry. 'What about the paint in the garage?'

'Without a pathologist being able to confirm homicide, we can't investigate the death. The coroner's likely to come back with an open finding and we're all hamstrung.'

'The Harbourns had a reason to stop her testifying.'

'Yeah, and the four with the best motive were in prison that day. The only better alibi would have been having breakfast with the police commissioner. Sure, anyone else in the family could have been at Giverny's house, but we don't even have enough for a search warrant. The most we've got is vandalism for the paint job and maybe trespass. But none of the neighbours saw a thing, and neither did Giverny's father.'

Anya could barely believe what she was hearing. Giverny hadn't just been raped, she had been tormented for the duration of the trial, and on the morning of the retrial had received a death threat. In blood red.

'What about the threat?' Anya raised her voice. '*Die Slut* isn't just vandalism. It's a direct threat to a key witness.'

A technician scurried past and the pair waited until he was out of sight.

Kate folded her arms. 'Look. Unless we can prove she was murdered, that's just a case of graffiti. I'm sorry, I know exactly how you feel.'

Anya doubted that. She felt ill in her stomach. What she felt was the erosive, gnawing ache of guilt and incompetence.

By trying – unsuccessfully – to resuscitate Giverny, she had effectively destroyed the crime scene. Her actions meant that the Harbourns wouldn't just get away with gang rape, they'd probably get away with murder too.

* * *

In bed that night, Anya's mind fought sleep and she tossed about restlessly. As a distraction from her racing thoughts, she opted for some relaxation music on her iPod. But tonight, Mozart's flute and harp concerto may as well have been screeching tyres for all the good it did.

She sat up, switched to a podcast of a lecture on cranial nerves. The lecturer's voice grated more than the topic.

Seeing the drum kit in the alcove of the room made her realise how much she had missed music on her trip. She pulled on her cotton dressing-gown and headed for the stool, picking up a pair of drumsticks. She switched the iPod to a salsa rhythm, counted in and began playing along.

With the hi-hat locked to minimise noise, she gently accented the beat using her left foot. For some reason, coordinating her left hand with the snare drum and cymbals was a struggle. Even with the sound-dampening skin covers, it sounded like a cacophony.

She checked the grip. Palm facing up, stick between the middle and ring finger. Maybe it felt awkward because she was out of practice. Switching the music to 'Rock and Roll High School' by the Ramones, she counted one, two, three, four. One, two, three, four.

By the fifth line she was out of time. She tried again and tightened the grip on both hands. The rhythm kept repeating through her arms, and her body was beginning to perspire.

For once she didn't care if the neighbour next door complained. The woman feigned deafness whenever Anya spoke to her, so the favour was about to be returned.

She unlocked the hi-hat then began an improvised solo, accentuating every second beat with a hit to the snare or cymbal. At first softly, then louder as sweat moistened the hair on the back of her neck, and her fingers.

Crash, bang, roll, crash. Anger released with every downward movement.

The right foot pounded on the kick drum pedal as her arms raised higher between beats, accelerating the rate and increasing volume to culminate in a prolonged drum roll, finishing with frenzied assaults on the snare, base drum and crash cymbal.

The sound left her ears ringing.

When the pounding of her heart slowed, she slid off the stool onto the floor, puffing from shortness of breath.

Damn it! Why couldn't she remember what Giverny had looked like when she found her? She'd pictured the girl's face so many times, she was more confused than ever.

Both hands were in a tremor when she finally relaxed her grip on the drumsticks.

9

At 8 am Anya cleared security and met Hayden Richards in the foyer of the department of public prosecutions.

'How's the cough?' he asked.

'Nearly gone.' The chest infection had improved quickly. Maybe Indian food was more therapeutic than she had thought. If she looked tired, it was for another reason.

'Do you know what Natasha wants to meet about?' She turned the focus back to work.

Hayden shrugged. 'We're about to find out.'

The prosecutor exited a lift and headed straight for them. 'I'll take you upstairs,' she said, barely looking at Anya. Judging by the crinkled shirt and pencil skirt, she had already been at her desk a while.

On the twenty-seventh floor she led them through a maze of desks with files piled high, stacks spreading onto the floor. The lawyers who chose to work here obviously had a massive workload. Compared to their defence and private practice colleagues, they were grossly underpaid. Phones rang unanswered as staff hurried to deliver files or took notes on their own calls.

They arrived at Natasha's office; surprisingly the desk was clear, despite every bench and shelf being filled with folders tied with ribbon. The only human touches were an apple and knife on a plate and a photo of a group of smiling bushwalkers on the windowsill.

'Take a seat.'

The visitors did as directed. Natasha seemed in no mood for polite conversation.

'I've seen the Hart PM report. Death by asphyxiation, due to a ligature. Nothing about homicide, signs of a struggle or interference by a third party. In other words, we've got *nothing*. Can someone please explain that to me?'

Hayden glanced at Anya. 'Well, as far as I could tell there were no defence injuries or bruising that might suggest she fought anyone.'

'What about the finger underneath the cord? Doesn't that tell us she tried to get the noose off?'

Anya sat straighter in the seat. 'It's possible she could have tried to hang herself then changed her mind. It does happen.'

'Is that what you think?'

'No,' Anya snapped. 'But it doesn't matter what I think. If you're asking me to stand up in court and deny the possibility, then I can't.'

The lawyer sat glaring at Anya and drummed her fingers on the desk. 'All right then, can you exclude the possibility that she was murdered and the killer staged the scene to look like a suicide?'

'I can't exclude that possibility.' Anya chose her words as carefully as she would on the stand in court.

Hayden cleared his throat. 'We have motive but not opportunity. We've gone through the calls the Harbourns made from prison, but they're all to family. As to the whereabouts of the other brothers, they all say the whole family was together all night and all morning. So far nothing we've found can break that alibi. We don't even know when the car and garage were painted.'

Natasha stopped drumming. 'If it's a two-car garage, why didn't the father see it when he drove off to pick up his ex-wife?'

'The garage door is clunky and he wanted Giverny to sleep as late as possible, so he left his car out in the street the night before,' Hayden explained.

'Did forensics go over the garage? What about fingerprints, footprints, anything?'

'There weren't any prints left behind on the Morris Minor,

or anywhere in the garage. Whoever did it must have used gloves. If any of the Harbourns was there, they didn't leave us much.'

'I want you to check speed cameras in the area, see if anyone was caught near the Hart house the night before or that morning. Check en route to the Harbourns' place as well. And petrol stations. Go over video loops in case one of them filled up a vehicle. The brothers in custody had a lot to lose if they were convicted of gang rape. With the new laws, they were each facing a possible life sentence for the abduction and gang rape.'

With a spate of highly publicised group assaults, the state government had legislated for mandatory maximum sentences for anyone involved in group rape. So far, multiple male gangs had been convicted. The guilty comprised various ethnicities and social backgrounds. Of course, the media only highlighted cases reflecting racial tensions, but the problem was not limited to one definable group. Far more victims presented to Anya's unit than the number who made police statements. Violence from the 'pack mentality' had been rapidly escalating; whether that was a product of young males and boredom, poor socio-economic circumstances or a disturbing societal trend wasn't understood.

Natasha turned her attention to Anya. 'I want you to think back carefully. Is there a chance you might not recall the haemorrhages to the face because you were ill that day and suffering from a fever?'

Hayden shot her a glance. Is that why he had asked about her health? She'd assumed he actually cared. Damn him. Her grip on the armrests tightened.

'If you're suggesting my judgement was clouded because of a temperature, you're mistaken. My priority was to save that girl's life. If I'd succeeded, we wouldn't even be having this conversation.'

'We all agree on that.' Natasha's tone was still accusatory. 'What I'm saying is that if you have a chance to review your initial police statement while well and temperature-free, is there anything you would like to correct? No one would blame you for making a minor error if you were sick.'

Anya hoped Natasha wasn't trying to coerce her into changing her statement. Her knuckles whitened with the grip. 'You aren't suggesting I lie?'

'No, but if you recall Giverny Hart's face having even a few tiny red marks on it, now would be an appropriate time to say so.'

Anya felt tightness in her chest. She looked over at Hayden. 'Are you involved in this ambush too?'

Hayden shook his head. 'Definitely not. With all respect, Natasha, you're treading a very thin line here. This could be seen as coercing a witness, and I'm prepared to state that – on the record.'

The prosecutor slapped the desk. 'Don't threaten me. If you people had done your jobs better, Giverny Hart would be alive and those raping bastards would be behind bars for the rest of their natural lives.'

Anya stood, no longer able to control her temper.

'I wish I could tell you exactly what you want to hear to make your case, but I can't. I don't remember. All I see is the cord around her neck. Her head was warm – I can tell you that because I cradled her when we struggled to cut the cable loose. I can tell you what her mouth tasted like when I tried to breathe air into her lungs. It was mint flavoured, like toothpaste.'

Hayden reached a hand out. Natasha was now on her feet, but Anya hadn't finished.

'And I can tell you what it felt like when one of her ribs cracked under the heel of my hand. And would you like to hear about the guttural howl her father made when I told him his child was dead?' Anya caught her breath and realised tears were streaming down her cheeks.

She looked at Natasha. She, too, was teary.

Hayden sat with an arm outstretched towards each woman. 'I think we should take a minute . . . and sit back down.' He cleared his throat and pulled a handkerchief from his pocket.

Instead of handing it to either woman, he rubbed it backwards and forwards across both eyes and the tip of his nose.

Anya sat down silently and the prosecutor followed.

'I'm sorry, Anya. This isn't a witch-hunt and I never wanted to compromise you. I know how hard you tried to save Giverny. You meant a lot to her.'

'It's common for sexual assault victims to feel close to their doctor,' was all Anya could think of to say.

'Right then. If there is nothing to prove Giverny was murdered, I want to reinstate the sexual assault charges, but not yet. We're better off waiting until we have an iron-clad case because we only get one shot at them for the gang rape. That's why the charges were dropped for the time being. But to nail the Harbourns I'll need help from both of you.'

Hayden turned to Anya for her response. Without the key witness, the case was weak and only hearsay. But at that moment there felt like no other option. 'Apology accepted. What do you need me to do?'

IO

After a welcome-back morning tea at the sexual assault unit, Anya retreated to her office. With so few doctors qualified and willing to be on call, taking leave became an accepted necessity. Despite absences increasing the load for the others, the knowledge and experience doctors brought back from overseas study and casework benefited them all.

Anya settled in and began checking files from a year or more ago. She remembered a young woman who had presented for an examination and morning-after pill. At the time she had refused to make a police statement and was quiet about the details of the assault. She did, however, let it slip that a group of brothers had 'taken turns' forcing her to have sex. One of them had been her boyfriend at the time.

That was the detail that had stuck in Anya's mind. She suspected that if brothers attacked one of their girlfriends, it was highly likely they had raped other women.

How many months since she had presented? Months blurred together in Anya's mind. She searched file after file, trying to recall specifics about the case. There had to be a good chance it was the Harbourns involved. There could not be too many sets of brothers raping women, or so Anya hoped.

Natasha Ryder had asked for help identifying any other cases that were 'similar pattern' evidence. If she could find another of their victims to testify against the Harbourn brothers, the prosecutor could present a pattern of assaults, thereby strengthening the case against them. Giverny at least deserved that much.

Mary Singer brought a coffee into the physician's office,

edging past a chair to deliver it. Rapidly running out of room in the unit, highest priority were more fridges in which to keep forensic specimens. Often victims chose not to make a police statement immediately following the assault, but had the option to do so later on. Sometimes that meant storing evidence for prolonged periods.

Office areas didn't rate improvement, especially when they required funding to do so. Anya didn't really mind. The room was too small for drop-in visitors and no one stayed longer than they had to. Most importantly, the door could be locked so she could work without interruption. As part-time director, hours in the office were limited.

The counsellor leant against the desk, a bench that ran the length of the narrow room. A filing cabinet in the corner filled the space quota after the two chairs. A pile of files lay on the floor, under the desk.

'Don't tell me you've been asked to do an audit?'

'No, but I could while I'm at it. I'm trying to find a case file but can't remember when the woman presented.'

'Can I help?'

'A young woman, raped by her boyfriend and his brothers.'

'That sounds familiar. Have you checked the rosters for when you were on?'

Anya leant back in her chair and sipped her coffee. 'That's the problem. I was on just about all the time between the others taking long service leave or maternity leave.'

'How about what she looked like?'

'Short, thin, long dark hair. She had a pierced eyebrow but didn't say much.' It was much easier to remember those details than names because each examination took at least an hour to complete. It wasn't easy to forget the person.

Mary stared at the floor. 'Halloween.'

Anya looked up. 'Pardon?'

'Halloween. Try end of October. I remember thinking the girl was dressed as if she'd been to a Halloween party. All black clothes and pale face. Is she the one?'

Mary was right. The woman had been dressed in black and had dark lips, giving her a gothic appearance. Anya flipped through the files to October/November. Nothing.

Then she checked October the year before. Relief filled her as she lifted out the folder.

'Got it! Thanks.'

Mary stood to leave. 'I suppose you know that Giverny's funeral is tomorrow. I'll be going if you'd like a lift.'

Anya did know and was unsure whether to attend. She had no idea if the Harts would appreciate her being there or if her presence would only upset them more.

'I'll see how tomorrow turns out. I could be caught up, and I'm still on call for the unit.'

Mary glanced over her half-glasses. 'If you ever want to talk, you know where to find me. It's worth remembering that carers need looking after too.'

Anya was already absorbed in the file and flipped to her summary. 'Appreciate the coffee,' she managed as Mary closed the door behind her.

Nineteen-year-old Violet Yardley had presented on 30 October. As was Anya's habit, notes of the conversation were scant, in order to protect the victim. If the assault ever came to court, even a minor difference between what Anya had documented and wording in a police statement could be used by a defence lawyer to discredit the victim.

She checked the address. The suburb wasn't far. Turning back to her laptop, she pulled up the Whitepages website. The address existed, listed under a W and P Yardley. Anya dialled the number.

A middle-aged woman with what sounded like an Italian accent answered.

'Hello, I'm hoping to contact Violet Yardley.'

The woman readily explained that her daughter was working at a shelter, packing boxes of food. When asked if it was possible to meet Violet there, the mother didn't hesitate to provide the charity's address.

It always disturbed Anya how much information people naively gave away over the phone, especially to a female caller. The majority of people still trusted, which is why scams and credit card theft were relatively easy to commit.

The inner-city area had little parking, so Anya hailed a taxi from outside the hospital. Within minutes she was at an old warehouse. A rollerdoor was raised in front of a sign marked *Deliveries only. No Parking.* Inside, a number of people filled boxes with tins of food and fresh produce that had been piled onto trestle tables.

Violet seemed thinner and more gaunt than before. The eyebrow piercing was gone, but her jumper and long jeans were still black. The young woman looked up and stopped loading a box when she saw her visitor.

'I'm taking a break,' she called to no one in particular, grabbing a pack of cigarettes from her bag on her way towards the open door.

Anya followed her outside. 'I don't know if you remember –'

'How am I supposed to forget?' She lit a match and struggled to light the cigarette in the breeze. Anya cupped her hands to shelter the small flame.

The young woman nodded in gratitude and inhaled. 'I didn't expect to see you again.'

'That's understandable. I hope you don't mind, but I rang your home and a lady told me you were here.'

Crossing one arm across her waist, she supported her smoking arm. 'My mother thinks I should bring more friends home, so she would have been happy that anyone phoned for me.'

Anya smiled. 'Mums care. It's their job. Which partly explains why I'm here. You didn't come back to the unit and I wanted to see that you were okay.'

Violet exhaled out the side of her mouth and watched the traffic. 'What can I say? Life goes on.'

A table-top truck pulled up, beeping as it reversed into the warehouse doorway.

'That's the leftover veg from the co-op,' Violet said, stubbing out the remains of her cigarette on a metal bin by the entrance. 'We do food parcels for the homeless and pensioners around here who can't afford to pay exploitative supermarket prices.'

'Before you go . . .' Anya managed. 'Please understand this is all still confidential, but there's an important reason I'm asking – were the men responsible for what happened to you that night named Harbourn?'

The young woman folded her arms and bit her bottom lip.

'I never told you that.' Violet searched Anya's face for an answer. 'How did you know?'

Anya felt a rush of hope. They could have another case to answer for. 'Because you're not the only one they've done this to.'

'Yeah, well, like I said, my life's moved on.'

Anya handed over a card, which the woman reluctantly took and stuck in the back pocket of her jeans.

'I know this isn't easy, but it's not too late to give a police statement if you decide you want to. The samples I took that night are still in the unit if you change your mind.'

'Give me one good reason.'

'One of the girls they raped is now dead. The police think they could have killed her.'

Violet's eyes flared. 'That's bullshit. I chose to go to their house. We all got drunk that night. They might have taken turns with me after Ricky and I had sex, but that was it. There's no way the Harbourns are killers. God, Rick was the nicest guy I've ever known.'

The young woman pushed past the volunteers unpacking the truck and quickly disappeared inside.

In disbelief, Anya walked back to the nearest intersection.

Almost a year and a half later, a woman who had been raped by a number of men could defend one of them as a nice man. Violet Yardley sounded as if she blamed herself for the assaults, never mind the unforgivable betrayal by her boyfriend. The woman was in complete denial.

If she stayed that way, there was little anyone could do to ensure her attackers didn't rape again.

11

After vacillating over whether or not to go, at the last minute Anya decided to attend Giverny's funeral. The afternoon service went longer than expected, with four hundred people spilling out of the church and its grounds. Old school friends paid their respects along with former teachers, extended family and community members.

Eulogies were accompanied by slideshows of Giverny as a smiling baby, a gap-toothed face in school uniform, with the bag almost as big as she was. Like other mourners, Anya struggled to fight back tears. As a mother, she could not help sharing the parents' grief, if only in the smallest of ways. Once the funeral was over, her life would go on pretty much unchanged. The Harts' lives were irrevocably changed, for the worse.

A white coffin covered in purple irises and cornflowers lay beneath the screen. Bevan Hart sat with his wife in the front row; both wore large dark sunglasses to obscure their misery.

Anya had hoped to slip in the back without being noticed, but a newspaper photographer recognised her and his flash alerted security guards who quickly removed him.

Bevan Hart moved across and invited her to sit with the family, given that, he explained, she had tried so hard to save his daughter's life and had been so kind throughout her ordeal.

Anya felt like a fraud, wishing there was something else she could have done to revive the teenager. It was her job to help victims like Giverny, nothing more.

Recorded songs filled the church, ones written to thaw the hardest heart. 'Amazing' prompted more tears in the crowd, as did 'Wind Beneath My Wings'. Eric Clapton's tragic tribute to his late son, 'Tears in Heaven', concluded the service.

Mary waited in the floral garden. Around the perimeter, Anya noticed a number of detectives, including Kate Farrer and Liz Gould taking note of who had attended. People who had been outside were being funnelled through a side entrance to sign a visitors' book. Those who had been seated signed another at the exit.

Immediate family were the only ones going on to the cemetery, so Mary and Anya waited to pay their respects to Devan and his wife. A woman who shared Val Hart's prominent nose and small chin thanked them for coming.

'My brother-in-law and sister speak highly of you,' she said, 'and all you did for our Giverny. Thank you for everything you did, right up until the last.'

Anya noticed Mary nodding self-consciously.

'We're so sorry for your terrible loss,' was all the counsellor could manage.

The relative took Anya's elbow. 'Is it true that the rape case against those animals has been dropped?'

Anya wasn't in a position to comment, but said, 'The prosecutor and police want justice for Giverny. I can promise you.'

'We'll be praying that happens,' the woman said before moving on to hug a bereft teenage girl.

Afterwards, Anya needed some solitude, so she retreated to her home office, grateful that Elaine was now on an extended holiday after managing the office alone in Anya's absence. Peeling off first her jacket then pantyhose, she hit play on the answering machine and flopped on the lounge.

Dan Brody had already left three messages. Each one sounded more urgent and asked her to call him the moment she got back. She groaned and sat up, flipped open her mobile phone, wondering why he hadn't called on that. The black screen confirmed the battery was flat – again. She plugged it into the charger. Usually, Brody's secretary called if there were cases to consult on.

She dialled his mobile number. He picked up on the second ring.

'Dan, it's Anya returning your –'

'Thank God. Can you come right over? It's an emergency.'

For once, the lawyer's voice was quiet and almost unsure. She checked her watch. With traffic, she wouldn't get to his office before seven. Despite the hour, she was loath to refuse work from the busy defence lawyer. He had already kept her in enough private consultancy work to keep her business afloat, cope with the mortgage and pay child support for Ben. Ever since a colleague in his law firm had tried to ruin her professional reputation Brody had, as if to compensate, increased the workload his firm sent her way. The effect had been to make her a more desirable expert witness for other firms and an expansion of her consultancy work.

'Is this a new case?'

'I can't explain over the phone, but I'm at home. I'll leave the verandah light on.'

Anya hesitated. She had expected him to be calling from his office. After taking down the details of his address, she agreed reluctantly to go. As she was pulling her pantyhose back on, her fingernail ripped through the nylon. Bare legs with the skirt would have to do. Before heading out the door, she collected the examination bag and checked the downstairs windows locks.

An hour later, she turned into the exclusive Hunters Hill street, highly curious about what sort of emergency Dan Brody had that couldn't wait until office hours.

She didn't usually do house calls to lawyers, and it wasn't about to become a habit. One of his high-profile friends had to be in trouble. But what required a forensic physician in an emergency?

Brody's reluctance to explain over the phone had been uncharacteristic, as was his distress, both of which surprised her. If she were being honest, the call had been slightly unnerving. She wasn't completely sure why.

Brody's street had mansions set back amidst lush, well-lit

gardens. As she drove up the hill it was obvious that each home outdid the last in landscaped glory – and value. Either this part of the city managed a lot of rainfall, or water restrictions weren't imposed or followed. She stopped at the top of the hill outside a red-brick home with wraparound verandahs. Double-checking the address confirmed this was Brody's house.

She pulled the handbrake hard and stepped out of the car. The fragrant smell of damp grass in the night air made her sneeze. Floodlights showcased late-flowering wisteria over a large arbor, immaculate lawns and topiary hedges.

She pushed open the gate and entered, following a stone path towards an ornamental pond adorned with statues of cherubs. Foot-long goldfish swam beneath waterlilies, while a jacaranda tree provided glimpses of shadow from the bright floodlights.

A closer glance at the water feature made her uncomfortable. The inviting scene was a potential tragedy. The surface should have been covered with metal grating, preventing little faces from becoming submerged. It probably had never occurred to Brody because he didn't have kids, but even a toddler could access the gardens, with potentially devastating results. She made a mental note to mention it at an opportune moment.

Up the stairs, Anya took in the harbour view and drank in the fresh breeze from the verandah. She straightened her shirt, checked her hair in the glass adjacent to the front door and knocked.

A few moments later, Dan Brody opened the door. He towered over her, even taller than his six foot four with him standing inside, one step up.

'Thanks for coming.' He ushered her into the house and locked the door behind her with the chain bolt.

Anya began to feel uneasy. 'What's going on?' she said, moving back towards the door.

'I just don't want anyone walking in on us.'

'You're beginning to scare me.' She looked around for signs of anyone else in the house. 'Unbolt the door and we can talk.'

The lawyer put two open hands out in front of him. 'I'm so

sorry. That was thoughtless. I just meant that I wanted to talk to you privately and in complete confidence. There's someone else with a key and I don't want to be interrupted.'

Someone with a key? His latest society girlfriend, no doubt. Before Anya had left for overseas, she and Dan had shared a celebratory meal when a case of Dan's ended with the acquittal of a homeless man accused of murder. Anya's evidence had been instrumental in the verdict. That night, Dan had been attentive and sweet, but two months were a long time in his fast-paced world.

'Fine.'

Usually immaculate, Dan's untucked shirt and jeans were creased, as if they had been pulled straight from the laundry basket. A crepe bandage barely hung on a bruised ankle and foot.

'Does this have anything to do with the first-aid attempt on your foot?'

'Yes, sort of. I stepped on some floorboards and went right through them. Wasn't easy getting a size fourteen out of that hole.' He glanced down at his attempt to cover the injury, then reached out to open a pair of sliding wooden doors.

Anya followed and took in the room as he hobbled along. Most amazing was the room's centrepiece – a walnut grand piano, flawlessly polished.

All the wall space was occupied by bookshelves stacked with hardcovers and leather-bound books. It was Anya's idea of a dream room, only hers would have a set of drums taking pride of place next to the piano.

'I didn't know you were that much of a reader.'

'I'm not,' he said, sitting on a brown leather lounge near a marble fireplace.

'This was my parents' home until recently.'

Anya knew that Dan's mother had died and that his father was in a nursing home following a stroke, but very little else about his parents.

'My mother was a voracious reader. Anything from

82

philosophy and religion to world affairs. It always surprised me that crime fiction was her true guilty pleasure. She was also an accomplished writer and artist.'

'Your father?'

'A couple of weeks after Mum died, Dad had a massive stroke. We tried to keep him at home but he needed twenty-four hour nursing and the house and garden aren't wheelchair friendly. To be honest, I think he found it hard to be here without Mum.'

He flicked something minute off the arm of the lounge.

'Anyway, we moved him into a nursing home but he had another stroke and lost all speech. I didn't like the care he was getting so I moved him a couple of weeks ago.'

Anya felt more comfortable now they were discussing his family. She had not met Therese Brody, but had heard wonderful things about her philanthropy and work with indigenous literacy projects; she had obviously been an intelligent woman with a strong social conscience.

'Has he settled in?'

'I believe so. Where are my manners – can I get you a coffee?'

'No thanks. I am curious, though, what you wanted to see me about. Please don't say it's just to check your ankle.'

Despite the warmth of the room and seeing Brody in a new, almost refined light in his home, she didn't feel the visit was meant to be social, particularly if he had a new girlfriend. Another woman arriving home and getting the wrong idea was the last thing she wanted tonight.

Dan sat straight and ran both hands down the thighs of his jeans. 'Maybe I should just show you.'

He limped out of the room and returned with a faded wooden box, not much bigger than average shoe size. He held the object with almost outstretched arms, as if frightened of the contents. After looking around, he opted to place it on the carpeted floor then stepped away and sat on the stool with his back to the piano.

'This is what I called you about. I didn't know what else

to do. I mean, I got one hell of a shock when I found it a few hours ago.'

'Don't tell me it's a live rat.'

'Trust me, it isn't alive. The lid was sealed tight. I had to pry it open.'

Anya didn't like dead rats any more than live ones, but she slid off the lounge and onto the floor. Out of the corner of her eye she saw Brody stand and move further away. Whatever was inside really had him spooked.

She tentatively wiped some dust off the lid with the back of her hand and revealed a detailed marquetry design. 'This is beautiful craftsmanship,' she said, but her host was staring out the window. She couldn't imagine what was inside that could be so disturbing. Undoing the clasp, she flipped open the lid and lifted what felt like wax-paper wrapping. She quickly sat back on her haunches, unable to believe her eyes.

'Where did you find it?'

Brody didn't move. 'Under the floorboards in what was my parents' bedroom. I was rearranging the walk-in wardrobe when part of the old floor gave way. When I eventually yanked my ankle out, the box was right there.'

Anya studied the tiny dead form, curled up inside the small chamber. The miniature body lay in a foetal position, knees resting against the chin. There was no doubt. This was a fossil-ised human baby.

The pair remained in silence for a few moments.

'I could do with that coffee now,' Anya said, returning the lid and closing the latch. 'After I wash my hands.'

'Of course.'

Brody moved to the kitchen area with a glass conservatory overlooking more gardens. A granite island-bench dominated the area, with copper pots hanging from a chained metal grid above it. Dan obviously had no trouble reaching the utensils that were out of reach of most people.

His hands trembled as he loaded a small machine with a metal capsule and placed a demitasse cup, the only size small enough to fit, under the nozzle. The smell of rich coffee filled the air.

He pulled a carton of full-cream milk from a serving door in the stainless steel fridge and placed some in a steel mug adjacent to the machine. Within seconds, he poured frothy milk into a china mug and repeated the process.

Anya washed her hands in the sink and dried them with paper towel from a dispenser at the wall. The mug warmed her hands. She could appreciate the lawyer's anxiety at the find. Despite dealing with criminal trials, he had probably never seen a human body before, let alone experienced the shock of discovering one in his parents' wardrobe.

'Do you have any idea whose child it could be?'

He offered his guest a cane stool, which she accepted.

'This house has been in Dad's side of the family since it was built three generations ago. It was always passed on to the eldest son.'

'Was there ever any scandal about illegitimate pregnancies?'

Dan shook his head and washed out the used steel mug. Apart from fresh basil in a small vase, the benches were empty of clutter.

'Do we need to call crime scene? I mean, will they want to photograph the . . .'

'Possibly. I'll check with them, but it's not as uncommon as you might think. With garden renovations, it's not unheard of for someone to discover tiny remains, particularly given the number of stillbirths and backyard abortions in the past.'

Brody nodded but didn't appear relieved in any way.

Anya excused herself to make the call. Moments later she returned, with a swab kit from the bag in her car.

'I just need to take some shots of the wardrobe with my mobile. I'll take the box with me if you like, and take it to the morgue. There'll have to be a post-mortem.'

'Of course. I'll show you where I found it.'

'I should probably take a DNA swab from you now, if you don't mind, for comparison to the child.'

Dan leant against the bench. 'It . . . it isn't mine.'

'I'm not suggesting that. We know it's old from the type of box and condition. But it would help us work out whether the child was born to someone in your family.'

'My grandparents always had servants. My grandfather had a reputation for being quite the ladies' man, before and during his marriage.'

The irony of his own reputation with women appeared lost on Dan Brody.

Anya knew it wouldn't have been the first time that a servant was impregnated by her boss and the results hidden. But to hide a dead child in the wardrobe wasn't the wisest move. It would have made more sense to throw the remains away or bury them.

She removed the cotton-tipped swab from her kit and Brody bent forward, allowing her to scrape the inside of his cheek. She felt his breath on her face as she removed the swab and returned it to its sealed container.

Dan reached forward enough to brush her hand.

'I'm just . . . well, grateful you're here. I didn't know who else to call.'

Anya felt a surge of blood to her face. She had never seen Brody like this and had never imagined that he could be so vulnerable. At work he was always in control and his arrogance was incomparable, even in the egotistical domain of law. Then again, if anything could rattle a person, an unidentified dead body in the house was it. His girlfriend would no doubt comfort him soon enough. For a brief moment, she felt jealous of the new woman.

With a permanent marker from her kit, she labelled the specimen before returning to the drawing room. Brody stood in the doorway, keeping his distance.

Anya bent down and collected the tiny body in its makeshift coffin. She hoped for its sake, and for Brody's, that the baby had died of natural causes.

12

The following afternoon Anya removed the wax-paper covering, held her breath and slowly lifted the remains from the box. Any uneven pressure could break off limbs. It was a wonder the body had survived the damaged floorboards and the subsequent car journey.

The white form seemed more delicate against the cold steel dissecting table.

Jeff Sales had been finishing off some paperwork and greeted Anya with something akin to excitement at her find. He was keen to examine the remains as soon as possible.

'It's an adipocere all right, not that I doubted you.'

Unlike the normal process of decomposition, this skin and soft tissue had undergone transformation. What once was skin was now a hard waxy substance – adipocere – most obvious over the buttocks, abdomen and cheeks, the fattiest areas of the body.

'It's a reasonable size and it's possible that it was delivered full-term.' Jeff switched on the overhead surgical lights. 'What do we know about it?'

'Only that it was found in a wardrobe, under the floorboards in an old wooden box. At the moment we have no idea who gave birth or how it got there, or whether it ever lived to take a breath.'

'So we're looking to see if any signs of homicide are present.' He moved the light directly over the abdomen. 'Remarkable, I think we can presume it's a female judging by the genitalia. I've never seen anything quite this preserved before. There's a stump of an umbilicus so at one stage someone cut the cord, post delivery.'

Determining whether or not the baby had taken a breath was not that easy. If the lungs had ever inflated, they were now collapsed and semidecomposed.

'Is there a chance you can rehydrate the umbilical stump and see histologically whether the child was freshly born or a few days old?'

'That's an excellent thought, I'll take some biopsies.'

The bright light highlighted splits to areas of the infant's skin. It would be difficult to determine whether they had occurred during the adipocere formation or were due to blunt-force trauma to the abdomen, thighs and upper arms.

John Zimmer wandered in with a female crime scene officer, both in their work overalls.

'The secretary said you were here.'

Zimmer had a sixth sense for unusual deaths. As part of his job, he frequently attended autopsies. 'Thought we'd get the heads-up on whether this one will be ours.'

'We still don't know whether the death was suspicious or not.'

Regardless, Jeff Sales invited them both in. 'The more the merrier, I always say.'

Zimmer dwarfed his younger colleague. 'This is Milo Sharpe, she's just transferred from down south.'

After introductions, Milo stood, hands behind her back.

'You have an unusual name,' Jeff said, glancing up over his half-glasses. 'What's the derivation?'

'It's a nickname. I have below average motor skills which came to the attention of fellow officers here, before I arrived.' She seemed to ignore Zimmer.

The senior CSO rocked on his heels. 'Well, it is our job to investigate and scrutinise.'

'Why Milo?' Anya dared ask. The rationale behind the name had to be obscure and less than complimentary.

'On January 26 I attended a car accident in the rain.' She spoke in a monotone as if tired of repeating the story. 'My gloves were wet and my superior threw me the car keys. I failed to catch them and they slid down the drain. I spent the next fifty-four minutes successfully extricating them.'

Milo, who didn't offer her real name, stopped without further explanation and turned her attention to the tools the pathologist had laid out for the post-mortem.

'Get it?' Zimmer said.

Anya raised her eyebrows.

'Venus de Milo. The armless statue. You've got to HAND it to her. It's a classic.' He grinned.

Apparently the officer endowed with the name didn't agree.

'It could be worse,' Zimmer added. '"Showbags" liked his nickname until he realised what it meant. He looks great but is full of shit.'

Anya hoped she hadn't acquired a nickname she was yet to learn about.

Jeff Sales refocused. 'What we have here, detectives, is an adipocere. It's a form of preservation.'

Milo's face was now centimetres from the table, studying the body. 'Is it a cultural phenomenon?'

'Good question. We're not talking mummification through embalming. This sort of preservation is mostly seen in bodies that have been immersed in water or left in humid or damp environments. It occurs where fat is present.'

'How?' Milo spoke without sounding either interested or bored.

'Bacterial enzymes and body enzymes alter the free fatty acids but don't cause the normal signs of decomposition, like bloating and discolouration. These remains had to have been protected from insects, or the story would be completely different.'

Obviously the box had been well sealed, as Dan Brody had described. The wax-paper wrapping would have contributed to the process.

The technician arrived with a portable X-ray machine and slid an X-ray plate gently beneath the fragile form. He had only one lead gown for protection, the one he was wearing.

Milo slowly circled the table, as if looking for clues. 'Who would just stick a baby in a box and hide it? The mother had to be mentally ill.'

Anya looked up. 'Not necessarily. We don't know how long the child had been in the box or how young the mother was. That box could have been in the wardrobe for decades. And if you think about it, babies buried in gardens weren't that unusual even a few years ago. Unmarried mothers were ostracised and received no government support. Backyard abortions were rampant. Some of the mothers were even sent to prison-like institutions or reform schools.'

The pathologist stepped back and ushered them out of the suite into the corridor while X-rays were taken.

'And,' Anya continued, 'in the past stillborns were buried in nameless mass graves or just thrown out with other hospital refuse. Maybe this mother loved the child and didn't want to see that happen.'

'Logically,' Milo added, 'landscapers and home gardeners should find these babies.'

It was unclear whether the CSO was being flippant or serious.

Jeff checked inside the room that it was safe to return and ushered them all back inside. 'There are other variables to consider. Foetal bones are far less resilient. They're relatively low in calcium so dissolve quite rapidly, particularly if there's lime in the soil. The most anyone would find is a couple of small bones they might assume are bird remains.'

'Any specific reason you're doing the X-rays?' Zimmer checked his watch as if he had to be somewhere else.

'Routine. The bones are so fragile, fractures don't necessarily suggest trauma, but if they're intact, it helps exclude significant blunt-force injury.'

'Is there any way of proving if the child ever took a breath outside the womb?'

Zimmer was asking if they could prove that the child had ever been legally alive. If it had, homicide could not be excluded; homicide had no statute of limitations. Their job would be a lot simpler if the child could be proven to have been stillborn. And Anya could let Brody know there would be no further investigation.

'I won't know until I examine the internal organs, which could be in any condition. If there's a chance, I'll test the stomach contents for milk. But after who knows how long, I won't lift your hopes. You can take the box with you, to examine it for blood, perhaps date it. Anything that can help with an approximate time frame.'

The female CSO had noticed it on the bench. 'Do you mean the chocolate box?'

Zimmer looked surprised by his new recruit.

'How do you know what it is?'

Milo stood, hands behind back again. 'My father collects boxes, amongst other things. This one would have originally had sweets inside. It should still smell like chocolate caramel.'

She took a long sniff. 'But it doesn't. It was a limited edition put out by an English company named Molly's Originals. My father will have the year recorded in his catalogue. From memory, it was late 1960s. He makes records of everything he owns.'

A limited edition box could pin down a possible year the baby was placed there.

'How sure are you that it's exactly the same?' Anya asked.

Milo replied, matter-of-fact, 'I have a photographic memory and an IQ of one hundred and forty-five.'

The comment was met with silence. Obviously, the CSO was capable of dropping more than just keys at an accident scene. The monotone speech pattern and lack of eye contact made Anya wonder whether she had a mild case of autism, perhaps Asperger's syndrome. It would explain the computer-like approach to facts, limited social skills and completely absent sense of humour. Then again, she was similar to any number of university professors or MENSA members who chose not to bother with 'trivialities' like interpersonal skills.

Obsessive-compulsive behaviours like box collecting could even run in her family.

Anya excused herself before Jeff Sales began the internal examination. Once she could have performed the procedure herself, but since becoming a mother she had found child cases especially difficult. Not having to stay made it easier. John Zimmer instructed Milo to observe while he headed upstairs.

'Milo takes a bit of getting used to,' he said as they left the suite. 'She's like an encyclopedia but you need more than that if you're going to last in this game. Put it this way, you'd never accuse her of being too sensitive.'

Anya almost laughed. John Zimmer was complaining about someone being insensitive. She would never have thought it possible. 'Give her a chance. I agree that she's unusual, but you took some getting used to as well.' At the elevator, Anya pressed the up button.

'I always thought women were more aware of people's emotions. I can't risk taking her upstairs for the interview. You're sitting in?'

Anya had intended to check on Sophie Goodwin but hadn't heard about any interview. 'You've lost me.'

'I assumed you knew. Sophie's defied all the odds and woken up. The detectives are on their way to get a statement.'

13

Kate Farrer and Hayden Richards were outside the ICU, along with a uniformed officer who stood guard.

'The father's asked for you. I was about to call,' Kate said. 'I didn't want to waste your time if she was drifting in and out of consciousness.'

Anya wondered why Mr Goodwin had asked for her when they had never even met. It gave her the opportunity to make sure that, if awake, Sophie was well enough to be interviewed. If not, she wouldn't hesitate to tell the detectives to come back when the teenager was more coherent and up to being questioned.

With Sophie's physically and emotionally frail state, she couldn't afford a setback like being upset by a grilling. She had also been hypotensive for a prolonged period due to blood loss, and the long-term effects on her brain still hadn't been determined.

'We've got a video camera on standby and a room to view from down the corridor. Just let us know when we're ready to start the interview.'

'Wait,' Anya said. 'If she's only just woken up, she could be disoriented and confused. Add to that, she might have just remembered what happened and may be too upset to—'

'We understand that,' Kate interjected. 'But she needs to help us catch whoever did this as soon as possible. If she can just give us an ID, that's all we need for an arrest warrant. Then we'll be happy to back off until we get the okay.'

Anya appreciated the urgency, especially given the brutality and violence involved in the attacks, but Sophie's wellbeing was the priority. Causing distress and setting back her recovery wouldn't bring her sister back. As with the doctors treating Sophie, having examined the young woman Anya had taken on a role as her advocate. That was her duty of care. The doctor-patient relationship always took precedence over any duty she had to the police. Even if the detectives didn't like it, they had to abide by any medical decision for now. She decided to see how Sophie was for herself.

Inside the specialised unit, Anya scrubbed her hands at a sink by the door and pulled on a white gown. Sixteen curtained cubicles contained patients. Three private rooms existed for patients requiring isolation.

Sucking noises from breathing ventilators filled the communal area around the central nurses' station. Occasional alarms beeped and nurses calmly checked the monitors before resetting the offending machines. A glance at the whiteboard on the wall told Anya which bed Sophie was in.

Usually reserved to quarantine infectious patients, room eighteen kept the teenager safe from prying eyes and opportunistic photographers.

A male nurse greeted her. 'Can I help you?'

'I'm Doctor Crichton. Anya. Apparently Mr Goodwin asked me to see him.'

'He did. He wants to thank you for the holy medal you gave his daughter – he's convinced it saved her life. Frankly, to have survived those injuries, something bigger than medicine had to be on her side.'

He gestured towards a single room close to the nurses' desk. Through the open door she could see the figure of a man sitting, face hunched over the bed as if in prayer.

'She's still ventilated but has woken for a few minutes at a time.'

'Does she know where she is?'

'She's not panicking or trying to fight the ventilator and seems to recognise her father. We're keeping the analgesia up because of her wounds and that'll make her drowsy.

Endotracheal tube will stay until that neck wound heals, so long conversations might have to wait.'

Anya took a breath and entered the room.

Mr Goodwin sat in the same clothes he had been wearing the morning his daughter had been brought in. Wrapped around his shoulders was a blue hospital-issue cotton rug.

An airconditioning duct pulsed cold air right on to the bed and Anya felt the chill in the room. The father stood but didn't let go of his daughter's hand.

A nurse sat at a mobile desk covered in a broadsheet filled with details about oxygen levels, urine output, fluid intake and blood test results.

'Mr Goodwin, I'm Anya Crichton, the forensic physician.'

The man let go of his daughter and wrapped both hands around Anya's.

'Please call me Ned. Thank you for coming to see Sophie. I heard you've been checking on her but were respectful of our privacy.'

Anya didn't have the heart to explain that she hadn't known how to face him, and with his surviving daughter unlikely to live, she had simply avoided any meeting as long as she could.

'How's she doing?'

Sophie lay semi-upright in the bed, covers pulled up to her armpits. The blood pressure and heart rate monitors showed stable signs, as did the pulse oximeter on her finger. Anya noticed the girl's petite hands and realised how hard she had fought to stave off her attacker. Every nail had been broken, but someone, probably one of the nurses, had filed them as a less obvious reminder. Defence injuries on her arms were covered with bandages, but she seemed even smaller and more fragile than the morning in emergency.

The medal and chain were wrapped around one wrist, placed carefully so as not to disturb intravenous equipment. Not exactly protocol for a unit obsessed with infection control and sterility, but the staff had made an exception for Sophie.

On the mobile drawers sat a photo of the sisters, presumably with their late mother. The life in each one sparkled in the image.

'She woke up and squeezed my hand a while ago, then went back to sleep. Every now and then she looks up to make sure I'm still here.' Ned reached over and stroked his daughter's forehead. She opened her eyes and he beamed.

'Darling, I'm not going anywhere. You're safe and a lovely doctor's come to see you.'

The girl's eyes moved to Anya. Her mouth moved and it looked like she was saying 'Hello'.

'The special Saint Jude medal came from one of the ambulance officers who saved your life. I just made sure it stayed with you, which I can see it has.'

'And for that we're grateful. The priest gave the last rites and we were told to expect the worst, and now look at Sophie. She's a real fighter, this one.'

His lower lip trembled. This was a man struggling to maintain any semblance of control.

'Thank you for what you did when she came in. I know you work with the police. The emergency doctors and surgeons told us how gentle you were with our Soph.'

Suddenly, tears filled his eyes and the grief overcame him. Anya moved forward and he grabbed her tightly. Her body resonated with each heave and sob.

The nurse moved slowly towards them and put her arms around Ned's shoulders.

'Let it out, it's about time you did. You've been through hell, but Sophie's doing better, you can take a break now.' She began to lead him towards the door, and turned back to Anya.

'Doctor will stay with Sophie while we have a five-minute break. We'll be right back if they need us.'

Like a child, Ned Goodwin accepted being led away, too exhausted and wrung-out to argue.

Anya nodded and sat in the chair by the bed.

Sophie opened her eyes and focused on her visitor for a few seconds before closing them again.

'Can you hear me? Your dad's just gone outside for a couple of minutes. I'll stay with you for as long as you like. My name is Anya.'

The girl licked her dry, cracked lips. A glass of water and straw sat on the bedside table. After checking the chart to make sure fluids were permitted, Anya offered Sophie a sip.

She responded by sucking up a small amount and letting it spill on her lips. Despite her youth, the girl had a strong face. Anya's mother would have called the square-shaped chin a sign of a stubborn child. Judging by Sophie's obvious determination to survive, the description would have been apt.

Anya offered some more water but her patient pulled a little to the side, opened her eyes and mouthed something. The first time it wasn't clear. Then it seemed obvious.

'Rachel.'

Anya felt her stomach tighten. Was Sophie asking where her sister was? Did she have any memory of what had happened?

It was impossible to read in the girl's eyes.

The grip on her hand tightened and Anya sat forward.

'Sophie, do you remember what happened? Why you came to hospital?'

Her spare hand reached for the breathing tube inserted into her windpipe and groped the bandages covering her neck.

The tired eyes closed again but the grip on Anya's hand remained.

Part of Anya hoped Sophie would never remember the vicious rape and stabbings, or the sound of her sister's dying screams.

'If you're tired, we can talk later. You need to rest.'

Sophie opened her eyes wide and the ventilator began to alarm. She seemed to be having trouble breathing. Anya cradled her forward while the male nurse hurried in. Snapping on gloves, he pulled out a sterile suction tube and inserted it through the tracheostomy opening.

Sophie coughed and wheezed as the nurse withdrew the tube. 'Just a bit of mucus,' he said. 'It happens now and then.

There you go.' The suction tube came out. 'You'll breathe easier now.'

He smiled, collected the mess and left Anya still supporting the girl in bed. Sophie's hand pulled on Anya's shirt collar until they were face to face.

'What is it?' Anya almost whispered.

The young girl licked her cracked lips and whispered.

'I remember.'

14

Outside ICU, Kate paced. Liz Gould stood texting on her phone while John Zimmer sat on one of the waiting room lounges, legs stretched in front and eyes closed.

'Sophie's awake,' Anya said, 'and she says that she remembers.'

'So we can do the interview?'

Anya held up her hands. 'She's barely conscious and keeps dozing off.'

'But she does remember that night.' Liz Gould clicked shut her phone and stood.

Zimmer opened his eyes.

'The breathing tube is in her neck and she can't speak properly. Her vocal cords are out of commission, but she is able to whisper. It just takes a bit more time and patience to understand. She'll tire very quickly.'

Kate shoved her hands in her pockets. 'We don't care if she blinks yes or no answers. We just want to find out what happened and whether she can ID whoever did this.'

Anya was concerned about pushing the young woman but the police needed to act quickly if they were to find any evidence of the attack on his clothes or in his car or home. If the examination she did had failed to yield firm physical evidence, they had little to go on, especially if Sophie didn't know her attackers.

'I'll talk to the father and the intensivist and be back. You might as well stretch your legs, get a snack. This might take a few minutes.' Anya wanted to make sure Sophie was up to the interview.

'We're fine.' Kate made it clear they weren't going anywhere.

A few minutes later, Anya returned. 'You can have a few minutes, but please, don't push her. Sophie's incredibly weak. The nurse is easing back on the analgesia so she'll be a bit more awake, but if she gets any pain, we'll have to stop.'

'We?' Liz asked.

Anya looked around the group. 'The father asked me to stay.'

Zimmer retrieved a digital recorder from his pocket. 'I'll try not to be too intrusive. The audio visual guys can set up for a more formal version once she's stronger.'

'Let's do this.'

The detectives entered the unit, washed their hands and greeted Mr Goodwin.

The nurse had brought some more chairs in, and suddenly the room felt crowded, almost claustrophobic. Sophie looked at each in turn and nodded.

Liz Gould took the lead. 'I know this is very difficult but we have to ask you a few questions. Anything you can tell us, no matter how small a detail, could help.'

Sophie nodded. Anya sat on one side of her, with Ned on the other. The nurse stood in the back of the room with John Zimmer.

'Do you know who did this to you?' Liz spoke gently, like a mother promising to look after an upset child.

'No,' she whispered. 'Never saw them before.' The machine breathed in, then out.

'Them? How many people were there that night at your house?'

The teenager closed her eyes. Her right arm twitched as she tried to move her hand. She showed three fingers against the blanket.

'Were there three men?'

Sophie nodded.

Anya swallowed. The sisters had no chance of fighting off three men at once. Across the room Kate's eyes were studying the only living witness.

Liz continued. 'Can you tell us what they looked like?'

'One had brown hair. Short. Cold dark eyes,' she whispered. 'And strong hands . . . Tried to fight.'

Anya touched her arm. 'We all understand how hard you tried. You fought for your life with everything you had, which is why you're here now.'

The grieving father stared at the wall. His hand gripped Sophie's but he couldn't look at his daughter when she spoke. Rachel's name had not been spoken, but remained on everyone's mind.

The nurse disappeared and returned with a plastic mug full of tea for Ned. 'I put in extra sugar. You need to keep up your energy,' she said. He appeared grateful for the temporary distraction.

Anya offered Sophie some more water, which she sipped.

Kate sat forward in her chair. 'Can you remember anything that could help us identify them? Tattoos, anything special about the haircuts, any distinguishing features?'

'Short hair, like in the army.'

Liz encouraged, 'You're doing really well. We know how tired you are, but we have just a few more questions. Did any of the men have a beard or a moustache? Maybe a scar or birthmark?'

Sophie's eyes widened. 'One had a mole. On his chin.' The heart monitor crept up and the blood pressure level rose. 'The one who took Rachel . . . with his brother.'

The detectives shared looks. Brothers, one with a mole. Sophie had to be describing Gary Harbourn and two of his brothers. They always hunted in a pack. Anya remembered seeing them clean-shaven the night of their release. The same night they had the street party. The same night the Goodwin girls were attacked. One had a mole on his chin.

'How do you know they were brothers?' Kate urged.

'One said their mum . . . would . . .'

She seemed to be fatiguing, struggling to get the words out.

'Would skin them if she found out.'

The monitor alarmed and the nurse moved forward. 'I think she's had enough for now.'

Sophie's eyes flickered then closed again, as if she could no longer keep them open.

'You have done a brilliant job,' Liz reassured her. 'We're going to catch the men who did this.'

Mr Goodwin held the mug without letting go of his daughter's hand.

Anya stood, to give the nurse space, and the detectives filed out.

As they stepped outside the unit, Kate's phone rang. She answered it on the second tone. 'We've just spoken to her and you won't believe—'

A few moments later, she clicked off her phone.

'That was Hayden. One of the pubic hairs collected from Sophie when she came in got a hit. It didn't have the root attached, so only one type of DNA, apparently. A few years ago, Noelene Harbourn was arrested for prostitution after bashing one of her johns, so her DNA's on file. Hayden says the hair has to have come from someone in her family.'

Anya explained, 'Mitochondrial DNA is different from the DNA inherited from both parents. It is only passed on from the mother. The problem is, mDNA isn't specific to an individual. What it can do is confirm that the owner was born to children from a specific maternal line.'

'Exactly,' Kate said. 'The hair has to be from one of the Harbourn boys.'

'Not necessarily.' Anya tried to make it clearer. 'Mitochondrial DNA may only be passed on by mothers, but that means the grandmother shares the same as her daughter. Males don't pass it on to their children, but they have it in their genetic make-up.'

'Yeah, but there's no question that it's Harbourn DNA,' Kate argued.

'The problem is that anyone born from the same family of women will have that same genetic code. Noelene Harbourn's mother, sisters, grandmother, maternal aunts, and any of their offspring. You could be looking at a large number of people descended from the same woman.'

The three police stood dejected. That meant they had nine children, not to mention how many cousins, second cousins who could have been in the Goodwin house that night.

Liz spoke first. 'I'll start with the family tree. Maybe we'll prove Darwin's theory and find out the rest died from natural selection.'

'All right,' Kate said. 'Thanks to our witness, we have reason to suspect Gary Harbourn was at the scene and the physical evidence matches the family DNA profile. That's got to be enough for a search warrant.'

'Let's hope a judge agrees.' Liz Gould had already begun to make the call. 'We can hit them first sign of light tomorrow.'

15

Noelene Harbourn opened the door in a pink chenille gown and knotted the tie at her waist.

'What the hell do you bastards want now?'

The verandah light was still shining. 'Do you know what fucking time it is? This is more bloody harassment.'

She turned to go back inside.

'If you're not off this property in one minute, I'm calling my lawyer *and* letting the dogs out.'

Kate assumed they were the same thing. The big-mouthed matriarch was the reason they were here and they had family DNA to prove it. Today she bore no resemblance to the suburban mother who flirted with the media while handing out home-made favours.

Liz Gould stood her ground. 'You might want to see this first. It's perfectly legal. A search warrant for this house and surrounding property.'

The grey-haired mother flattened her unruly hair with her hands and turned around.

'You've got nothing on me or my boys. Why don't you just piss off and catch a real criminal.'

Kate turned to the uniformed police in the marked car and waved them to come in. The older woman snatched the warrant and studied it.

'This is bullshit,' she snarled. 'My boys have been with me since they got out of jail.'

'Is that so?' Liz pushed past and led the search party inside. 'We have reason to suggest they can assist us in our enquiries.'

'Whatever this is, it's a set-up. Don't any of you move. I'm getting my lawyer.'

One of the uniforms began videoing the scene. 'Ma'am, I'll be taping the search and you're welcome to observe, but you are not permitted to interfere or remove any items from the house.'

She pushed past to the corridor off the main room. 'Gary! Kids, get up! The pigs have a search warrant.'

A slow stream of bleary-eyed faces appeared. The youngest two looked like they'd slept in their clothes. Of the nine offspring, supposedly seven lived at home in between sojourns in prison.

Kate counted heads. So far four males stood in the hallway along with two young girls, aged about ten and twelve.

'We've got a runner. He's jumping the back fence,' Liz called from further inside the house.

Gary, the one with the mole on his chin, was missing.

A uniformed officer raced out the back door and easily vaulted the paling fence in chase.

'Why did Gary bolt?' Kate demanded.

Noelene Harbourn puffed on a cigarette. 'Got me stumped. You people have harassed him enough, probably thought you'd plant something on him if he hung around long enough.'

She took a slow, deep inhalation then blew smoke in Kate's direction.

'Maybe he had an appointment to get to. I've got my hands full with this lot. I can't be expected to keep track of every child every minute.'

Good to know, Kate thought. If the matriarch admitted that in court, it could blow holes in any alibi that claimed she knew where the boys were at all times.

The team searched under beds, between sheets, anywhere that Rachel's missing underwear could be hidden as a trophy of the kill. Kate checked inside the washing machine before pulling out the cord and moving it half a metre forward. Nothing had been hidden underneath either.

She moved to the bathroom and ran an angled dental mirror

in the narrow space between the toilet cistern and the wall. Next step was removing its lid and making sure nothing was hidden in the water reservoir. Rust stains marked the bowl.

Liz Gould moved around the walls with a stud finder, looking for signs of metal behind the plasterboard. It wouldn't be the first time criminals had stashed weapons and evidence in the space between walls. The uniformed officers examined the rubbish bins while another checked the outside garage.

The family milled about in the lounge room, remarkably unperturbed by the intrusion. Kate assumed the house had been searched numerous times over the years, which meant the chances of finding anything to connect them to Rachel's murder were pretty remote. The Harbourn brothers would have to be unbelievably stupid to bring evidence back to the house.

Then again, she thought, they were serial criminals who'd been caught too many times to remember.

Kate learnt a lot about the house inhabitants from a search, but mostly she saw squalor and complete apathy to house cleaning. From the state of the kitchen, with dirty plates piled high on the benches, grease stains behind the stove, it was a surprise that Noelene Harbourn's biscuits hadn't poisoned the journalists.

She checked inside and behind the stand-alone stove and oven, the fridge and freezer and inside every cupboard and drawer. She collected two carving knives for examination. The officer filmed the find.

John Zimmer arrived with his latest sidekick, Milo, carrying the crime scene equipment behind him.

'We're here with the luminol.' He squinted through puffy eyes. The early hour wasn't affecting only the Harbourns.

'Going to clear out the cockroaches while you're here?' Noelene hovered behind them. 'I'll sue if you damage my expensive china,' she announced, then cackled.

Nothing in the house looked cared for, or worth much.

'Love what you've done with the place,' Zimmer replied.

'The peeling wallpaper is all the rage again. Remind me to get the name of your decorator.'

'Fucking smart-arse,' she muttered.

Seemingly oblivious to the banter, Milo indicated that they would begin.

'Ma'am, we're going to ask your family to step back into the bedroom while we spray parts of this room with luminol. We're looking for traces of blood and need to darken the room.'

'No one moves. My lawyer's on his way. He'll be here any minute.'

'I'm afraid he'll have to wait outside as well, ma'am, civilians in darkened rooms is against occupational health and safety regulations.'

Noelene Harbourn stared at the CSO. 'Health regulations? Now that's priceless. Where the hell did you beam down from?'

'Sorry to cut short this little chitchat, but we've got work to do,' Zimmer said, and headed for the first bedroom. Liz Gould joined them. The family moved into the corridor while Milo examined the lounge room.

After about ten minutes, Zimmer emerged with a bag containing something. 'Two shirts and a singlet in the wardrobe had a hit.'

Maybe the Harbourns were more stupid than they had thought.

As they moved on to the next room, the uniformed officer returned through the front door, accompanying Gary Harbourn, who was dressed only in red underpants.

Kate folded her arms. 'Why did you run?'

'It's a nice morning. Felt like a jog.'

If he did kill Rachel, he wasn't remotely fazed about being caught.

'In your underwear, without shoes, over the back fence?'

'I'm a spontaneous kind of guy,' he grinned.

'Good to know,' Kate said and stepped closer, as if confiding in him. ''Cause impulsive people tend to leave evidence at crime scenes. Where were you the night of the fifteenth?'

Gary didn't react. The arrogance and smugness was

unbelievable. If he was at the Goodwin house that night, he was facing a murder charge and knew it.

Noelene Harbourn moved forward. 'All the children were home with me. That was the night they got out of prison.'

The same day Giverny Hart died. Kate tightened the grip on her own arms. 'I thought you had a street party. You mean to say that none of you left the house that night?' She had seen the news footage of them in the street celebrating Giverny's death. So would a jury.

'No, but they stayed on the street, and I can produce at least ten people who can say exactly the same thing.'

'I'll be needing their names,' she said and pulled out her notebook.

Noelene rattled off the names of her other children, who remained silent in the lounge room. Including her, that made seven family members who would give Gary an alibi.

Kate knew that's why prosecuting them had been so difficult. So far, the family bond had been unbreakable, even if it meant serving time in prison for a crime a sibling committed – a perverse honour system for the utterly dishonourable.

Two hours later they had just about finished the search without finding anything else. Frustrated, Kate took one last look, in case they'd missed something – anything – that could incriminate the killers. The place was deteriorating, but Gary's room was worse than the others. Dirty fingermarks covered and surrounded every light switch, but in his room, the power points at floor level had scratches in the paint around them. She called Liz, who ran her stud finder around it.

It buzzed, as if metal was behind.

Kate pulled out her pocketknife, knelt down and levered off the cover. In the recess behind, she carefully reached in, and felt the plastic bag. She slowly pulled it out and held it up in almost disbelief. Inside were a knife and a pair of women's underpants.

Liz Gould used the dental mirror and shone a torch inside. 'There's another bag.' Inside were two hand guns and boxes of ammunition, all stuffed into the secret hideaway.

Rechecking the other power points revealed various quantities of hash and tablets in sealed plastic bags.

Kate held up the stash and stared at the faces of the males in the lounge room. Gary was definitely at the Goodwin house, Sophie had confirmed it. But which other family members took part in the rapes and killing?

They all stood defiant. Despite the evidence, the Harbourns were sticking together.

16

Anya pulled the document from the fax machine. Jeff Sales had completed his report on the fossilised baby.

She switched on the desk lamp, sat and read. The internal organs had undergone some degree of deterioration but it had been possible to biopsy sections of liver, brain, stomach, heart and kidney. Understandably, after many years and no history to go by, it was difficult to establish much about the cause of death. However, there appeared to be no evidence of physical trauma to the skeletal remains.

The attempt to collect milk from the stomach had been unsuccessful. So it wasn't possible to establish whether the baby had lived long enough to feed. One section of the report immediately caught Anya's attention.

Behind the left eye was an unidentified retro-orbital mass. It was unclear whether or not it extended from the brain tissue given the state of internal deterioration. X-rays revealed minor asymmetry of the orbit, with thinner bone on that side. Histology could take weeks to complete, given the fragile state and special fixative processes required to make a definitive diagnosis under the circumstances.

It appeared the infant had some form of intracranial tumour, which could well have been the cause of death.

To be noticeable on gross examination, the tumour had to have been significant. In that case, probability was, the baby had died of natural causes. She may never have taken a breath.

At least Dan Brody would be spared a homicide investigation involving someone in his family. The mystery of whose baby it was remained, but the answer was now academic. There would be no police involvement or public coronial inquest. She reached for the phone to call him when a new page arrived through the fax.

DNA analysis from the private testing facility confirmed the remains were those of a female. The DNA provided by Dan Brody bore similarities to that of the sampled remains. That wasn't surprising if his grandfather had had an illegitimate child.

The next sentence explained in more detail. Mr Brody and the remains shared mitochondrial DNA. In other words, they both had the same mother, aunt or grandmother. One of them had carried a child and hidden its dead body in a box in the wardrobe, and if Milo was right about the age of the wooden box, it had to have been Dan's mother.

Anya wasn't sure how to explain that to Dan. He spoke of his mother as if she were a saint, and had mentioned his parents were childhood sweethearts – first and only loves.

DNA may have proven a different story.

She rubbed her temples and dialled Brody's number.

Half an hour later he pulled up in his red Ferrari. Only Brody would personalise his numberplate with LAW4L, as if the car didn't attract enough attention on its own. The sound of big band music blaring from the speakers let her know he had arrived. Thankfully, for the neighbours' sake, he had chosen to lower the bass levels.

She poured two glasses from a bottle of red wine and answered the door. Her neck began to itch from the hivelike rash she got every time she was nervous.

'Thanks for coming,' she said, and ushered him in.

'Couldn't keep me away, that is if the body is still at the morgue.' He quickly glanced around and Anya wondered which of them was more uncomfortable.

'I've poured a glass of wine if you'd like.'

'That would be great. It's been a long day in court.'

When Anya returned from the kitchen, Dan was holding a picture of her son, Ben. 'He's really growing.'

Ben was and she couldn't wait to see him the following Friday and hear about the rest of the trip. She suddenly remembered the bookcase still in pieces upstairs. It would have to wait.

Dan took off his tailored jacket and draped it lining side out on the end of the lounge. He accepted the wine and sat. 'How are you and your ex-husband getting on?'

'One of the cases I worked on over the last few weeks involved a cruiseliner, and as a thankyou the company flew Martin and Ben over for a holiday.'

Dan looked almost disappointed.

'Ben stayed in my cabin and Martin did his own thing in the day. We'd meet up for dinner for Ben's sake, but nothing's changed. Martin still has a lot of growing up to do.'

'Sorry to hear that.' He studied the colour of the drink before taking a sip. 'You need someone who's on the same level. I mean in terms of age and maturity.'

Anya was never sure how to take Dan's personal comments. What had started out like a compliment ended up sounding as though she were matronly.

'Are you saying I'm old before my time?'

He sniffed the top of the glass. 'No, of course not. I just meant—'

Seeing a verbose lawyer tongue-tied made her smile. 'It's okay. Did you tell your girlfriend about the box?'

This time it was the lawyer's turn to blush.

'Not yet. I don't know if I want to, to be honest. We met while you were away and things happened so quickly. But there isn't the trust there yet that comes from really knowing someone. I don't feel I can trust her the way I can you.' He took a sip. 'I mean, she really wants to make this work and I owe her that. Guess I need to give it time.'

She felt the rash on her neck redden. 'Would you like to read Jeff Sales's report or just get the summary?'

Dan sat forward and pulled a handkerchief from his pocket and placed it on the coffee table. Anya had never felt the need for coasters on cheap furniture, but appreciated the courtesy.

He placed his glass on top. 'I'll read and you can translate if necessary. By the way, this place is really nice and this couch is far more comfortable than mine. Want to swap?'

Anya shook her head; although a leather sofa did have appeal compared to her second-hand lounge, she had to admit that sinking into this one took the edge off a long day. She handed him the envelope in which she'd placed copies of the post-mortem results, minus the DNA profile. She sat close enough to track the words as he read.

It took a few minutes for him to comment.

'The baby died of some kind of cancer? Nothing suspicious?'

Anya sat back and folded her arms. 'That's what it looks like. There's no need for an inquest.'

He breathed out. 'It's kind of sad, but it is good news, under the circumstances. Thanks for doing what you have. I owe you.'

He leant back and locked his hands behind his head. 'As far as I know, my dad's father had six kids and neither they nor my cousins have any kind of hereditary diseases to speak of. The old man died of lung cancer after smoking fifty a day for most of his life.'

Anya rubbed her neck. The only way to tell him was to just give him all the facts.

'The DNA sample showed you and the baby, a little girl, are related, but it isn't through your grandfather. You share the same mitochondrial DNA.'

He didn't react.

'Dan, mitochondrial DNA only comes from the mother's line. What I'm trying to say is that the baby had to be from your own mother's line. It could be from women on your mother's side – cousins, for example.'

'That can't be right,' he said. 'My mother was adopted. She was orphaned in England during the war. Apparently my grandparents on Mum's side weren't able to have kids so they visited an orphanage while on holiday there and adopted Mum. Mind you, I sometimes wonder why they bothered.

There wasn't a lot of love in that family. By the time I was born, Mum had no contact with her parents. First time I saw my grandfather was in law school when he gave a lecture. Guess Mum felt like an accessory – all their high-powered friends had children – so they had to have one, and a girl could marry into a legal dynasty, increasing their status. By marrying my father, who was never going to be a judge, she ruined their ambitions.'

In that case, there was only one possibility. 'Dan, you understand what that means? The baby has to be your mother's.'

He reached for his drink and quickly emptied the glass. 'No one ever mentioned a stillborn. If I had a sister I'd know. My parents didn't keep secrets.'

He stared at the glass in his hand. Anya stayed silent, giving him time to absorb the news.

'If what you're saying is true, the only explanation has to be that it was just too painful for them to ever talk about.'

Anya took a deep breath. She didn't want to be the one to shatter Dan's image of his late mother but she had no choice.

'There's a chance your father doesn't even know about the baby. The DNA test shows that he cannot have been the father.'

Dan immediately stood, handed Anya the empty glass and grabbed his jacket. She couldn't read what he was thinking, or whether he was angry or even believed her.

'The only way to sort this out is to talk to Dad. If you don't mind coming, I could pick you up next Sunday, say about three and we can clear this up. There has to be a mistake somewhere and a simple explanation.'

'Sorry, I can't go with you. I've got Ben for the weekend.'

'No problem. Bring him along. There's a park next to the nursing home. He'll love it. Tell you what, I'll even bring a football.'

Anya tried to protest, but the lawyer was used to winning arguments. Ben would go with them and get to run around a park as a bribe.

She closed the door, surprised at how well Dan had taken the news, but doubtful he had accepted the truth about his mother.

She couldn't see how the visit could end well for Dan or his unsuspecting father.

17

Anya fumbled for the phone in the dark.

'Doctor Crichton,' she droned, eyelids too heavy to open.

No one spoke back.

'Hello,' she mumbled, hoping the caller had changed their mind.

As she was about to hang up, she heard what sounded like someone crying in the background.

'It's Violet Yardley.' The voice was high-pitched. 'You told me I could call. I didn't know what else to do.'

Anya reached over and turned on the bedside lamp. The clock showed 12:15 am. No wonder her limbs and head felt like lead as she tried to sit up.

'Are you all right?'

'I'm scared and I need your help. Someone's in trouble.'

Anya was suddenly alert.

'Where are you? The police can be there—'

'No, no police.' Violet became more shrill. 'That'll make everything worse. She's hurt. It's bad this time.'

'Wait, Violet.' Anya needed to know how severely injured this unknown person was. If she needed an ambulance, they could be wasting critical time. The image of Giverny Hart's body and what a difference a few minutes made flashed through her mind.

'How badly hurt is she? Was there an accident? Do you need an ambulance?'

'No. No ambulance, no other doctors and no nurses! We want you to look after her.'

So far Anya had no idea what had happened to the friend.

She hadn't ruled out a drug overdose or attempted suicide or an accident. Fear of police and hospitals suggested she'd done something illegal, possibly drugs or drink driving. Then again, she could have been sexually assaulted. She needed a lot of information quickly, if she was to help in any way, without Violet becoming histrionic and panicking.

The background had gone quiet.

'Can you tell me if your friend is still awake?'

Anya heard muffled crying in the background. At least the victim was conscious and breathing.

'If I'm going to help I have to know what I'm dealing with and how badly she's hurt.'

Violet waited before answering. 'She's beaten up, her face is swollen and she can't move her left arm. Please help, she's in a lot of pain.'

Asking for pain relief over the phone instantly aroused a doctor's suspicion. It could be a ruse to get hold of narcotics. It wouldn't be the first time an addict had feigned injury, although that usually entailed stories of miscarriage, ectopic pregnancy or a bone disorder.

Anya spoke slowly and clearly, trying to quell Violet's rising panic.

'I don't carry pain relief in my bag or at the assault unit attached to the hospital. If she needs something strong, I can't give it to her. Hospital's the best place for her.'

In case drugs were the reason for the call, it should be enough to discourage an addict from continuing with the sham.

Instead, Violet became more frantic. 'She's straight-edged – she doesn't even take headache tablets. And she isn't drunk. I'm really scared, you've got to help us. There's no one else we can turn to.'

'Is the person who did this near you?'

'No. He's gone for now.'

Committed now to seeing the girl and her friend, Anya climbed out of bed and pulled on a pair of jeans. The crumpled oversized T-shirt she slept in was replaced with a bra and shorter, ironed version. She glanced past Ben's empty bedroom on the way downstairs.

'I'm on my way to the hospital, the same place you saw me the first time.'

'I remember.'

'Let's meet out front and I'll let us in.'

'Please hurry.'

Violet hung up and Anya dialled Mary Singer, to keep her informed of what was happening. Mary, who sounded surprisingly alert for this time of night, wanted to come along, citing a policy to always have a counsellor in attendance, but Anya promised to call back if Mary were needed.

Twenty minutes later she pulled up outside the centre and immediately saw two small figures in the shadows of the street-lamp, one bent over. She rushed over to offer support but Violet urged her to take them somewhere safer.

Once inside, Anya locked the entrance and quickly glanced out the glass door to make sure no one was outside. She switched on the light and led the girls to the examination suite.

The girl with Violet staggered to the lounge chair, her friend at her side. Anya would not have recognised the face even if they'd met before. The cheeks and eyes were swollen, and blackened. Blood stained her pale shirt. With one hand, she held a blood-soaked towel to the back of her head. The other showed a deformed wrist and forearm, which on a quick glance had to be a displaced fracture.

Anya immediately pulled on latex gloves and grabbed a thick surgical pad along with a pillow. Violet made way as she moved over to the lounge.

'That's a pretty nasty gash to the head. Can I take a look?'

The girl seemed to defer to Violet, who nodded.

Anya carefully lifted the broken forearm onto a pillow on the owner's lap. The woman grimaced but did not resist. Next came a cursory examination of the scalp wound.

'Looks like someone really did a job on you. This might sting a bit.'

Anya pressed around the seven-centimetre split in the skull, feeling for boggy swelling, anything to suggest a fractured skull beneath. Relieved not to find any abnormality, she then studied the jagged laceration more carefully.

'Can you tell me how this happened? It's pretty obvious someone wanted to hurt you.'

Violet had folded her arms and sat on a single seater, bent forward, with her long black skirt stretched over her knees. 'Is this confidential? Like you promised when you saw me?'

Anya looked across. 'Yes, but if someone's life is at risk, that confidence may have to be broken.'

The two women exchanged looks. 'Told you she was all right,' Violet said. 'We're safe here. Go on, tell her.'

The laceration had temporarily stopped bleeding but would need stitches, so Anya sat, gloved palms facing upwards on her lap.

The unknown woman spoke through a split bottom lip.

'My name is Savannah. Savannah Harbourn.'

18

Anya had heard a great deal about the crimes of the Harbourn family, but never any mention of Savannah.

Violet appeared agitated while she explained, 'We used to be friends. That's how I met her brother, Rick, the one I was going out with when . . .' She picked at the skin framing a thumbnail. 'The night I came here.'

'She means the night she got pissed and had sex with my brothers,' Savannah said, matter-of-fact.

'Do you know whoever did this to you?' Anya asked. 'You and Violet look terrified.'

Savannah breathed through her puffed-up mouth. The bridge of her nose had already widened with swelling.

'I went over to see my two younger sisters. I moved out, but go back to help them with homework and stuff. It was after eight and no one was cooking for them, so I started making spaghetti.'

'Their mother has never given a shit,' Violet said. 'If it wasn't for Savannah, they'd live on potato chips and Coco Pops.'

'When I was in the kitchen, Mum and Gary, my oldest brother, started arguing about the police and what they had on him this time. He just kept saying he had it covered. I ignored it 'cause they argue like that all the time. It's why I left home.'

Anya could imagine the scene in the crowded, squalid home full of teenagers and adults in constant trouble with the police. If criminal behaviour was learnt, the family home was the ideal schooling ground. Savannah was wise to move away from it. With this family, though, violence seemed to have been inescapable.

'What happened then?'

Anya stayed seated, allowing Savannah to tell her whole story before suturing and cleaning the wounds. She had numerous questions about what Savannah knew about the family's criminal acts but wanted to gain the sister's trust by letting her speak freely for a while. She hoped something – anything – would come out about Giverny and the attack on Sophie and Rachel Goodwin. Even though this conversation was in complete confidence, Anya just might be able to persuade Savannah to speak to the police about what she knew.

'Gary started screaming and then Bruce, Peter and Paddy came home. They joined in and said Peter got rid of the paint that night, and that's all he and Bruce did. But Mum didn't believe them and started slapping them around the face.'

Violet spoke again. 'They would just take that from her, no one would dare hit back.'

Anya wondered if the violence they inflicted on women was a surrogate way of getting back at their mother. Abusers had often been abused themselves, but it was no defence – moral or legal. It didn't make the victim's suffering any more bearable.

'I stayed out of it, but half the street would have heard. They kept telling Mum that they got rid of the paint, that's all. Eventually she took off in her car. There's this bloke she goes to when she's pissed off with us lot.'

The paint. Was it the red paint they had used to scrawl threats on Giverny's car? That meant the Harbourns were involved in what happened at the Hart home, despite four of them being in jail at the time. Anya wanted to know exactly what they had said to incriminate themselves, but had to be very careful in dealing with Savannah. At the moment she was a patient, not informant.

'Can I get something for the pain? This arm is killing me when I move.'

Anya didn't want her to have anything orally, in case the arm had to be reduced under a general anaesthetic. And she didn't carry injectable narcotics, to protect the unit from attacks and break-ins.

'That arm may need surgery, so you can't have anything by mouth until we get an X-ray.'

Violet moved to stand but when Savannah tried to lift her arm to do the same, she recoiled into the lounge.

'Hold on,' Anya explained. 'I can walk you across the road to X-ray and give you an anonymous code, which we have permission to do. No one has to know your name, or what happened. But that arm definitely has to be sorted, or you could lose function in it. If it's an unstable break, it could cut off the blood supply to your hand, which would mean something a lot more serious.'

With a fresh head injury, Anya also wanted the girl to remain conscious and lucid. Painkillers could sedate and cause even more problems. Immobilising the arm was as effective as pain relief for now. She rechecked for the wrist pulses. The fingers were pink and still receiving adequate blood flow. She then repositioned the pillow closer to Savannah's body, so the arm was better braced against even the slightest movement.

Anya locked the unit when the three of them walked across the road to the emergency department. Violet wanted a cigarette and waited outside. She could have been keeping an eye out.

The triage sister kindly fast-tracked them with an anonymous code and soon they were in X-ray. Anya put on a lead gown to stay with her patient.

Two ribs had been broken, but thankfully hadn't managed to puncture a lung. Above the wrist was fractured but the skull was intact. The emergency physician on duty put in a local anaesthetic block in that arm and pulled it back into place. Another X-ray showed it back in alignment. They then moved into a treatment room and waited for the same doctor to return.

He opted to stabilise the forearm with a plaster backslab and bandage. It wasn't the ideal treatment, but under these circumstances could be easily removed if Savannah needed to be seen by her family and didn't want them to know she'd been to hospital.

As they waited together for the plaster to set, the doctor left to get a suturing kit for the scalp wound. Savannah began to open up.

'Why are you being so nice?'

'It's not nice, it's my job. Just like the doctors in here.'

Savannah began to cry. 'No one's ever been this kind to me before.'

Anya put an arm around the girl, who had grown up with abuse and beatings. The smallest amount of compassion could set off an avalanche of emotion in someone like Savannah.

'Mum reckons I waste air when I breathe. She hates me.'

Ordinarily, that would sound like an immature reaction to an argument, but Noelene Harbourn had some serious psychopathology. Savannah may well have been right about her.

With the plaster in place, it was time to suture the head wound. Hair could hide the stitches, if she washed it carefully when she got home.

As Savannah sat bravely throughout the procedure, Anya thought about the dysfunctional family.

Social commentators and clergymen lamented the demise of the family, but whether nature or nurture caused criminality was irrelevant. Families like this should be broken up and separated.

Savannah had deserved much better.

'What happened after your mother left?'

Savannah paused and lowered her head. 'Gary told me to find his baseball bat and got wild when it wasn't there. My sisters called me into the bedroom and said the police had been around asking more questions. All Gary cared about was what Bruce and Paddy told the police, but Amber said they'd already taken off somewhere with the bat. Gary lost it and started laying into me. First with his fists, and when I went down he started kicking me.'

Anya's mind raced. Was it the brothers taking the baseball bat that sent him into a violent frenzy? Or what they were going to do with it? Gary was capable of turning on anyone, except, it seemed, his own mother.

'What did they do with the bat? Why did he care so much?'

Savannah stood up, cradling her arm. 'It's what he used to beat people up with. Anyone who owed him money or double-crossed him, he reckoned.'

They headed outside to where Violet was sitting on a step, still smoking.

'Did she fix you?'

Savannah nodded. 'Thanks, I feel a lot better.'

Anya said, 'This time you were lucky. How did you get away from Gary?'

'I didn't. He just left. Rick had been out with his mates and at least he helped me off the floor when he got home. The others had got home and passed out on the lounge.'

'It isn't the first time. Those arseholes would belt her up if she didn't get them a drink or bag of chips or do some shit they told her to.' Violet flared. 'Tell the doctor what happened when your mum got back.'

Savannah rubbed the bandaged arm with her good hand.

'She'd been drinking. She has been even more since Ian got locked up. I could smell it. When I told her what happened, she started yelling at me for making Gary angry. Then she slapped me really hard in the face and went to bed.'

19

Martin brought Ben over to stay and agreed to have dinner with them. Over schnitzels, vegetables and chocolate-chip ice-cream, the three chatted for hours about the trip and their adventures. It was almost like earlier times. The holiday had done them wonders.

Martin barely mentioned his girlfriend and Ben thrived on the attention from both parents. Past bitterness seemed to have been forgotten. Both parents kissed their sleeping child goodnight.

The Saturday with Ben passed in a blur of hugs, laughter and games. Anya could have sworn he had grown in the days since she had seen him.

Sunday morning had him up much later than normal. Anya checked to make sure he was all right, and watched him sleep, so peacefully, so innocently. Disneyland and the trip home had exhausted him. Even so, he'd hung a display full of badges by his bed, collected and swapped in Anaheim.

Anya looked at the unmade bookcase at the back of the room. Ben hadn't even asked about the boxes; all he wanted was his mum. She couldn't help but smile. Last night they'd snuggled on the lounge and watched *Ratatouille*. Days, and nights, with Ben were precious and too few.

She slipped downstairs and boiled the kettle while he slept. In retrospect, the divorce with Martin had been inevitable. Except Anya hadn't counted on losing custody because she had become the working parent supporting them all while Martin stayed at home as the primary carer.

Anya placed two teaspoons of leaves and another 'for the

pot' as her grandmother had always done, and filled the teapot with boiling water before turning it three times, just like Nanna used to.

She sat and felt the sun on her skin through the kitchen window. This was her favourite time of day. No phone calls or meetings, and the world felt temporarily calm. And Ben safe upstairs, as if he lived there permanently.

Anya thought about how much of Ben's schooling she had already missed, and it was only his first year. Other mothers did reading and canteen duty, but she had to work to pay child support on top of the mortgage and Elaine's wage. Business had improved, but a lot of the government work went unpaid. Even so, it often led to paid jobs, which always helped.

A mug of tea later, Anya heard quick steps on the wooden stairs. 'Good morning,' she said and met him in the doorway with a hug.

Ben, still sleepy-eyed, wrapped his arms around her without a word. When he didn't move, she checked to see if he had fallen asleep standing up.

'How about some breakfast? I can do orange juice, scrambled eggs and toast.'

'Can we go out for waffles? I like waffles with maple syrup like we had in Disneyland.'

'How about we see what cereal's left in the cupboard, after you ate two big bowls yesterday?'

Ben grinned with pride.

Anya was always conscious of wanting to make sure Ben enjoyed his visits, but tried hard to make sure he ate something nutritious for each meal.

He yawned and scratched his belly underneath his pyjama top. For a moment Anya saw a mini version of her former husband. Ben opted for some muesli with banana and milk and sat himself in his usual spot at the small table, across from his mother.

Within moments of the first mouthful, he was back to

his chattering self, regaling her with funny moments from *Ratatouille*, interspersed with more tales about the airport and plane food. Sometimes the stories he told took longer than the actual scenes, but that was one of the things she loved about him.

After he'd finished, he asked if they could colour in together. In a flash he was back with a pencil case and colouring book full of animals. He flicked open at a page of a mother tiger and her cubs, handed her the orange pencil and began with blue for himself for the sky.

'Mrs Henry says I need to practise staying in the lines. She says I am good at writing letters but go too fast colouring. Did you do that when you were in kindergarten?'

'I don't remember, it was a long time ago.'

He had managed to colour over clouds but Anya chose to let him go.

'Hey, after this we can go to the park then come back here for lunch. We have to go out with a work friend this afternoon to visit his sick dad.'

Ben glanced up through his curly mop of a fringe. 'Are we going to the hospital?'

'No, sweetie, we're visiting a place called a nursing home, where people go when they're not well enough to look after themselves, but not sick enough to be in hospital.'

He swapped the blue for a green pencil and began tracing the outline of the grass. 'Why don't their mums and dads look after them?'

'Because their parents are usually in heaven.'

'Do they have families?'

'Sometimes.'

'So why don't they live with them instead of the nursing place? Mrs Henry says families are supposed to look after each other. That's why we have a family.'

Mrs Henry, Ben's kindergarten teacher, featured a lot in his conversations. Anya loved the way she made learning a game for him.

'Some families can look after their older members, but most can't.' Like everything in life, the issue was complicated.

'Why not?' The grass merged with a cub, which was fast becoming green and black.

The questions never ran out with Ben. 'Why' had to be his favourite word.

Anya thought about the number of reasons. Smaller families, longer working hours, distance from relatives, selfishness, family problems; the list was endless. She opted for a practical answer. 'Well, if your nanna was in a wheelchair, she couldn't live here because the bedrooms are upstairs. Where would she sleep?'

Ben considered this for a moment. 'You could bring her to our house and you can come and live with us too.'

Anya would love nothing more than being with her son full-time, but Martin had a girlfriend. Besides, she couldn't live with an adult who thought surfing was more important than paying bills. Even so, looking at Ben, she had to admit that, as a father, Martin was doing a great job.

'Hey, as far as I know, Nanna's pretty happy seeing her patients and looking after her garden. Now, what about the park?'

Ben placed his bowl by the sink and trotted off to get dressed. While washing up, Anya wondered what sort of a father the Harbourn children had had. Chances were he hadn't fathered all of the children, if Noelene's 'profession' continued throughout the relationship.

Had he been inherently bad, abusive or violent? Was he even literate? Was he strict, or morally void?

It can't have been easy raising nine children, but large families could be perfectly functional, or at least appear that way. She headed for her office and clicked on her laptop to check her emails. There was nothing further from Dan Brody. They would still expect him this afternoon.

Ben reappeared in a new Buzz Lightyear shirt and shorts. The navy made his eyes an even deeper blue. 'Mum, why don't you have the same name as Dad and me? There's a boy in my class whose parents didn't get married and they have different names.'

'Your dad and I got married but when we got a divorce, you kept the name Hegarty, and I changed my name back to what it used to be.'

He manoeuvred onto her lap and dangled his legs beside hers. The computer was an instant magnet for her son, but she wasn't about to turn down the affection it encouraged. 'Why?'

That word again. 'It's far too complicated.' A five-year-old couldn't understand her need for autonomy and independence and she was not about to explain why she had changed her surname from Reynolds to Crichton either. She tried to change the subject. 'So are we going to the park?'

Ben stayed sitting and reached for a paperweight. 'Why do people have to have different names?'

Anya kissed him on the cheek. 'It'd be pretty funny if poor Mrs Henry called the roll and said the exact same name for every child. Imagine if you all were called Ben.'

'The girls would look pretty silly being called a boy's name.' He giggled at the idea, then opened the drawer and rummaged until he found a pencil. 'But why do we have to have last names?'

Anya put the pencil back and closed the drawer, mindful of his fingers. 'Names go back a very long time and tell you things about the family. Some names tell you where a family came from, like Crichton. It comes from a place in Scotland where my great-great-grandfather used to live. Other names can tell you what someone did for a job. Someone called Smith was related to a person who made things out of metal or could have even made things out of gold.'

'Is Josh Smith rich?'

'No,' she laughed. 'But his great-grandfather could have been a jewellery maker.'

'What's a Hegarty?'

'Well, Benjamin Hegarty, let's find out.' Anya called up

Google and searched. The site described it as meaning 'unjust'. Knowing Martin sometimes that could fit. 'It sort of means one-sided.'

'You mean like the goodies? That should be you because you help catch the baddies with Auntie Kate.'

'Something like that,' Anya said and lifted him off. 'Time we cleaned your teeth and I got dressed. Can you find some shoes and socks in your bag?'

Ben was off. Before switching off the computer, she typed in *Brody*. 'Muddy place' wasn't what she had expected, but was pretty appropriate right now, given the discovery of his mother's baby.

Curiosity led her to type one more name: *Harbourn*. She sat back when the result flicked on to the screen. The family moniker couldn't be more telling.

'A polluted, dirty stream.' With a family labelled polluted, they either lived near contaminated water or were known for generations as vile people. She suspected the criminality displayed by the current family members wasn't due only to events in their childhood. At least some of it was probably in the genetic make-up. She had always thought that environment was more important than genes, but many of Ben's mannerisms and his easygoing personality were more like her father, whom he didn't see very often, so the traits could hardly be learnt. Having a child had forced her to reconsider the influence of inherited traits.

She decided to perform a literature search on the latest research to help her better understand criminal families.

In the Harbourns' case, she had a gnawing feeling that evil and violence were quite likely blood born.

20

A nya glanced at the minuscule back seat and offered to take her own car. Even with the front seat as far forward as possible, Ben would only just fit into his booster, feet tucked up. Without much of a window and limited ventilation, she hoped the tuna pasta he'd had for lunch wouldn't reappear on Dan's upholstery.

'It'll be fine,' Dan reassured. 'It's just a car.'

Ben gently stroked the red paintwork. 'My dad says that fast red cars are for people with baby willies.'

Anya felt her face brighten as she squeezed Ben's hand tighter. 'I'm so sorry, Dan, I don't know where that came from. I'm sure he doesn't even know what it means.'

Dan stood hands in his back pockets, then moved them self-consciously to his front. 'That's okay, having met your ex-husband, I can imagine he might say that.'

She bent down to her son's eye level. Martin did have a habit of mouthing off, especially about people who intimidated him for one reason or another. 'We don't say rude things like that. Apologise please.'

'Sorry, Mr Brody,' Ben uttered, and raised his eyebrows at his mother. 'Why is it rude?'

'Sometimes it's not polite to repeat what grown-ups like your dad say.'

Despite Anya's reservations, Dan remained insistent that they take his Ferrari to the nursing home. With Ben in his booster and Anya in the passenger seat with her knees almost touching the dash, they accelerated out of her street, faster than she had expected. Ben sat quietly, having quickly forgotten his reprimand.

'This is a cool car!' he exclaimed.

'Glad you like it. Thanks for agreeing to come,' Dan said. 'I don't get the chance to visit my dad very often.'

Anya wondered whether Dan couldn't or *wouldn't* make the time. Like most people, he managed to do the things he enjoyed, like socialising and attending A-list parties. Was it guilt about placing his father in a nursing home, or discomfort at seeing someone he loved so disabled? She knew his father had suffered at least two strokes. To be institutionalised as a result meant the overall disability had to be severe.

The car hugged a tight corner on an amber light. Anya placed her hands by her sides to brace herself. 'How long ago was his first stroke?'

'Happened just after Mum's funeral. Doctors thought it was the stress of losing her. He was one of those men who never had to see a doctor or take medication.'

Anya knew the type. Usually they were men who had been active in their youth and clung to those memories. While they were healthy, they stayed away from doctors, even for routine check-ups. By the time they had their strokes or dropped dead of a heart attack, it was too late.

They pulled up at a set of lights, next to a P-plater whose eyes widened at the sight of the Italian car.

Dan revved the engine then backed off the accelerator when Anya turned to him and raised her eyebrows. 'You know you'd make that teenager's day if you let him take off from the lights first.'

The lawyer shrugged. 'You're always thinking of other people.' Still, he hesitated when the lights changed and the P-plater disappeared with smoke blowing out the back of his faded Cortina.

'Satisfied?' He changed gear and revved the engine again.

Anya smiled.

'You know, you're like my mum in that way.' He held the gearstick while he spoke. 'Dad used to say that Paul Newman had it right being so proud of his wife. Why go out for a hamburger when you've got steak at home? Even after fifty years together.'

Anya's grandparents were like that. She had tried to imagine sleeping next to someone for fifty or more years then suddenly waking up without them. The world empathised with the grief of a newlywed whose partner had died. The reality was that, in time, young people moved on after the death of a spouse. For a couple who had been together decades, the grief of losing their life partner could be too much to live with.

She moved her hands to her lap as they overtook a bus. 'Do you share his steak philosophy?'

'In theory.' He grinned. 'But in Dad's day they didn't have lamb burgers, gourmet vegetarian, organic meat or duck to choose from.'

'You and my ex-husband have more in common than you think.' She turned around and saw that Ben had fallen asleep.

'Are you close to your father?'

Dan glanced at his passenger. 'I was closer to Mum. Dad has always been pretty opinionated about community service law and didn't really approve when I went into private practice.'

'You said he was always healthy. It can't be easy going from that to a nursing home.'

Dan slowed the car a little and checked road signs. 'It's not easy seeing him so helpless. He isn't the father I know, he's a shell of a man now. Hell, we can't even argue, so how am I supposed to know when I've disappointed him again?'

Suddenly Dan's behaviour with women and his aggressive approach to winning cases made more sense. Even intelligent, successful adults still desperately wanted approval – and love – from their parents, and could overcompensate in the process.

After thirty years, Anya still wanted to hear her mother tell her that she wasn't to blame for Miriam's abduction.

Dan pulled into the gravel driveway leading to the redbrick complex and parked in front of a grassed area. He pulled a backpack from the boot as Anya reached back and stroked her son's arm, waking him from a shallow sleep.

Inside the grounds of Pine Lodge, they pressed the buzzer and waited. The jangling of keys preceded the staff member's appearance.

'Good morning. How can I help you?' The older woman pushed the sleeves of her navy cardigan up to her elbows. Beneath, her corporate patterned shirt hung out over navy trousers. This was a nurse who was more hands-on than usual administrators. The white walking shoes confirmed it.

As she wiped her hands on her trousers, the sleeves slid down again.

'Now, you would have to be William Brody's son. You are the absolute spitting image.'

Dan lowered his head and tentatively extended his hand.

'Oh, it's only water, I've been helping bath one of our residents who thinks cleaning once a month is excessive. Sometimes it's just like being with toddlers, the fuss some of them make.' She shook hands with each of them, making a special fuss of Ben.

'I'm Rhonda Gillespie, nursing unit manager. I was on holidays when your father was admitted, which is why we haven't met. The old wag is doing really well.'

'Is it convenient to visit?'

'We'll make it convenient. Nothing like some lovely family to cheer you up. How about in the garden? He likes it out there and it's a gorgeous day.' She showed them in and pointed to the doors past the corridor. 'Nothing extravagant, but there's a courtyard with outdoor furniture, potted plants and a birdbath.'

'Excellent,' Dan said.

Ben held his mother's hand.

Sister Gillespie locked the front door behind them and loped off, shoes squeaking on the lino floor with each step.

'You'd think this was a prison,' Dan whispered.

'They probably have some demented patients who wander.

They have a duty to stop them getting lost. No doubt some lawyer would sue them for neglect if that happened.'

'Valid point, I suppose.'

Dan opened the external door for Anya and Ben. They walked down a ramp to a wooden bench by a half-filled water feature. The lawyer fidgeted with his shirt, tucking it further in multiple times before curling his top lip at the oversized birdbath.

'That's a disgrace, it's stagnant. You'd think they would have gone to the trouble of putting in a pump and fountain instead The rates they charge . . .'

Anya wondered if the sound of running water would have been advisable in a home for the elderly infirm.

'I'm guessing you've never had prostate trouble, or urinary incontinence.'

'Ah. No.' He sat and straightened his legs before pulling them back in.

'Can I look for insects?' Ben asked, squatting down near one of the plants near the brick wall.

'Sure, but don't touch any spiders.'

'Mum.' Ben raised both hands in the air. 'Spiders have eight legs. Insects only have six legs.'

'Just don't touch any, please.' As he wandered off Anya asked softly, aware of her son's proximity and acute hearing, 'How are you going to approach him about the box contents?'

Dan leant in closer. 'Planned to wing it, depending on how he is today. The doctor tells me he has bad days and sometimes worse days. It's not the sort of thing you just drop into a casual conversation. "Hi Dad, how are they treating you, what's the food like, oh and did you know there was a dead baby in the walk-in wardrobe?"'

At that moment the door opened and the sister pushed her patient along in a wheelchair. The man sat slumped to the right, but his frame was large.

The senior Brody was clean and neatly dressed in a checked shirt, corduroy trousers and a hound's-tooth squire's cap. By the gnarled fingers and flexed wrist, William Brody had suffered an extensive stroke paralysing the whole of his right side.

The nurse turned the chair to face away from the sun and placed the brakes on. Bending over to make eye contact with the old gentleman, Nurse Gillespie said, 'I'll leave you to catch up with your son and his lovely girlfriend. If you need me, just press the buzzer around your neck. Okay?'

She waited for a response.

William Brody stared at her with his pale blue eyes and raised his left hand, but not in a dismissive way.

'Oh, and here's your notebook so you can write things down.' She explained to Ben. 'William can't speak words any more, so he writes them down. That's pretty impressive, isn't it?'

Ben ran over to check the pad then returned to a pile of stones near the wall.

With that, the nurse straightened and headed back inside.

Dan moved forward and awkwardly hugged his father.

'It's great to see you settled in. Hope you're not giving the nurses a hard time.'

The older man reciprocated with his good arm for longer than Anya had expected. Dan was the one to break the hold.

'Dad. I've brought someone with me to meet you. This is Doctor Anya Crichton.'

Mr Brody looked across at Anya and smiled, revealing a droop to one side of his mouth. He removed his hat, placed it in his lap and extended the functioning hand. Anya shook it and felt the strength of his grip. Despite his disabilities, his eyes had a rare sparkle to them. She liked him already.

Dan reached into his daypack. 'I've got some fresh pyjamas and toiletries and a copy of the latest Edinburgh military tattoo on DVD. The staff told me over the phone you can watch DVDs in the common room. Maybe we can watch it together next time. Oh, and I was going through some of Mum's things and found this. Thought you'd like to keep it by your bed.'

He placed the silver frame in his father's lap. Anya could see that it was a photo of the couple's wedding day. In it, a young couple smiled with the promise of a new life together. William Brody touched the photo and Anya thought she could detect a slight tearing of his eyes.

'I found something else, Dad, and I'm not sure how to explain it. I asked Anya to come along to help.'

The senior Brody frowned and his eyes darted from Dan to Anya and back again.

'There's no easy way of saying this. I found an old sealed box under the floorboards in the wardrobe.'

William tightened his grip on the photograph and looked down.

His son bent forward to meet his father's eyes. 'Did you hear what I said? It had been there for years.'

The old man resisted looking up. For a moment Anya wondered whether the recent stroke had affected his ability to understand. She decided to try a more gentle approach.

'Mr Brody, I'm a pathologist. Dan asked me to take a look at what was inside because it was so unusual. I had to notify the police—'

With that, William looked up, eyes wide open, and shook his head. Anya realised he understood exactly what they were saying. *NO POLICE* he wrote on the pad before reaching out for Dan, clasping at his arm.

'Dad, are you all right? Do you understand?' The lawyer looked at Anya for support. 'God, I wish you could just talk to me.'

'It's okay,' Anya said. The part of the brain responsible for speech was separate from the writing centre. Mr Brody still had the ability to write his innermost thoughts. She held the paper and replaced the pen in his bony fingers.

The new words he wrote were shaky, but clear.

NO POLICE.

'Why? Dad, are you trying to tell us that you know about the box and what was in it?' Dan stood and ran his hand through his hair. 'I can't believe you kept this a secret. A real skeleton in our closet.'

Ben had found a small lizard to distract him and, to Anya's relief, was paying no attention to the conversation.

Dan whispered. Mr Brody's hearing had to be better than most elderly people's.

'What were you thinking, keeping a dead baby quiet? I grew up in that house and am supposed to be an officer of the court. So were you.'

Anya studied Mr Brody. 'Notifying the police is just procedure. There isn't going to be an investigation, or media attention, if you're worried about a scandal tarnishing the family name.'

William looked down at the photo again as Anya continued, 'We ordered a DNA test on the remains.'

Dan bent down, seemingly more aware of Ben in the background. 'Dad, we know it was Mum's.'

Again, the left hand tried to hold the pen steady.

THERESE
GOOD WOMAN.

Dan returned to the bench, read and reread the note. His jaw tensed.

'Please, no more secrets. We know that you weren't the father.'

The old man stroked the photograph and tears dropped on to the glass. Minutes passed before he picked up the pen and wrote.

GOOD WOMAN.

Dan sat forward. 'I can't believe it. You always said that you two were childhood sweethearts, never been kissed by anyone else. And now you're saying she got pregnant to another man? And you knew she buried the baby? God, Dad, what other secrets have you been keeping? When I think of all the self-righteous lectures you've forced me to listen to.' Dan's voice grew louder, as if trapping a suspect in a trial. 'Does the real father know?'

The old man shook his head but looked at Anya, almost pleading with his eyes. There had to be more to the story and his son wasn't giving him a chance to explain.

138

'Dan, would you mind taking Ben inside for a few minutes, I'd like to talk to your father, and I'm sure you could use a drink of cold water.'

The lawyer hesitated, but breathed out. 'Ben, how about we see if they have any jelly in the fridge?' Ben stood up, wiped the dirt from his knees and, after a nod from his mother, grabbed Dan's hand and headed inside.

Anya knelt close to the chair. 'Do you know who the father was?'

Mr Brody blinked his eyes and nodded.

He wrote again. *BEFORE WE MARRIED.*

'Is this man still alive?'

He nodded again.

So William Brody knew the mother had a relationship before him, and married her anyway, perpetuating the story that they were both first loves.

'You don't have to answer, but your son will want to know. If the baby was buried in your home, you must have been there when it was born . . .'

The old gentleman touched Anya's shoulder and tried to mouth something. Words would not come. The pain and frustration in his eyes were obvious.

A breeze picked up some leaves and whirled them in a circle.

'Some say love has no beginning and no end,' she ventured. 'You must have loved Therese a lot to marry her, knowing she was pregnant to another man.'

He clawed the pen and tapped the pad for her to hold. *JUDGE HIM, NOT HER. SHE LOVED ME.* He scribbled over the word *JUDGE* and circled *LOVED ME.*

'I don't doubt that. You look very happy in the photo, like soul mates.' Anya wanted to be supportive. This man had buried his life partner, then lost his ability to walk, talk and stay in the home they had made together.

He brushed Anya's chin with his hand before adding the words: *DAN LUCKY.*

She felt the heat in her face and neck. 'No, no. We're just friends, we work together sometimes. And don't worry, Ben's my son. We're not going to spring anything else on you.'

More scribbling followed.

DAN IDIOT.

Anya found herself laughing and a smile unravelled across the healthier side of William's face. She could see how handsome and vibrant he would have been in his youth. This was a good man.

'I think Therese was one very lucky woman.'

Dan lurched down the ramp and Ben trotted behind, finishing off an ice-cream cup with a tiny wooden spatula. Half of the contents were smeared on his face. Sister Gillespie followed.

'Not getting burnt out here, are we? Don't want to prematurely age that peaches and cream complexion of ours.'

Mr Brody looked up at her and rolled his eyes at Anya, then smiled again.

'Who's that gorgeous-looking man in the wedding photo?' The nurse helped herself to the framed image. 'You were a bit of all right in your day, and so was your bride. She was stunning.'

With that, the picture was back in Mr Brody's lap and the chair had been turned around.

Anya checked her watch. It was nearing five, probably dinnertime for the residents.

'We should go, it's getting late and I have to get Ben packed up,' she said. 'It was a pleasure to meet you, Mr Brody.'

The old man doffed his cap and reached out with his hand.

'Would you mind if I came back some time to visit?'

He squeezed her fingers tightly. In any form of language, that was a definite yes.

They all said goodbye and then left the way they had come in.

Ben folded himself into the back seat again and Anya made

140

sure he was strapped in securely. Dan paced around before getting in. Once on the road, he accelerated and braked, jerking the car with every gear change. Still jetlagged from the trip, Ben quickly dozed off, much to Anya's relief.

'Would you like to talk about it?' she said, unsure whether she should leave him to brood.

'It's just that they lied to me all these years. Mum has an affair, gets pregnant and they don't think to mention it?'

'Will you be proud to tell your children about every woman you ever slept with?' As soon as the words were out, she regretted them.

Dan pulled over to the side of the road.

'I get it, but this isn't just a fling. She had a baby then buried it. For all we know, she could have murdered it, or Dad did out of anger at what she did.'

Anya realised they hadn't asked how the baby had died. That, she thought, would be better asked without Ben or Dan around. 'We know the baby had a tumour and was unlikely to have been born alive.'

Dan placed his forehead on the steering wheel. 'Unlikely doesn't mean it was stillborn.'

'Your father said it was before they were married, so she hardly betrayed him. What are you so angry about really?' He had spoken about his mother as if she were a saint. 'Is this because your mother wasn't "pure" when she married your father?'

Dan turned his head and Anya recognised the flash of guilt. 'Oh my God, that's it, isn't it? That's what has you so churned up. Not what was in the box, but your mother's history.'

Anya had never been so disappointed in a man. With all the sexual relationships the lawyer was reputed to have had, his double standard didn't extend to those women, any of whom could be a mother one day. Even more annoying was that he wasn't mature enough to see his own mother as a complete person with her own desires and needs.

'That's the most ridiculous thing you've ever said—'

'Mummy,' Ben said sleepily from the back. 'I don't feel well.'

Anya turned around just in time to see her son vomit curdled ice-cream across the Ferrari's back seat.

21

'That's my boy,' Kate laughed. 'All over the back seat?'
'It wasn't funny!' Anya exclaimed. 'You should have seen Dan's face.'

'What on earth were you doing going out with him anyway, and with Ben? Is there something going on you should tell me about?'

'Nothing like that. It was just a favour to help him with his father. Ben was fine up until the trip back.'

Kate's laugh was infectious and Anya had to admit the incident was now funny, even to her. The owner of the Ferrari might take some time to feel the same way, though.

'I can imagine the smell. What did Mr Pompous do?'

'His face pretty much said it all, but he was polite. I cleaned it up with wipes and he tried to help but, honestly, it was easier to do it myself. Ben was pretty upset.' Anya felt another laugh bubble up. 'But he did feel better once he'd emptied his stomach . . . again . . . all over the place.'

By the time Hayden Richards arrived at ICU, the pair were buckled over like schoolgirls. Neither saw him coming.

'He must really have the hots for you,' Kate teased.

'Is this a private conversation or can I join in?' Hayden hitched his trousers and raised an eyebrow.

Anya cleared her throat and hoped her cheeks didn't give away the embarrassment she was suddenly feeling.

'Oh,' Kate said, 'just a funny story involving Anya's son. He's a real little character.'

Hayden frowned and glanced at an elderly couple walking past the unit, then spoke to Anya.

'Sophie has asked for you to be with her for a further interview. You can tell us if her injuries are consistent with what she remembers.'

Anya pressed the buzzer to the unit.

'Audiovisual's set up in a consulting room down the corridor, they'll record everything again,' Hayden said. 'We'll need to get as much as we can from her, even if it takes all day with breaks in between.'

Anya hoped the teenager was up to the stress. Reliving that night in minute detail wasn't going to be easy. She entered the intensive care room alone first.

Ned Goodwin wasn't ready to hear every brutal detail of what had happened to his two daughters. He assured Sophie that he was going out for air but wouldn't be far away if he was needed.

With the neck wound far from healed, Sophie placed slight pressure on the bandage as she whispered, 'I'm scared.'

Anya pulled her chair closer. 'That's okay. Anything you remember is helpful, and if you want to stop for a while, just say so. Your wellbeing is the priority here, no matter what the police may like to think. And if it is too painful to remember or you need more time, tell us.'

The patient pressed her neck again. 'Thank you for being here.'

Anya wasn't sure why Sophie felt the connection, but she shared it too. The Saint Jude's medal remained pinned to Sophie's gown. The smallest of gestures made an enormous difference.

'You're in good hands.' She glanced at the shelves on the wall. 'And look at all the beautiful flowers.'

Tears welled in Sophie's eyes and the breathing machine accelerated.

'I know you didn't ask for this, and we can't change what happened.' Anya leant forward; instinct told her the girl needed a hug, but she moved the fringe from Sophie's eyes instead. Tears had changed them from grey to an almost bright blue.

'I miss Rachel. Have to be brave for Dad.'

This was too much to expect of a fourteen-year-old. Not only was Sophie still dealing with life-threatening injuries, she felt the need to support her father.

'You have to grieve as well. He understands that and is trying to be brave for you.'

The young girl seemed far more frail than at the first police interview. She buried her face into Anya's shoulder and cried. It was no surprise the emotion was coming out. It had to. Physical healing was one thing. Emotional wounds took a lot longer.

'People say I'm lucky . . . to be . . . alive.' She lifted her head and glanced around the room. 'Strangers sent all this.' She paused for a couple more breaths. 'I'm not lucky or grateful . . . Don't understand why this happened.' More tears flowed. 'Dad cries . . . when he thinks I'm asleep.'

A torrent of pain, from that night and since, poured out of Sophie's traumatised body. Anger was a large part of grieving, and she had every right to be angry.

Nothing Anya said would make a difference right now, so she just held Sophie. Never good at meaningless platitudes, she was better at listening. Which was what this girl needed more than anything at this moment.

'I should have died, not Rachel.'

'You can't think like that.'

Anya pulled back and dabbed Sophie's eyes with a tissue from a box on the bedside drawers.

'No one understands.'

Anya hesitated before deciding to explain why she understood part of what Sophie and her father were going through.

'When I was five, my little sister was abducted by a stranger. She was never found, but I spent years feeling guilty that I wasn't taken instead. I was supposed to be looking after her and didn't.'

Sophie's eyes glistened as she listened.

'I understand what it's like to be the survivor. But there was absolutely nothing you could have done. It was out of your control, just like my sister was with me.' She brushed a strand of hair out of the young girl's eye. 'Your father is so grateful that you're here. Do you think he'd be any less hurt if Rachel were in your place, or if you had both died?'

She shook her head.

They sat hugging for a few more minutes until a nurse checked to see if the police could come in. 'Give us another minute,' Anya said, and wiped Sophie's face with a damp facecloth.

'You can do this later if you don't feel up to it.'

'If you stay . . . I'll be all right.'

'Deal, but remember what I said earlier. If you want to stop tell us.'

Hayden Richards and Liz Gould entered and sat on vinyl chairs provided by the staff.

A video camera was set up, and switched on by the cameraman before he left. The red light on the front glowed. Kate had opted to stay in the AV room, monitoring the recording. If anything else happened to Sophie – medical complications – it was important to have any evidence she gave on tape for potential jurors.

Hayden began by announcing the date, time and location of the statement.

Sophie sat with the bed more upright. If Anya hadn't been present she never would have believed the degree of composure and maturity in someone so young.

Hayden asked if she could describe what had happened the evening of the attack. They heard how Rachel had cooked dinner: lamb chops and mint sauce. Sophie had just cleaned up the kitchen and made two cups of tea before their favourite TV show, *Home and Away*, came on. As they sat down to watch, someone knocked on the front door.

Rachel looked through the window and saw a ute in the drive. She opened the door and the men just pushed inside. There were three of them. One just started yelling at her to get him the money.

'Can you point to where exactly this was?' Hayden showed her a line map of her house. No crime scene photos were necessary.

'There. The living room. The one yelling had a baseball bat and smashed the cups off the table. Rachel told me to run.' She spoke, head lowered. 'I was too scared to move.'

'Do you remember anything about the man with the bat?'

'He was the one with the black mark on his chin. He was really angry and just kept shouting, "Tell us where the money is." Rachel kept saying we didn't have any and begged them to leave us alone.'

Sophie's face became void of expression. 'The one with the bat punched Rachel with his fist. She hit the wall, hard. He started shouting that he was going to kill us.'

Liz Gould shifted slightly in her seat. 'Was Rachel conscious after she hit the wall?'

Sophie licked her lips. Anya offered her a sip through the straw, which she took before answering.

'I think she was dazed. I reached for her handbag, which was next to the lounge. She had twenty bucks. But that's when the one near me hit me hard in the head. My ears started ringing. Rachel told them we didn't have much money. They wouldn't listen.'

Liz asked, 'Did they mention anything that you can remember, guns, cars, drugs or places? Or call each other by names?'

'Not that I remember. We don't use drugs. We promised Mum before she died.'

'Did Rachel have a boyfriend?' So far, the police had no motive.

'Only one since school.' The breathing machine was becoming less noticeable. 'They broke up after Mum died. She loved hairdressing and was too tired to go out with anyone after work.' A small smile appeared. 'She said nagging me about homework and the phone bill was more fun than a boyfriend.'

Liz commented, 'She sounds like a pretty good big sister.'

Sophie thought for a moment. 'Sometimes she was a pain but so was I.'

Rachel Goodwin and Savannah Harbourn came from different worlds, but cared the same way for their younger siblings. Anya shuddered to think that Gary Harbourn and his brothers had hurt both of them so much.

'What happened next?' Liz asked.

'The one with the bat grabbed her by the hair. It was pretty long, she had a weave done at work . . . She squealed as he dragged her into the bedroom. One came over to me with a knife and told me to shut up and stay still. He said I was next. I started crying. I begged them not to hurt us.'

'Do you remember anything special about the man with the knife?'

'He was sweating a lot and wiping his face with his sleeve. He had a cap on. I didn't see his hair or eyes.'

'Where were the other two?'

'They went in the bedroom and closed the door.'

Sophie looked down and her shoulders tightened. The breathing machine accelerated, along with rises on the heart rate and blood pressure monitor.

'Take your time,' Anya offered. 'If you need a break . . .'

Sophie shook her head, closed her eyes and spoke.

'I could hear Rachel crying and someone yelling. The room was getting dark. It felt like hours. Then Rachel screamed really loudly. It sounded like she was in so much pain. After that, she didn't make any more noise.'

Anya felt a cold wave across her skin. Sophie was describing the moment when her sister had been stabbed and killed.

'What happened after that?' Liz asked gently.

Sophie touched the intravenous drip taped to the back of her hand.

'Two of them came out and the one who had the bat had blood all over his clothes and hands.'

'Was he holding a knife?'

A pause.

'I don't know. I didn't see it until after the other one started swearing and screaming, "Why did you have to do it? Mum's going to skin us." The other one must have still been in Rachel's room.

'The man with the mole told him to shut up, that we could have fingered them. That's when I tried to run for the door but someone grabbed me and slammed me into the wall.'

She pointed to the diagram in her lap. 'That was here. I hit my back and couldn't breathe. The others came out and held me down. The one with the mole told one to pull my jeans off. I tried to fight, but they were too strong. It really hurt but he wouldn't stop. Then one of the others raped me. That's when I saw the knife, in my face. I knew they were going to kill me, just like Rachel.'

Sophie faltered and asked for another drink of water. Anya held the cup and felt the tension in the room. No one wanted to put a victim this young through further trauma, but it had to be done, and it might even help Sophie deal with what had happened to her.

'You're doing really well, take your time,' Anya encouraged.

'After they finished, they let me go. I tried to pull up my jeans, but the one with the mole grabbed the knife and I felt pain in my stomach. I tried to protect myself. But there was more pain in my chest. It was worse. I rolled over and saw blood on the floor. Then I held my breath and pretended to be dead, like when we were kids.'

The detectives looked at each other.

'What did they do?'

Sophie closed her eyes and seemed exhausted. The monitor's readings had slowed.

Liz and Hayden remained perfectly still, knowing what came next.

'Someone said to leave me, that I was dead anyway. I didn't look but heard the footsteps going to the front door. Then someone came back, pulled my head up by my hair, and said, "This is how you make sure there are no witnesses."

'I saw the knife flash and heard something tear. I didn't know my throat was cut until I woke up in here.'

Anya signalled to the detectives to end the interview. Without hesitation, Hayden stood, announced the time and turned off the camera. After the others had left the room Sophie dozed off and Anya stroked her hair for a couple of minutes.

She thought back to the morning in casualty where one surgeon argued that Sophie would not survive an anaesthetic, and the emergency doctor rushed to insert drips, give blood transfusions and pack the neck wound. They were concerned that if they tried to move her neck the slightest amount, the fragile veins in her neck would tear.

There was such incredible strength and resilience in this young girl. With extensive injuries she had crawled the length of the drive down towards the road, where she had lost consciousness again.

Something about Sophie made everyone want to fight for her, the way she had already done.

If Savannah Harbourn understood what had happened at the Goodwin home that night, she might change her mind and help stop Gary and the brothers from hurting anyone else ever again.

22

With Ben and Martin back home, Anya sat down to the late news with a spinach cannelloni from the local delicatessen. Depressing vision of terrorist attacks in India led the bulletin, followed by doom and gloom forecasts about the latest global financial crisis. Footage of families sleeping in cars accompanied a reporter using cliches like 'tough times ahead' and 'belt-tightening'.

She ate the meal and scraped every morsel of the cheese sauce from the plate with her fork. If it had been chocolate, she would have happily licked the plate clean while no one was there to watch. One advantage of living alone was that she could eat whatever whenever, even dessert first if she wanted.

Breaking news reported a fatal smash and subsequent road closure. Police in fluorescent vests examined a compacted white vehicle that had crashed head-first into a tree.

A number flashed on the screen, urging witnesses to contact police. Anya immediately felt for the family that would receive a knock on the door with the heartbreaking news, and the police who had to deliver it. Without speed and alcohol, most road trauma could be avoided.

She switched off the television and headed for the kitchen to boil the kettle for a cup of peppermint tea before bed. In the morning she would phone Violet Yardley to see how Savannah was doing. She wanted to give the women a bit of time, without pressuring them too quickly. The doorbell interrupted her thoughts.

Looking through the peephole, Anya saw two uniformed police. Her heart lurched. All she could think of was Ben.

God, no! Please don't let anything have happened to him.

Pulse quickening, she undid the chain and opened the door.

'Anya Crichton?' the junior officer asked.

Anya nodded, her mouth suddenly dry.

'Sorry to disturb you at this hour but you might be able to help us regarding the victim of a fatal accident this evening.'

Anya felt her knees buckle and the senior officer stepped forward. 'We're not here to break bad news,' he quickly added and gave his colleague a scathing look. 'We should have made that clear the moment you opened the door.'

He held up one of her cards and she took a long, relieved breath. 'There's been a fatal motor vehicle accident. The deceased female had only a driver's licence and your card in her purse, suggesting you had something to do with her, possibly recently.'

Anya felt her pulse slow and invited the officers inside. It must be about the smash she had seen on the news.

'I'll help any way I can. Please come in.'

The men removed their caps and wiped their feet before entering.

'Do you know the name of the victim?' Anya asked, offering them a seat in the lounge room.

The junior officer flicked open his notebook as if remembering the name was too difficult. 'A Savannah Harbourn of Miller Avenue.'

Anya sat down on the edge of the lounge as if she'd been winded. Only nights before the young woman had confided about a life of abuse. She was one of the Harbourns' chronic victims, silent and unrecognised. Now she was dead. Her mind raced back to how frightened Savannah was of being caught telling anyone what had happened.

'Was anyone else hurt?'

'No, ma'am. Did you know Ms Harbourn?'

That meant Violet wasn't in the car as well. 'I met her once last week and gave her my card.' Anya placed a hand on the lump that was now in her stomach. 'What happened?'

'So far we haven't located any witnesses, the road's fairly quiet this time of night and poorly lit. The car appears to have been travelling on a straight stretch and hit a tree at high speed. Skid marks suggest she tried to brake suddenly before colliding with the tree.'

The senior officer sat quietly, rotating his cap between his knees. 'Can you tell us how and when you came to meet?'

Anya was careful not to mention Violet Yardley but the coroner and pathologist performing the post-mortem would need to know about Savannah's injuries prior to the crash. 'She had been badly beaten and I examined her at the sexual assault unit.'

The note taker scribed. 'Had she been raped?'

'No, she was the victim of a violent assault and needed medical attention. Before you ask, she was referred by someone who attended the unit previously but I can't give you that name.'

The men exchanged glances. 'Don't suppose we could trouble you for a coffee?' the older one asked. 'It's been a long night.'

'I could do with one myself.' Herbal tea would not help now. Anya returned from the kitchen with a tray. She was still stunned by the news of Savannah's death. The Harbourns were known for sticking together, no matter what. But would they kill one of their own to protect the rest?

After what Savannah had said about the mother thinking she wasted oxygen by just being alive, it was a distinct possibility. Like so many victims of chronic abuse, Savannah had broken down that night. All it had taken was the smallest show of compassion.

The doorbell rang again. Kate Farrer didn't wait for an invitation inside.

'I guess you know that one of the Harbourns died tonight and she had your card in her purse.'

Bad news travelled at breakneck speed in the police network.

'Are you investigating the crash?' Anya asked quietly in the hallway.

'Should I be?'

Kate moved through to the lounge room and the officers stood. After waving them to sit again, she helped herself to another mug from the kitchen and returned.

Anya briefly described Savannah's injuries and her broken left arm which emergency had reduced and plastered, the bruises to her face and the scalp wound that needed suturing.

The younger constable referred to his notes again. 'It appears that the woman who crashed tonight didn't have a cast on her arm.'

'Could we be looking at mistaken identity?' For one moment, Anya hoped that it was not Savannah in the car.

Kate sat on the coffee table facing the lounge. 'Family already identified the body.'

Anya felt her stomach tighten again. 'It's more likely she took off the cast to hide the fact that she had seen a doctor. It's not uncommon among abuse victims when they go back home. I assume the car was an automatic. But if she had to turn the wheel suddenly, she couldn't have done it with that left arm.'

Kate poured herself a coffee. 'She's the only one of the Harbourns to fly the coop. Are you saying the old couple she boarded with beat her up?'

Anya knew what Kate was getting at. 'No. But what I know is only hearsay and won't hold up in court.'

The detective sipped her coffee. She was now running the discussion. 'I want crime scene to go over that car for any signs of a collision before it crashed. We could be looking at a homicide.'

'The accident team is still at the scene,' the younger officer announced.

His partner spoke next. 'We can check speed cameras in the area, see if they captured the Colt. It could give us an idea as to how fast she was going before the accident.'

Kate tugged the back of her hair. 'She may have been driving with a broken arm but that doesn't mean this was an accident. She was part of a family of psychopaths. We're looking at three of them for the Goodwin homicide. The fourteen-year-old almost had her head cut off after being raped.'

Both men lowered their heads as if humbled.

Kate finished her coffee. 'You could also help out by checking surveillance of service stations, ATMs, banks and anyone else in the area with a security camera. We might get lucky and see if another car was following Savannah.'

The three stood, thanked Anya and left. As she closed the door, Anya remembered the fear when she had seen the uniforms at the door. Had Noelene Harbourn experienced the same terror, or had she already known that her daughter was dead? She had no way of understanding a mother who could hit her already beaten daughter for 'complaining'.

She remembered seeing an interview of a bushwalker whose arm had been trapped under a rock in a remote location. He described amputating his own limb with a pocket knife in order to live and get to safety. Sacrifice one arm for the rest of the body.

The Harbourns had an incredibly strong survival instinct for which Savannah may have just paid the ultimate price.

23

From the images of Savannah Harbourn's car on the news, the make and model of the vehicle were unrecognisable. The engine had been driven back into the front seat, a four-door car reduced in length by half. It was no surprise the driver had been killed.

A more recent model would have had airbags, but they were unlikely to have saved anyone with crushed legs and severe chest or head trauma.

In spite of Savannah's broken arm, Anya refused to accept this could have been an accident.

Unable to sleep, at first hint of daylight she drove to the crash site. Turning into the road on which Savannah died gave her an eerie feeling.

Parkland lined with trees was on one side, with a school the length of the block on the other. No wonder there were no witnesses to the crash. At night, the area would have been deserted save for passing traffic.

Round a bend, black skid marks were visible on the opposite side of the road. Twenty metres long, they veered to the left on a verge then disappeared.

This was where Savannah had been killed.

School didn't start for at least two hours, so Anya parked her car and crossed the now quiet road. She walked down the small dip to where the Colt had hit the tree outside the park, a distance of only ten metres from the road. The trunk showed little damage apart from an indentation around hip level.

Even at low speed the Colt would have been crumpled on impact with an immovable object. The surrounding ground had been disturbed by the accident squad, ambulances and police. The foliage had all but been destroyed.

At the base of the tree sat two bunches of flowers. One, daffodils; and the other, plastic poinsettias, the type that are all over gift shops before Christmas. She photographed them with her phone and bent down to see if either had cards attached.

The daffodils had a letter wrapped in cellophane.

> *I'm so sorry. I finally understand, and forgive you.*
> *No more pain or hurt.*
> *You can rest in peace now you are free.*
> *White light forever, Violet.*

Anya had to admire Violet Yardley. Despite being raped by Savannah's brothers and not being helped by the person she considered her best friend after the ordeal, Violet could forgive. Anya doubted if she were capable of being that generous in similar circumstances.

The plastic poinsettias had one printed word on a card. *WHY?*

The flowers could have been placed there by anyone, family or friends, even a child. Presumably plastic flowers were meant to last as a permanent reminder of what had occurred, but the base of the tree wasn't visible from the road. The solo word was haunting.

Anya couldn't get the same question out of her mind. She checked the GPS on her mobile and plotted the route between the elderly couple's home where Savannah boarded and the Harbourn family home. They were only eight streets away.

Back in her car, Anya followed the route to the Harbourn home. Turning right at a set of lights, she noticed broken orange plastic, again on the opposite side of the road. She pulled over outside a house and parked. The pieces didn't look as though they had been run over, and may have been fresh.

She called Kate, who was already up. 'I'm near last night's accident site and I think she could have been rear-ended at a set of lights about a kilometre away. It could explain why she was speeding.'

Kate was silent for a few seconds. 'If she were rear-ended, she'd be more likely to stop because it wasn't her fault. She was caught speeding so we know how fast she was travelling. Even you said she had a broken arm, which was an accident just waiting to happen.'

'I understand that, but bear with me a moment. What if she were being pursued? Was anyone else photographed speeding at the same time?'

'Unless you can find someone who saw the accident, there's nothing to suggest anyone else was involved. The squad was all over this last night. There was only one set of skid marks. One car. Hell, maybe the one responsible Harbourn tried to avoid hitting an animal and crashed.'

'Fine.' Anya felt anger rise. This was a woman who had been assaulted, feared for her life and was now dead. How difficult was this to understand? She took a deep breath. Getting angry with Kate wouldn't help. 'Can you just check if there was any recent damage to the back right of her car? Please. This girl was terrified, and for good reason. On a busy night, even the squad could have missed this.'

More silence.

'I'll make a call and get back to you.'

Anya performed a U-turn, pulling up short of the intersection with her hazard lights on. Morning traffic began to flow, and cars moved around hers without too much inconvenience. She then stood on the footpath, waiting. After honked horns and a few words of abuse as irritated commuters passed, the only person to offer assistance was a tow-truck driver. She politely declined. This was clearly not a place to break down if you wanted a good samaritan's assistance.

Minutes later, the phone rang. It was Kate's number. 'You were right. There was damage, but without any glass or plastic on the road, it was assumed it had happened before the crash. The old, "You know what women are like in car parks" line.'

'Thanks for this.' There *could* have been another car involved with Savannah's last night.

'I'll get the accident guys back, but in the meantime can you secure the scene?'

'Already done,' Anya announced as another motorist hurled abuse through his window. She gave Kate the intersection location and didn't have to wait long.

Detective Sergeant Owen Hollis, head of the accident investigation unit, was the first to arrive, in a police van. He immediately introduced himself and donned a lime-green fluorescent vest

'Thanks for the call. The rest of the unit is at a pile-up on the M4. They're still trying to evacuate the injured.'

He shook hands with the sort of grip that almost invited an arm wrestle. There was no hint of resentment at being recalled. Despite accident investigation detectives dealing with death, they tended to behave differently from their Homicide colleagues. They had to be more relaxed about getting forensic evidence at scenes. Often they worked in the midst of a main road while peak-hour traffic still had to flow, or while storms raged around and over them. It made survival sense to be less obsessive about protecting the scene.

Hollis had already placed detour signs at the end of the street to divert traffic to the next set of lights. He pulled out a camera and photographed the plastic on the road. He then removed a tape measure and began recording distances of the broken plastic from the kerb, to the middle of the road, and to the line that stopped traffic at the lights.

He squatted to take a closer look at the plastic. 'It's an indicator light, and we've got part of a headlight as well. And here,' he pulled out a thin metal spatula and collected something small, 'flecks of white paint. We can compare them to any found on the Colt and see if these two did collide.'

There didn't seem to be enough plastic to go on. Anya wondered what the chances were of being able to connect them to a specific car. 'Is there enough of any of the damaged lights to work out a make and model?'

He methodically collected each tiny fragment in an evidence bag. 'Never underestimate the power of sticky tape. You'd be surprised how much detail these tiny bits can reveal.' He looked up. '3-D jigsaw puzzles are my specialty.'

Kate pulled up behind them in her unmarked car, with Shaun Wheeler. This time the junior officer had full colour in his cheeks and was chewing gum.

'What have you got?' Kate asked.

'There was definitely a collision – the paint's fresh. I'll see what I can put together. There was some damage to the rear end of the Colt, so we'll see if we get a match.' He glanced up at the red-light camera to their left. 'Worth checking that one, too. If your driver was pushed through the light, or took off after being hit.'

Kate nodded a look of approval. 'Call me as soon as you know anything.'

The accident investigator saluted. 'You'll be the first. I'll start working on these as soon I get back to the office.'

The detectives left and Anya remained behind.

'I'm about to review the crash site if you'd like to come along,' Hollis said. 'Don't get to see forensic physicians that often on this job, and a second pair of eyes is always better than one.'

'I wouldn't mind. The driver who died had been recently assaulted and had reason to fear for her safety. If I can help, I'd like to.'

He opened the van passenger side door and handed her the original reports submitted by the uniformed police who were first on the scene. 'Just need to collect the detour signs and we'll be on our way. I'll follow if you like.'

Anya returned to her car and read the forms while she waited. Portions of the information were missing, due to absence of witness statements. Weather and terrain conditions were unremarkable and unlikely to have contributed to the smash. Being a single-vehicle accident, most of the form's sections were irrelevant. It was designed as a one-size fits all approach and intended for use in court and insurance claims.

They provided no information she didn't already know, apart from the year of the car's manufacture – 1988. That meant no airbags or power steering, which would have made controlling the vehicle in an emergency more difficult, especially with a broken arm. She couldn't imagine why Savannah had chosen to drive that night, at that time, with the fractured, unplastered arm.

Unless she had gone back to the family home to make sure her younger sisters were fed and safely in bed.

The police van appeared behind, and she led the way. About fifty metres from the site, Hollis stopped and switched on a *POLICE ALERT* flashing sign on his roof. He placed a series of emergency cones along the road, and gave Anya a fluorescent protective vest when she met him halfway.

'The skid marks are recorded as twenty metres long, but that's only the visible ones.'

Anya didn't know there were more than one type. 'How can you differentiate between marks that are and aren't visible?'

He took photos of the unmarked road from various angles and again laid out a distance-designed tape measure. Anya had no idea what he was documenting.

'There is always a shadow skid. Skid marks happen when the driver brakes hard and the tyres stop rotating. They start light and typically get darker as the skid progresses, until the car stops. It also takes time for the tyre to heat up enough against the road to leave visible marks. With sudden braking, the wheels begin to slow and don't lock up the instant the brakes are applied. That's when very faint shadow marks appear, before the black skid marks.'

'But do they help determine the speed or if the car was forced to change direction, say by being bumped or forced off the road by another car?'

'If the car had anti-lock brakes, we wouldn't be having this discussion. The problem is that when the wheels lock, it's impossible to steer. But if the car were hit by something else, it could have forced a change in direction. In this case, however, the skid marks are all in a straight line. Looks like the driver braked, locked the wheels and couldn't steer around the bend and so ran off the verge, down into the tree. Pretty straightforward.'

A furniture truck drove around them and Anya felt the gust of wind. She instinctively turned her back to avoid the dust in her face. Hollis did the same.

'In terms of speed,' he continued, 'there is a multitude of variables to factor into calculations. Things like road surface, level, defects, drag factors, wind conditions. If you're wondering about the speed of impact in this instance, it could have been as little as sixty kilometres an hour, the limit for this particular road.'

Anya was aware that even speeds that low could be fatal, particularly when small cars hit solid objects like trees. If only more people understood that.

A car sped past, clearly exceeding the speed limit.

The question that remained in Anya's mind was, why did Savannah brake that hard, fifty metres back, on a straight stretch of road?

There had to be another car on the road with her. The fragments of plastic had to hold the key to who ran into her before she crashed.

24

With two separate court appearances in the next two weeks and reports to write, Anya planned to hibernate in her office for the rest of the day.

She would review Violet Yardley's file, in case there was anything that could help the police further. But the first priority was to document everything she could remember about Savannah Harbourn. What she had said, how she had acted, her state of mind, her injuries. From what she had said, her life was spent trying hard not to draw attention to herself.

Violet had even described her as 'straight-edged', drug- and alcohol-free. So the toxicology report should come back negative.

This was a woman who went back to the family home to make sure her younger siblings were being fed, looked after, and even helped with their homework. She feared for what would happen to them if she left.

Anya did, too, now the sisters had lost their only protector.

The broken arm would have been a significant hazard driving, though. Without the strength of one arm, she had little control if she needed to swerve or avoid an accident. That word again. The term 'car accident' was completely misleading when most involved substance abuse, speed or breaking road rules – all illegal acts. Working in the morgue had proven that more often than not, innocent people were victim to what was nothing less than criminal behaviour.

Paperwork filled the rest of the working day. After a hot bath and a plate of pasta, Anya settled in to watch some television, to get her mind off work and sort through some of the photos from the trip. They'd make a great scrapbook for Ben.

Just before nine, Kate Farrer knocked on the door.

'Slimy bastards!' she said, storming into the hallway with a thick file in her hands.

'Who?' Anya followed Kate to the kitchen.

'The bastard Harbourns. The ringleader, Gary, the one with the mole. He's admitted himself to a private psychiatric hospital and the shrink there thinks he's too unwell to be interviewed about Rachel Goodwin's murder.'

Kate threw down the file, shoved the sleeves on her shirt to her elbows and slapped both hands on the counter.

Anya considered the possibilities. If the police had physical evidence from the scene and Sophie's statement, it could be a stunt to avoid being arrested. 'What's the reason for admission. Is he claiming to be suicidal or depressed?'

'He's already going for an insanity defence. He drove himself over there and walked in the door saying he's hearing voices telling him to hurt people.'

Schizophrenia wasn't an easy state to fake, although some criminals assumed it was. Anya flicked on the kettle. 'You can't just wake up one day, say you have schizophrenia and deny responsibility for all your actions, it doesn't work like that.'

'Want to bet? He's already got one psychiatrist convinced.' Kate stretched and cracked her neck. 'This has got to be a bad joke. What are we supposed to tell Ned Goodwin? "We know who raped your daughters, killed one and left the other barely breathing, but he's hiding in hospital and we can't get to him."'

Anya could see Kate's point of view, but hiding in a psychiatric facility was risky. 'You can ask for an independent assessment—'

'That's why I'm here.'

Anya should have known this wasn't a social visit. She grabbed two mugs from the cupboard and began to make a pot of tea.

Kate hauled herself up to sit on the bench. 'As one of our favourite forensic physicians, the department formally requests you assess Gary Harbourn for any injuries he could have sustained when he attacked the Goodwin girls, and tell us if you think he's fit to be interviewed.' She grabbed the last apple and placed a card in the now empty fruit bowl. On it was the hospital's contact details and the name of the treating psychiatrist.

'The doctor says Harbourn's not going anywhere, so you can go any time tomorrow if that suits.'

'I can do a physical assessment and look for injuries, but my usual role is to make sure a suspect isn't intoxicated, suffering drug withdrawal or some physical or mental illness that will impair his ability to answer questions at that time. A diagnosis of schizophrenia, even if he has it, doesn't automatically mean insanity. Incidentally, "insanity" is a legal, not a medical term.'

Kate groaned. 'As far as I'm concerned it's an insult to the victims' family to have that bastard parading as someone with a real mental illness. He's gutless and can't even face up to what he's done. He's taking the piss out of all of us. It's just a bloody great game to him and his family. All you have to do is catch him out faking it.'

No pressure then, Anya thought. The timing of the hospital admission was highly suspicious, given Savannah's death, but she had to maintain an open mind. When Kate left, she'd have to brush up on everything she had on schizophrenia.

Even so, a diagnosis could explain Gary's rapid escalation in violence. Progressing from thug to rapist was one thing, but as far as they were aware of there had been no gradual increase in aggression in his sexual crimes. More violence could have been a natural progression if each rape didn't live up to his fantasies, but the number of stab wounds in the Goodwin girls suggested something dramatic had occurred.

'What did the forensics show from the evidence you collected in their home?'

Kate chomped into the apple, juice trickling down her chin, which she caught with the back of her hand. 'Gary's prints were on the knife handle. When questioned, they said that Gary was off his head on drugs and alcohol and Rick and Patrick followed and tried to stop him hurting anyone, but he was too strong.

Gotta love the imaginative lies these guys come up with. Oh yeah, and the "invisible man" who mysteriously does all their crimes was at the Goodwin house and raped the girls. The underwear was Rachel's and both girls' blood was on the knife. We've got Gary but we need to nail down the others. We have three other possible suspects. It'll come down to whether or not Sophie can ID her attackers, even though she said she didn't see the face or eyes of at least one of them.'

Anya couldn't forget what four of the brothers had done to Giverny. 'What about the red paint on the kids' shirt?'

'It came from the same batch as the paint on Giverny's car. But the best we've got is a shirt belonging to Rick that was used while he was in jail. Nothing was stolen from the Hart house so we've got nothing but vandalism given the post-mortem findings. Even if we find out who wore that shirt, it wouldn't be worth prosecuting.'

Kate jumped down and headed for the door, chomping into the apple as she left. With a full mouth she managed, 'I've got to go. We can tie Gary to Sophie with the knife and underwear. Somehow we've got to put a wedge between the Harbourn brothers and get one to crack.'

Anya closed and deadlocked the door. At least the department would eventually pay her for the assessment. She poured a cup of strong black tea and traipsed upstairs to change into her pyjamas. She returned and curled up on her comfy lounge to read the file Kate had left.

It resembled a hospital file on someone with a lifetime of admissions. A series of charge sheets outlined a litany of offences. By eighteen, Gary had spent four years in and out of juvenile detention for armed robbery, breaking and entering and assault.

Kate had summarised a number of incidents and outcomes. At eighteen, he was arrested for sexual assault, but was acquitted at trial. The victim suffered from agoraphobia and was terrified of leaving her home. She gave her evidence by video link and had an anxiety attack in front of the jury.

According to Kate's notes, the jury thought she was mentally unstable and an unreliable witness.

It was possible that Gary targeted women with a mental illness. They were among the most vulnerable, and their credibility could be shattered in court, if they were even capable of testifying. It was easy to pick up the basics about psychiatric disorders through prison and defence lawyers.

By nineteen, he was in court again, with Ian, one of his younger brothers. This time the charge was ram-raiding a gun shop with a stolen car. Each claimed they had been framed by a third person, Simon Vine, who had committed the robbery and planted guns at their home. The complete cache was never retrieved.

A witness said one of the men had a beard during the robbery, but couldn't identify Gary or his brother, who Kate had noted were both clean-shaven for the court appearance.

Despite the doubt, Gary was convicted and served eighteen months. Ian Harbourn spent seven months in prison.

Anya rubbed her eyes. The words began to blur, with charges and trials all reading alike. Simon Vine was named as the mastermind in most of the family's crimes, but the police had been unable to locate anyone by that name. She doubted they ever would. This was Kate's 'invisible man'.

Flicking through the medical history proved more interesting. Four years prior, Gary was admitted to the same psych facility for depression and suicidal ideation, claiming fuguelike episodes in which he supposedly 'lost' periods of time.

This defence failed when he used it to fight a charge of grievous bodily harm. He had bashed a former employer with a baseball bat, and set fire to his business. She underlined the words *baseball bat*.

Anya recalled what Savannah had said. The night she was beaten, Gary wanted her to find the baseball bat and then flew into a rage when he found out two of the brothers had taken it out. The bat was for bashing victims. Ironically, the fact that the brothers had taken it might just have saved Savannah from being killed by Gary, who had only his fists and feet to lash out with. Then again, if the bat were home, Savannah may never have been hit at all. That night.

The episode with the employer scored him a four-year sentence, of which he served two. The record stated that he had agreed to be treated with antidepressants and attend regular counselling and anger management sessions in jail. Anya suspected it was a criminal's career move, bargaining for a more lenient sentence.

She dropped the pen on the floor and put the papers back into the file. It was almost incomprehensible how many times family members had been in and out of prison with short penalties given the severity of the crimes. They were beyond rehabilitation. And yet all had been released, to rape, torture and kill without any fear of the consequences. No wonder they weren't threatened by the justice system.

The pendulum had swung in favour of offenders, to the detriment of victims. By benefiting recidivists like the Harbourns, it had failed to protect Giverny Hart and the Goodwin sisters and even one of their own, Savannah. She couldn't begin to estimate the number of people who continued to be affected by their crimes.

Despite being limited in the scope of her interview and examination, if Gary was faking psychosis she was determined to catch him out.

25

The following morning, Anya arrived at Saint Stephen's Private Clinic. The entrance, with its marbled floors and floral centrepiece, resembled an expensive hotel rather than an acute psych facility.

The 'client liaison officer' sat at a desk and greeted her. Within minutes of being buzzed, Doctor Kyle Temple appeared in the foyer. No white coat in sight, the young psychiatrist wore an open-neck business shirt and tailored trousers.

He extended his hand. 'I hoped we might have a brief chat before you see our patient.'

Our patient? she thought. This was a short assessment to determine whether Gary Harbourn had physical injuries to connect him to the Goodwins. Her questions would be limited, and in the presence of a member of staff. She had no role in his management.

They headed along a corridor that featured an indoor rainforest along one side and the piped sound of birds punctuated by a rhythm of flowing water. Presumably the rainforest provided a calm and private environment, but Anya was struck by how extravagant the setting was, and how expensive it must be to maintain. With the state of public psychiatric wards, this place must have a long waiting list for admission.

She wondered how Gary Harbourn could afford to stay here, or how he had managed to secure a bed at short notice. Drugs, robberies and standover tactics were clearly more profitable than unemployment benefits.

They walked past an empty communal area with a large plasma screen television. That room was empty. Further along was a double door marked *Theatrette*.

'We have a holistic approach to treatment and try to give our clients the most relaxing, least pressured routine. In the evenings we show movies and encourage families to come along on themed weekends.'

The place was more like a luxury resort than a mental health facility.

'This is quite impressive. How many beds do you have?'

The doctor ran his hands through his fringe and smiled. 'We can accommodate up to seventy, but at the moment we've thirty-one inpatients partaking in programmes which include alcohol and substance abuse, eating disorders, self-harm, post-traumatic stress disorder and depression. Then, of course, we have our section for those with acute psychosis. Naturally, a large part of our business comprises regular outpatients, often after an intensive programme.'

They passed a glassed area comprising a gymnasium and massage therapy centre. A man and a woman worked out on treadmills to the sound of Britney Spears.

'The economic downturn and increased unemployment rates have left many people reconsidering private health insurance, but we refuse to cut back our services. Our programmes achieve excellent results.'

Whoever believed crime didn't pay should have visited Gary Harbourn in this luxurious setting.

Doctor Temple stopped at a door and scanned his ID. They entered the consulting room, which contained a desk and office chair, an examination bed behind a curtain and two armchairs facing each other. The psychiatrist chose to sit at the desk, as if interviewing Anya. So much for the brief chat.

'I've treated Gary Harbourn for a couple of years now and am very familiar with his case. This latest tragedy, the death of his sister, has really rocked him. He isn't coping well at all.'

Having been through the extensive file last night, Anya felt familiar with his history as well. 'Am I able to see him?'

'Yes, of course, but there are some things that concern me

about the timing of your visit. At the moment he is in a very fragile state.'

'In what way?' Anya was interested to hear about Gary's behaviour up until now, and the doctor's reasons for concern about her presence.

'He was brought here by his mother the night before last in a terrible state, around three in the morning. He had felt under stress, it seems, and had smoked a fair amount of cannabis and drunk a lot of alcohol over the preceding weeks. He had also neglected to take his antidepressants over this period.' The doctor swept his hair to one side. 'As you know, the combination of a pre-existing mental illness and intoxication can precipitate a psychotic episode. When he arrived he was talking about voices in his head telling him to kill women. He was convinced that he would harm someone so his mother brought him in.'

The timing of the admission coincided with Savannah's death and anyone would have been stressed facing a litany of charges beginning with homicide. Anya nodded, keen to let the doctor share his opinion and the diagnosis he had made for Gary Harbourn.

He placed his elbows on the desk and clasped his fingers beneath his chin. 'This is a very troubled man. There is a childhood history of physical abuse compounded by the nightmares he still has about seeing his father's body covered in blood in their living room.'

Doctor Temple paused, presumably to test Anya's reaction. She needed to stay objective and be seen as such. She did not respond.

'Mr Harbourn was stabbed to death, you know.'

Anya knew. Noelene Harbourn had never been charged because the family all touched the murder weapon and no one could refute her statement about being abused by the victim or her having to save herself and the children. 'I'm aware of the family background.'

'Forgive me, but I checked you on the internet. You're a forensic pathologist turned physician, so you cannot be expected to know all the subtle psychometric consequences of such a traumatic event. To a child, even if his mother killed in self-defence, this was an enormous betrayal of love, and one he was always unlikely to recover from. The relationship with his mother is complex and she continues to have inordinate control over all her children.'

Anya hoped he couldn't read what she was thinking. The siblings had conspired with their mother to disturb the crime scene. Gary would have known right from wrong even back then.

His mother didn't make him rape Giverny, nor make him mutilate and kill Rachel Goodwin. Why did this psychiatrist have complete disregard for the victims? Gary Harbourn was a violent perpetrator. Sophie and her father and the Hart parents were the real victims. She moved in the seat, checking her watch, hoping he would let her see Harbourn now.

If Doctor Temple noticed her sense of urgency, he ignored it.

'Gary's history of recurrent crime is textbook. He has been sexually and physically traumatised in prison and even refers to sex in terms of either prison style or free style.

'He is incapable of holding down a job and demonstrates numerous signs of antisocial personality disorder on top of his depression and drug-induced psychosis.'

The counterargument was that he couldn't hold down a job because he kept being imprisoned for criminal acts and he had burnt down the business of a former employer.

Anya always knew that a large number of people in prison had antisocial personality disorders, so it wasn't a reason to avoid prosecution. Nor was low intelligence or psychiatric illness. If that were the case, prisons would be virtually empty.

'Do you think there is any chance he could be feigning psychosis?'

Doctor Temple scraped his fringe to the side again. 'I'm sure you are aware of studies in which psychology students were briefed to enter public hospitals claiming to be hearing voices.'

He used the term 'public' with a hint of disdain.

'They were all caught out as fraudulent by the psychiatrists before they could gain admission. In fact, it's extremely difficult to fake psychosis.'

Anya had read other studies in which students were admitted because they heard voices but displayed no psychiatric symptoms once in hospital. In those instances, psychiatrists failed to diagnose the normal behaviour they exhibited. The other inpatients recognised the fraudsters, but the staff continued to document all behaviour as abnormal, reinforcing the diagnosis.

The field of psychiatry was reasonably subjective, which left room for manipulation by people like the Harbourns. Another reason why Anya preferred pathology.

Deciding not to challenge Doctor Temple, she nodded. 'May I see Gary now?'

Seemingly pleased that he had argued his case on behalf of his patient, the doctor stood up. 'He's learning how to use the computer but I'll bring him back here.'

As Anya waited she glanced around the room and noticed two framed panoramic prints of the Tasmanian wilderness – Cradle Mountain and Freycinet Peninsula, two of the most picturesque places in the world.

A few minutes later there was a knock on the door and Doctor Temple returned with a thickset man dressed in jeans, T-shirt and larger than needed slippers. Both feet were bandaged and he limped into the room.

'I'm Doctor Crichton.' Anya stood. 'Please take a seat.'

Gary Harbourn tentatively moved to the spare chair and turned back to Doctor Temple. 'Is it safe for her to be here with me? I don't want to hurt anyone.' He spoke like a frightened child.

'It's okay, Gary, the medication is starting to work. I'll stay in case you need me.'

'Thank you, Doctor,' Gary said and sat. He bowed his head and stared at his knees.

'Do you know why I'm here?' Anya asked.

'You think I'm insane and am going to hurt people. You want

173

to lock me up in jail.' His hands began to shake and he clamped them between his thighs.

Anya glanced at the ceiling corners and lights, wondering if the interview was being monitored or recorded. There was no sign of a camera.

'I'm here to have a look at you. There are some police who would like to have a chat with you when you feel better. I need to check you out to see if you've been hurt recently.'

The hands shook uncontrollably, even between his legs.

'What happened to your feet?' she tried.

'I cut them. The voice was telling me to hurt people. It wouldn't stop ordering me to hurt . . .' he looked across at Anya for an instant, '. . . women.' His gaze returned to his lap. 'So I cut them to stop me from getting away from the doctors here.'

'May I see how they're healing?' Anya tried to sound sympathetic. Temple was listening. She didn't want to appear combative in any way. This interview had to be unbiased.

Gary Harbourn unwrapped one bandage, hands struggling to cope with the simple task. He tried to cross one leg to show the sole of the foot and took two attempts before managing it. She wondered how he had coped with a computer keyboard before their meeting.

Spontaneously he announced, 'The Bible says that if your eye causes you to sin, cut it out; it is better for you to enter the kingdom of God with one eye than keep the bad eye and be cast into hell.'

Anya wondered if that was an admission to killing Savannah. She tried not to show any reaction, even if he had misquoted the passage.

'What do you think that refers to?' she asked, still looking at the feet.

'You can't die for a cause unless you're prepared to kill for it.'

That wasn't exactly Anya's interpretation. She documented the comment.

Although Gary Harbourn had multiple horizontal lacerations to his foot, none was deep enough to warrant stitches. In other words, they were all superficial and parallel, which would have been difficult to achieve with a genuine hand tremor.

'Can you tell me why you think you might hurt someone?'

Gary stared at her with dark cold eyes, the ones Sophie had described.

'It's the voice in my head. He keeps telling me to do bad things.'

'Can you tell me a little about the voices. Do you know who is talking to you? What do they sound like?'

'It's always the same. My step-father. He's telling me to kill women. Stab them, cut their throats before they kill us both. Can you make him stop?'

Anya studied his face, trying to see a smirk, or anything to suggest Gary was faking his symptoms. 'Do you know what happened to your father?'

He hesitated before answering. 'He's inside my head. He says I'm the only way he can stay alive.'

'Do you see him?' She hoped he would try to describe extravagant hallucinations and slip up, overdoing the symptoms and detail.

'Sometimes.'

'Does he appear to you in colour or black and white?'

Gary's tremor stopped. He appeared stumped for a few moments. 'No one's asked me that before. Why do you want to know?'

'Just curious,' she said, aware she had rattled him.

'I can't remember.'

'Can you hear his voice now?'

His little boy tone disappeared, replaced with a deeper, more controlled voice. 'He doesn't like you. He thinks I should hurt you because you're out to get us.'

Anya ignored the threat. 'Doctor Temple mentioned that you were improving on medication. I'd like to ask you a few questions and I need you to give me honest answers.'

Gary nodded. 'I want to help.'

Anya moved forward to examine his arms, chest, back, hands

neck and legs. There were no signs of scratches or bruising. He was clean and there was unlikely to be any evidence left from the night at the Goodwins on his body.

'Can you recall the night you had the street party after being released from prison?'

Gary shook his head and the hand shaking returned. 'All I remember is having some drinks and smoking a couple of cones. After that, it's all blank.'

Anya let a silence hang between them, choosing to observe overtly while taking notes. He didn't take the opportunity to initiate conversation.

'One more thing, did the voices ever want you to kill your sister, Savannah?'

He clenched his teeth. 'She died in an accident.'

Anya kept eye-contact. 'I was hoping you might like to talk about how she died. It could help.'

Gary quickly stood and pulled down the picture of Cradle Mountain, smashing it against the wall and screaming incoherently.

Doctor Temple stood up and pressed a red buzzer above the desk. Swiftly, Anya moved closer to the door. A nurse arrived with a trolley and two wardsmen. The psychiatrist drew up an intramuscular sedative and injected it into his arm with his staff's help.

After watching Gary Harbourn's sedation take effect, Anya excused herself and left the room.

Doctor Temple followed, like a nervous parent.

'No one could deny that Gary is very disturbed.'

'I agree. He is extremely troubled about a number of things, as you mentioned; his sister's death is one of them. However, he should still be able to be interviewed by the police about the night Rachel Goodwin and her sister were attacked – with your approval and presence, of course.'

26

Natasha Ryder downed a grape from the plate on the table and rocked in her chair.

'The insane defence? You've got to be joking.'

Anya handed the prosecutor her report of Gary Harbourn's assessment.

Natasha pulled on rimless glasses and read while Hayden Richards and Kate Farrer sat quietly.

'Hearing voices, that's original. Is there an "Idiot's Guide to Faking Insanity" that we don't know about?' Natasha mumbled as she turned the page. 'Let's get to the crux. Is he faking?'

Anya had to be honest. 'From that short interview, I can't be sure. His psychiatrist is convinced but Harbourn was reasonably lucid when I saw him, until I mentioned Savannah's death. That's when he went berserk.'

Kate slapped the arms of her chair. 'How can he be insane and lucid? He's taking the mickey out of all of us.'

'It's not that simple,' Anya explained. 'He claims to have been in a psychotic state when the Goodwins were attacked. One induced by depression, cannabis and alcohol. It's irrelevant whether or not he's thinking clearly now. My purpose was to assess any physical injuries he had and whether he was fit for police interview. That's it. The rest is my non-expert opinion.'

'I appreciate that,' Natasha said, 'but what's your gut telling you?'

Anya had to be careful what she said. This was outside her field of expertise. 'Sorry, but I'm not qualified to judge.'

Hayden Richards stroked his moustache with one finger.

'How about we show you his behaviour at the house search and you can compare that to the impression he gave you?'

'I want to review that tape anyway.' The prosecutor stood and turned on the portable television. 'Maybe you missed something. These guys aren't that smart.'

Anya could see Kate grip the chair. 'We even had a stud gun looking for metal hidden behind the walls, which is how we located the knife, which is consistent with the girls' stab wounds. We've established that the underpants in the bag belonged to Rachel. We believe we were thorough.'

'Let's see.' Natasha hit the play button and returned to her seat with the remote.

The DVD began with Noelene Harbourn in view wearing her gown. It quickly fast-forwarded to the room searches. A few minutes later, Gary Harbourn came into view, wearing nothing but underpants.

Bare-chested, it was possible to see a torso, biceps and triceps that had only developed from weight-lifting, with or without steroids. He may have had strength, but the shortened hamstrings and bulked quadriceps meant he was unlikely to be fast or flexible.

He didn't appear to be in any distress from his feet, which were bare and bandage-free. From his comments and wise-cracks, this was a man who didn't fear the police. He had cut the soles of his feet some time between the search and her inter-viewing him at Saint Stephen's.

Natasha paused the footage of the smirking Gary, who seemed to be daring Kate to arrest him.

The behaviour was arrogant and taunting, not what she would expect from someone in psychosis, with no memory of an event. Experience and instinct told her Gary Harbourn was faking to avoid prison.

'He's pretty smug, the bastard.' Kate scratched at the arm of her chair. 'As if he's sure we wouldn't find anything on him in the house that day.'

Natasha agreed. 'Not exactly Einstein, this guy.'

'What about the baseball bat? Any prints or blood on it?'

The conversation she had with Savannah and mention of the baseball bat had been confidential, but then she remembered Sophie mentioning the man with the bat going into Rachel's room. Gary's over-reaction to the brothers borrowing it the night Savannah was beaten meant it was probably incriminating.

Natasha played then paused the recording again. When Milo sprayed the luminol in the living area, there was no bat. A few minutes later, a baseball bat and tattered mitt were by the sofa.

'For occupational health and safety reasons the CSO wouldn't spray with members of the public present.' Kate sank in her chair. 'She got them to leave the room then re-enter it.'

Natasha forwarded through more images. The cameraman moved to the next room and followed Liz Gould and the CSOs.

The lounge room, where the family had waited, was only searched with the naked eye once the bat appeared. If an object had been in contact with blood then washed, it wouldn't have been obvious to anyone doing the search.

'Where did the bat come from?' Anya wanted to know if it had been there or brought out by one of the family when they moved back into the room.

The prosecutor moved closer to the screen and paused the image. She forwarded slowly. The cameraman had recorded each of the children filing out from the bedrooms.

One of the elder boys entered the room with something at his side, then the children huddled together. A few frames later, the youngest sister was standing near the bat, the handle now covered with a mitt.

They watched Liz Gould checking the walls with the stud finder, to knee level. Kate explained, 'Anything metallic, like the knife, would register. We got lucky in Gary's room.'

'Smart,' Natasha commented. 'It should become part of the routine. So we think this could have been used to threaten Rachel?' Anya could not admit knowing that the bat had been used for other assaults.

'We need to check it for traces of blood,' Hayden shook his head at the mistake.

'That leaves us with a few problems.' Natasha tapped the desk with her pen. 'Were Rick and Patrick the other Harbourns at the Goodwin home, and do we have anything to link them to that house, or even to Rachel and Sophie? And what about this Simon Vine character? If we can only prove Gary was there and he claims insanity, we could lose. If there's nothing to suggest he deliberately planned the attack on the Goodwins, he might get away with insanity as a defence. Without motive or a logical reason for him attacking the girls, it's hard to challenge a drug-induced psychosis. If a jury sees his act, they'll acquit. A good defence lawyer could tear Sophie to shreds on the stand given her severe blood loss that night and inability to ID the others.'

Kate flicked through her notebook. 'The singlet and shirt that showed positive for luminol were Gary's, and they'd both been washed. Lab's trying to get DNA from the blood in the seams, but hasn't had any luck yet.'

'We're still canvassing friends and acquaintances about who left the street party, but so far no one's talking. It seems everyone we approach thinks of the Harbourn brothers as folk heroes beating the system by getting out of jail, or else they're too scared of being bashed, or worse.' Hayden sounded more frustrated than the prosecutor.

'What about the knife? Do we know where it came from?'

Kate answered, 'Patrick claims Gary took the knife from him that night. Wait for it, to carve up roast chickens for the street party. Funny how he could hand Gary a knife and not leave his own print on it.'

Hayden added, 'There's no obvious link between the Harbourns and the Goodwins, so we don't have a motive. The pubic hair found on Rachel's body could belong to a number of extended family members, but so far all but one has a sound alibi, some interstate and others overseas. It seems that even the cousins want nothing to do with Noelene's bad brood.'

The prosecutor turned to Anya. 'This isn't enough. We need more on the family.'

Giverny's rape and death, Rachel's murder and Sophie's brutal assault should have been enough, she thought. But the legal system put the onus on the prosecution to prove beyond reasonable doubt. Giverny was dead so that case was compromised. Natasha Ryder was placing all of her hopes for a conviction on the Goodwin case, or any other they could prove. Yet despite physical evidence linking Gary Harbourn to the Goodwins, he could avoid prosecution by pleading insanity.

'I have spoken to a woman who came to the SA unit. She was raped by some of the Harbourn brothers over a year ago.'

Natasha sat forward and flicked open a folder containing a legal pad. 'What's her name? When can I see her?'

'Hold on.' Violet's name had to remain confidential. 'At this stage she still refuses to make a statement, but the forensic evidence from her attack is kept locked in the SA fridge. I've spoken to her recently but until she officially comes forward, there's nothing I can give you. She was involved with the family and is still terrified of them.'

The prosecutor tapped her pen on the pad. 'Not good enough. If she knows the family, maybe she can fill us in on some of their dirty secrets, give us something to go on. Can you put pressure on her?'

Anya's first thought was Giverny Hart and how she had been threatened with the weight of the law if she refused to testify. Violet didn't deserve that treatment either. 'I pushed my luck tracking her down in the first place.'

Hayden considered, 'Can you make a statement to the effect that there was a similar pattern of evidence in the attacks between this woman and Giverny?'

'Everything was different. Giverny was randomly snatched off the street, this girl was linked to one of the brothers and was drinking with them when the rapes took place.'

Natasha dropped the pen on the pad. 'We're back to having nothing. Even if she does agree to talk to us, it sounds like a disaster to prosecute. It would be her word against the family's, no matter what the evidence shows. It always comes back to "he said, she said".' She swivelled around to the window. 'We have the murder weapon, but we also need something to connect the Harbourns to the Goodwins *and* the names of exactly who else was present. Without all of those things there's virtually no chance of prosecuting.'

Anya remembered the cropped top Zimmer found at the scene. It had a bloodied fingerprint on it. 'What about the print on Rachel's pink top? The one we think was used to gag her?'

Hayden shook his head. 'Fingerprint's not on file. It doesn't match anyone in the system.'

'Aren't all the brothers on file? Each of them has a criminal record.'

'They should, I'll double check that. Maybe someone else was at the scene that night, like Simon Vine, our phantom friend. So far we've only looked at the Harbourns.'

'That's because they only ever travel and hunt in a pack. The family's like Medusa's head,' Natasha said. 'You cut one of the snakes off by sending it to jail and another one slithers up to take its place.'

Hayden's phone rang and he moved away to answer it. A minute later he returned to the table with a large grin.

'We just got two breaks. It seems Noelene Harbourn's been telling lies. Two of her sons were filmed at a bottle shop that night, nowhere near the Goodwin house when the girls were attacked. With Ian still in prison, that only leaves Patrick and Rick with Gary at the Goodwins. And Rick's prints weren't on our data base. It seems he had a juvenile file sealed at the mother's request. We got a court order to access it. The print on the top was definitely Rick Harbourn's.'

'So we've just narrowed down which three were most likely to be involved.' Natasha smiled for the first time that day.

'Now we crank up the pressure and see which one loses his head first,' Hayden said. 'We'll bring them in for questioning then charge them.'

Anya asked Natasha about prosecution for Giverny's rape.

'If we successfully prosecute the Harbourns for Rachel and Sophie, it will be easier to argue that pack rape is their specialty. But if we fail on the first trial, the chances of ever making them pay for what they did to Giverny Hart are too low to even contemplate. It all rides on convicting Gary, Rick and Patrick.'

27

Monday morning, Natasha Ryder strode into court and placed her briefcase on the prosecutor's table. She looked formidable in her dark trouser suit and mauve shirt for the hearing to establish whether Gary Harbourn was fit to stand trial for the aggravated sexual assault and murder of Rachel Goodwin and the rape and attempted murder of Sophie.

The bail hearing for Rick and Patrick hadn't gone to plan. Both had been released on bail, their lawyers arguing that they had tried to stop their psychotic brother hurting the Goodwin girls. Rick's juvenile file was not admissible and he gave some sob story about needing to support his family. Anya couldn't believe he claimed his fingerprint was on the cropped top because he had removed it from Rachel's throat, trying to save her life. With passports confiscated, both brothers had been released pending trial.

It may have been clichéd, but glasses made Natasha look wiser, and somehow softened her features, which no doubt made her look more sympathetic to juries. This hearing was to be heard in front of a judge, however. Natasha's role was to convince him that Gary was mentally fit to stand trial. Whether he was insane at the time of the attack was for a jury to decide if the case went to trial.

Trailing behind the prosecutor was a lawyer carting a trolley of files; he took a seat at the table.

Across the aisle sat two lawyers, almost clone-like in appearance. Charcoal suits and single-coloured ties that at least were each a different colour.

Gary sat unshaven, in dishevelled clothing, no doubt to look the part of a mentally unstable character, despite the luxury of his psychiatric facility. It also hid the mole that had incriminated him.

The press gallery contained a smattering of journalists, and the public gallery was empty apart from Noelene Harbourn and her supporters. Bevan Hart sat in the back row, with the junior Homicide detective, Shaun Wheeler. It didn't surprise Anya that Giverny's father had come to witness the trial, and his appearance with the junior detective was not unusual. Kate and Liz Gould would be testifying, not Wheeler, so there was no reason for him to be excluded from observing. Besides, victims and their families often relied on ongoing support from police to face the legal process.

The court rose for Judge Philip Pascoe.

Anya's heart sank. He had a reputation for being old school but strongly advocated rehabilitation programmes in lieu of tougher sentences, without appreciating that few such opportunities for prisoners existed due to funding constraints. Nevertheless, he continued to err on the side of minimum sentencing, even for repeat offenders. She had no idea about his sympathies towards cases involving the possibility of mental illness.

From the number of age spots and deep lines on his face, he had to be near seventy, the compulsory age for retirement.

Natasha's confident appearance seemed to evaporate as he entered the room. She fidgeted with a pencil on the desk.

The judge's assistant outlined the reason for their presence, to establish whether Mr Gary Harbourn was in fact fit to stand trial for the aforementioned crimes. After a lecture on the significance of the hearing and the responsibility of legal parties, the judge began to hear evidence.

Natasha argued that Harbourn had been calculating and aware enough to flee a search at his home, and the defence played up the fact that he had been in his underpants, jogging at the time – hardly rational behaviour.

Anya was stunned to be called by the defence to recount

what had happened when she had seen Gary in the hospital, and how he had behaved. All she could do was state the facts and hope the judge would pick up on the tremor not affecting Gary's computer skills but preventing him from functioning in the presence of a psychiatrist.

Natasha tried to lead Anya into stating her opinion, but the judge instructed the prosecutor to keep her questions relevant to the expert witness's area of expertise.

By the end of the day, Judge Pascoe had heard the evidence and retired to his chambers.

The next afternoon, Kate called with good news and bad news. Pascoe had decided Gary Harbourn was fit to stand trial. The bad news: because of the severity of Sophie's injuries and potential for further acute complications, he wanted to make sure the defence team had a chance to cross-examine her, the key witness. It meant a rushed trial, making the prosecution's work more difficult. Besides that, Pascoe was due for retirement in three months so he wanted the trial completed by then.

He brought the trial forward to four weeks from Monday. Kate didn't think it gave them enough time to prepare all the evidence for trial.

Intentionally or otherwise, the judge's decision had favoured the Harbourns.

Anya didn't tell Sophie that when she went to visit her the next day.

The morning of Rachel's funeral, Anya had cancelled appointments and stayed with Sophie so Ned could attend. Sophie had been too ill to go, even with a nurse and portable ventilator. Drifting in and out of consciousness, she had been unaware of what she was missing, using all her reserves to heal her shattered body.

After that, Anya had made the effort to sit with Sophie Goodwin at least three times a week. With her breathing tube continuing to block, she had further surgery to replace and secure it. Then came collapse in the base of her lungs, which led to bilateral pneumonia over the following week. Despite making good progress, she was still battling to get through each day without further complications.

Anya's visits gave Ned a chance for a shower and a meal outside the ICU, which had become his second home. He slept in a recliner rocker that had been moved into Sophie's room. Without enough rest, Ned Goodwin was facing becoming ill from exhaustion. Giving him a short break was the least Anya could do.

She always took along a book to read, something she had loved as a girl herself. Sophie closed her eyes and drifted in and out of sleep as Anya read aloud from the story of Helen Keller, *Pollyanna* or *Alice in Wonderland*. A.A. Milne poems were a definite favourite.

Sometimes Sophie would talk about her mother, and things she remembered from childhood. Rachel featured a lot in the conversations, but Sophie avoided becoming maudlin. If she had enough energy, they might watch TV. Inevitably, Sophie would fall asleep and Anya would sit and work on her laptop.

Anya found herself growing fonder of Sophie, and the relationship had nothing to do with pity.

The fourteen-year-old girl was naturally positive and managed to laugh at herself, even lying in an ICU bed. Sometimes she would remember something about the attack, or ask about the surgery or want more details about her injuries. Anya always answered honestly, even questions about whether any man would want to marry her, and what sex with someone you loved felt like. It was like having a little sister, one who had grown up far too quickly and painfully.

As days passed, the fear of the trial and testifying occupied Sophie's thoughts more and more. Although Anya tried to prepare her for what was to come, there was no escaping the trauma Sophie and her father were about to endure in the name of justice.

28

The morning the trial began, Anya listened from the back of the courtroom. Charges against the three accused were read out and each was asked if he was entering a plea. One of the defence lawyers stood and buttoned his suit jacket.

'Your honour, my client, Gary Harbourn, wishes to plead not guilty on the grounds of insanity at the time of the offence.'

The remaining lawyers stood in turn, declaring 'not guilty' on behalf of their clients.

Natasha arched her lower back, as if preparing for a physical battle.

Judge Pascoe asked why the Crown intended to prosecute the three accused in the one trial. Despite his wearing glasses, Anya noticed his unnerving squint. The right eye deviated outward when he spoke.

'Your Honour, we intend to argue that in the aggravated sexual assault and attempted murder of Sophie Goodwin, the three accused acted in a joint criminal exercise by committing the offences together. In doing so, all of the participants are guilty of the same crimes, regardless of the individual parts played.'

The defence lawyers argued for separate trials, no doubt to wear down the key witness. If she faltered or varied testimony over the course of several trials, they would have cause to discredit her. For Sophie's sake, Anya hoped there would be only one. Repeated examination and cross-examination on the stand was more than any victim, particularly one who had suffered so much, should endure.

Pascoe licked his top teeth. 'In the interests of justice, I am granting the request to have a separate trial for Gary Harbourn. Rick and Patrick Harbourn will be tried together.'

Natasha stood and objected. 'Your Honour, we strongly object to separate trials. For the key witness, the possibility of appearing in separate trials will be devastating. She remains in intensive care following the attacks and is clearly traumatised by the violence perpetrated against her and the murder of her sister.'

'I have made my decision,' Pascoe announced. 'First on the agenda will be Gary Harbourn.'

Before Natasha had a chance to respond, Pascoe turned to the bailiff. 'You may excuse the other defendants and bring the jury panel in.'

Before the pool of potential jurors entered, the judge turned to Natasha. 'Ms Ryder, I expect women in my courtroom to dress appropriately. You will wear a knee-length skirt when you next appear before me, not trousers as you are wearing today.'

Natasha turned to her assisting attorney who widened his eyes in surprise.

Anya chose to leave the courtroom then, bowing first to the judge before exiting. She couldn't believe that Pascoe could be so brazen in his sexism. Mind you, she had seen senior surgeons behave the same way to junior female doctors, demanding they wear skirts for ward rounds. Equality still had a long way to go in the legal and medical professions. It didn't make his comments any less offensive.

Anya's phone rang as soon as she turned it back on; it was Dan wondering if she'd been to visit his father again. Anya felt bad about it, but she hadn't been able to fit it in yet. She told him about the trial starting.

'Who's your judge?' Dan asked.

Anya answered and his prolonged silence said more than she wanted to know.

'I have managed to avoid him so far, but he and Dad had

some kind of run-in years ago. There's no love lost between them now.'

Anya promised to visit Dan's father very soon and explained she had to go.

Kate Farrer met her outside. 'Are they stalling or going ahead?'

'They're starting on the jury pool.'

Kate punched the air. 'I was worried. Pascoe is hard on police and prosecutors. Knowing the Harbourns, I was sure they'd use every possible trick to stall again.'

'He ordered separate trials for Gary and the others.'

Kate's elation was short-lived. 'Can't he see what that'll do to Sophie?'

'I'm not sure. Natasha has to prove Gary's malingering and has never suffered from a psychotic episode.'

Just then the prosecutor came out of the courtroom.

'We've got a ten-minute recess. One of the jury panel's absconded,' she said, pacing on the gravel outside the Supreme Court. She ignored cameras standing by, looking for the day's scoop.

'I'll need you in there, Anya, as first witness. I want you to give your evidence while the jury's fresh, and brace them for what they'll see in Sophie's first statement. We'll play the tape before setting up the video link with her hospital room.'

'Why separate the trials?' Kate pressed.

The prosecutor glanced around before answering. 'Pascoe's not far from retirement and my guess is he's going to give the defence a loose rein, to limit their chances of appeal. That way he'll finish up with a clean slate. That'll be pretty tough on us. We'll have to prove the case beyond any possible doubt.'

Kate glanced at Anya and knew she was on notice. No stuff-ups or mistakes.

'I'll need you tomorrow, Kate, all things proceeding,' Natasha added. 'Make sure everything you found on that search warrant is within the terms of reference and legal. Anything less than kosher and the case will be thrown out of court. If the Harbourns get an acquittal, we fail and they walk away, immune from further prosecution for what they did to Rachel and Sophie.'

29

After opening arguments, Anya took the stand and swore the truth oath. Natasha asked her to define her professional qualifications.

Gary Harbourn's lawyer, Joseph Stilton, interjected, 'Your Honour, we accept the witness is an expert in the field of forensic medicine.'

This was a common tactic employed when the defence didn't want the jury to hear the full extent of an expert witness's qualifications and experience.

Anya looked across at the jury, comprising five women and seven men, all watching her intently.

Natasha continued, 'Can you please tell me how many clinical vaginal examinations you have performed?'

'Through work at sexual assault units here and in England, I've seen over nine hundred alleged sexual assault victims. Prior to that, I reported vaginal injuries on over eighty female homicide victims who had been sexually assaulted.'

'In your own words,' Natasha stood firmly behind the bar table, 'could you please tell us what you found when you attended the homicide scene and observed Rachel Goodwin's body?'

Anya made eye contact with the prosecutor and described what she had seen when she arrived at the Goodwin home the morning after Rachel's murder. She observed two jurors taking notes, while a middle-aged woman winced when she described the naked young woman and the way she had been tied to the blood-soaked bed.

'I'd ask you, Doctor, to read from the post-mortem report and explain the injuries for the benefit of the jury.'

Anya read the description of tears, lacerations and large contusions, and simplified descriptions and explanations of the terms.

Natasha moved forward and pulled back a sheet from a chart.

Anya was given permission to step down and describe the extent of the external and internal injuries.

'And in your opinion were these injuries caused by consensual or nonconsensual intercourse?'

Rachel's injuries and vaginal tears were most probably the worst she had seen. 'I believe that these injuries were caused by nonconsensual sexual intercourse.'

Stilton objected. 'The doctor was not present and is in no position to state whether the bruising occurred without consent. Plenty of people within the population participate in vigorous consensual sex.'

Some snickers came from the public gallery. Anya noticed Noelene Harbourn cover her mouth with one hand as if shocked. With the other, she pulled the pre-teen daughter beside her to her breast, blocking her ears from the supposed vulgarity.

It seemed ridiculous that the description of the injuries didn't shock her enough to protect her daughter, but mention of sex did. It was obviously meant to suggest that Gary Harbourn came from a sheltered home, with an innocent and protective mother. What else but insanity would drive him to commit such a horrible crime? She was playing to the jury at every opportunity.

The judge immediately asked the jury to be excused for legal arguments.

Once they had filed out, Pascoe turned to Anya. 'Doctor, I don't believe that you can unequivocally state that these vaginal injuries could only have been caused by nonconsensual intercourse. Mr Stilton has a point.'

Anya glanced at Natasha in disbelief. She was unsure where the judge was going with this.

Stilton interjected again. 'Your honour, consent is an issue that is yet to be established in this case. And one that the deceased is not in a position to verify. The suggestion that nonconsensual intercourse took place is highly prejudicial to my client.'

'Your Honour,' Natasha said, 'Rachel Goodwin did not consent to being stabbed multiple times or murdered. We accept that as fact. In terms of nonconsensual intercourse, the witness is expressing an opinion based on the severity of injuries. The defence has accepted she is an expert in this area and, as such, perfectly qualified to provide that opinion.'

'Your Honour,' Anya tried to appease his desire for semantics, 'these sorts of injuries are more commonly seen in rape cases. I have never seen anyone with injuries like this sustained from consensual intercourse.'

The defence lawyer wasted no time. 'Again, Your Honour, I am concerned by the issue of nonconsensual sex. This is an erroneous argument because women sustaining those types of injuries following consensual sex would not seek out Doctor Crichton's medical expertise.'

Anya chose her words carefully. 'I liaise with casualty and emergency departments and have worked in those areas over many years. Never have I seen injuries like this, which would require urgent medical treatment for anyone participating in consensual intercourse.'

The judge scratched his broad nose. 'This troubles me. A jury will be swayed by your opinion, and yet you have failed to prove beyond reasonable doubt that every one of these injuries would have occurred solely without consent.'

Natasha Ryder placed her hands on the bar table, fingers splayed. 'The severity of the injuries must be evidence in itself of nonconsent. They would have caused significant pain, which would have compelled the victim to request any consensual activity to stop. In other words, this degree of pain would lead to withdrawal of consent if it had in fact been prior given.'

'That doesn't necessarily follow,' Stilton declared. 'Otherwise there would be no industry in sadomasochism.'

After a further half-hour of debate, the jurors were allowed back in.

Natasha compromised by altering her original question.

'Were the injuries you saw on the body of Rachel Goodwin consistent with nonconsensual activities?'

'Yes, the genital injuries were consistent with an absence of consent, as were the stab wounds to her torso and abdomen.'

'Could the sexual injuries have been self-inflicted, for example by attempts at self-stimulation?'

'Not with the victim's hands tied tightly to the bed.'

Someone in the gallery scoffed and drew the ire of the judge's good eye.

'Have you ever seen a sexual assault victim survive with the severity of injuries you described on Rachel Goodwin?'

'No, I have not.'

It was the best Natasha could do. She had planted the notion of rape strongly in the minds of the jurors. Motive was important to establish, and a sex crime provided a motive to permanently silence the victim. It also provided the opportunity to introduce previous histories of rape, if they fitted within the bounds of similar pattern evidence.

Despite the surprising challenge of the judge, who seemed to be guided by the defence, Anya hoped that Natasha had scored a major win for the prosecution.

'Pascoe may be preventing grounds for an appeal, but he's going to make my life hell for the next few months,' she said, as they left the courtroom for the day. 'Fancy a drink?'

Anya had found the testimony gruelling. She hoped the rest of the trial would be smoother.

'Just one. I've got a lot of work to catch up on.'

They walked across the road into a cafe and sat at the bar. Court finishing at four o'clock meant plenty of seats were available inside. Natasha flicked her hair off her shoulder and removed her glasses. 'A gin and tonic and . . .'

'Lemon, lime and bitters, thanks.'

Natasha paid with a credit card before the pair chose a table at the window, out of hearing range of other diners.

Anya spoke first. The rash on her chest and neck was fading, but her disbelief at what had occurred in the courtroom had not. She felt like breaking something. Anything.

'How are the victim's family and friends meant to feel, hearing that garbage about painful sex? And poor Bevan Hart, I saw him in there as well.'

'Afraid I suggested he come along, given the charges involving his daughter's assault are temporarily on hold. He knows that if we get this conviction, there's a better chance of successfully prosecuting them for Giverny's rape.'

The drinks arrived and Anya placed hers on a coaster.

'I can't believe Pascoe supported the defence. Is he going to sit back and let Stilton suggest that Rachel injured herself masturbating, then Sophie came in, tied her sister up and stabbed her multiple times? Oh yeah, then went outside, interfered with herself and cut her own throat.'

'Maybe Stilton's hedging his bets to get Harbourn acquitted, in case diminished responsibility fails. I wouldn't put anything past Pascoe. Being one-eyed isn't just physical with him.'

Anya glanced around to make sure no one was listening. Mocking a judge within earshot of other lawyers wasn't a wise move.

'Was he seriously supporting the concept that pain and sex are compatible?'

'Afraid so. He always gives the defence much more room than us, even if it means the victim is violated all over again.'

Anya wondered how long it would be before judges with archaic views, many of whom seemed far removed from modern reality, would die out. 'Judges like Pascoe are on borrowed time. He's close to retirement.'

She sipped her drink and noticed a well-dressed man at the bar watching Natasha.

'Not our old "Unsinkable". Philip Pascoe would have

survived the *Titanic*. With his arcane attitudes to women, he probably did.'

'Why Unsinkable?'

'Apparently he survived a rare childhood cancer and lost that eye.' She ticked off on her fingers. 'Then he was in a car accident years ago that completely mangled the car, but he walked away without a scratch. He's just back from time off. He had part of his leg amputated for some obscure kind of bone cancer. Old boy looks stronger than ever. If you ask me, he's got some deal going with the devil.' She took a sip from her gin and tonic.

People in suits filed into the cafe. The man Anya had noticed greeted some of the newcomers but kept an eye on Natasha in between conversations and bouts of laughter.

'Do you know the guy at the bar, dark suit, silver tie?'

Natasha looked around. 'Met him once or twice. From what I hear he's a pretty good litigator.'

'Well, he's been watching you since he got here.'

'Really?' Natasha finished her drink, pulled a compact out of her purse and fiddled with her hair.

As if on cue, the lawyer approached their table and offered to buy them a round.

Natasha smiled and gestured for the man to take a seat. Anya waited for an introduction, but suspected the prosecutor didn't remember his name. He reeked of cigarette smoke, and that alone would have been enough to put Anya off staying.

Still fuming from the judge's comments, she grabbed her bag and stood to excuse herself. There had to be another way to make the judge and jury see sense.

At that moment Natasha's phone rang. After muttering 'Yes', then 'No', then 'Right', she hung up and gave a wry grin.

'Who'd have thought? Harbourn must have figured he took a decent hit today. He's just fired his lawyer. We'll find out in the morning if the trial's on hold.'

For someone claiming diminished responsibility, Gary Harbourn was proving pretty adept at using the system to his advantage, holed up in a cushy private psych hospital instead of prison while he delayed the trial with legal games.

Anya left, wondering how she could support a system that catered to the Harbourns at the expense of people like the Harts and Goodwins and lauded judges like Pascoe.

She thought about Natasha's comments about the unsinkable judge and decided what she had to do.

Outside the cafe, she dialled Dan Brody's number. The call went to voicemail.

'Anya here, please call me as soon as you get this, it's urgent.'

She noticed a message from Hayden Richards. Damn. Her phone was still on silent after court.

There had been a female sexual assault. She pulled out a notepad to document the address and recognised the street name. It was Saint Stephen's Private Clinic.

30

Anya was greeted by a nurse who quickly ushered her down the corridor, past the gym, towards the consulting room. Doctor Temple stood outside, in jeans and a striped shirt, hand on his chin.

Hayden nodded at her. 'Thanks for coming so quickly. We have a female inmate—'

'Inpatient,' the psychiatrist corrected. 'This is a medical facility.'

'She says she woke up and found a man on top of her. She screamed, but he covered her mouth until he'd finished having nonconsensual intercourse with her, then ran off.'

This wasn't Anya's first call-out to a hospital or clinic. She'd attended sexual assault victims at elderly nursing homes and facilities for the severely intellectually and physically disabled. This was her third psych clinic. In previous cases, members of staff routinely preyed on society's most vulnerable.

'What's her medical condition like?'

'She's stable and as far as I can tell there are no signs of her having been assaulted.'

Anya tried to remain calm. If the psychiatrist had already examined her genitally, without collecting forensic specimens, he may have ruined any chance of her collecting physical evidence, and traumatised the patient further, making all of their jobs far more difficult.

'As you know, Doctor Temple, in sexual assaults there is often no physical sign of injury.' Hayden put his head down. He looked as frustrated as she felt right now. 'What's her background and mental state?'

'Schizophrenia since the age of eighteen, with severe psychotic episodes. She's had numerous admissions for violent behaviour associated with treatment cessation and substance abuse. Her parents admitted her when the police picked her up for urinating in public. Prior to this episode, she'd held down a clerical job for three months. She is, however, something of a fabulist, which is why I have to question whether or not she really was assaulted. She is delusional. This isn't the first time she's reported something like this.'

Anya put down her bag. A woman suffering delusions would never have her claims taken seriously, so was the perfect victim for a sexual predator. It was possible she had been sexually abused before, rather than just imagined it.

'What about cameras?'

'Privacy prevents us from having cameras in the rooms or private areas. This corridor isn't monitored either.' Doctor Temple was pleading for something from Hayden and Anya. 'Our patients are voluntary and we've never had anything like this happen before. There hasn't been any need for cameras except in the gardens and entry foyer.'

'In other words, something like this getting out could ruin this place's reputation,' Hayden said. 'And you're telling us the woman is unreliable as a witness.'

'That's correct.' Temple seemed to relax.

'If you don't mind, we have our jobs to do. I need to speak to whoever was on duty this afternoon and get the names of any visitors, delivery staff or kitchen hands, and I'll need to talk to the other patients.'

The psychiatrist stiffened again. 'I'm afraid that is fraught with confidentiality issues.'

'Rest assured, Doctor,' said Hayden, 'I won't be telling anyone unless we find out one of your patients committed rape under your watch. No amount of privacy can stop me charging whoever did this.'

'Where was Gary Harbourn when this occurred?' Anya

wanted to know. With his history of sexual assault, he had to be the prime suspect.

With a diagnosis of diminished responsibility, he could use it as an excuse for raping other patients. Even better for him if the police doubted the victims' stories. It was the perfect set-up for his sick, violent attacks.

Temple's colour faded. 'There is a police guard at each end of the ward, but he's free to come and go within those parameters.'

'Do the other voluntary patients know they're in with a gang rapist and murderer? What would that do for your reputation?' Hayden hitched up his trousers. 'Now, where can Doctor Crichton examine this patient, whose name, by the way, Anya, is Lydia Winter.'

Lydia twisted a handtowel around her wrist and crushed it between her fingers. The nurse helped her into a backless gown; her ribs protruded beneath stretched skin.

Anya explained who she was and what she was here for, but Lydia barely acknowledged her presence. 'We don't say much, do we, Lydia,' said the nurse as she tied the gown at the back.

'This is a lovely doctor, who wants to make sure you're all right.'

Lydia clung tightly to the handtowel.

Anya asked the nurse to collect the panties Lydia had been wearing, along with the sheets from her bed, and placed them in paper bags from her kit.

'Lydia, can you tell me what happened to you this afternoon, after you fell asleep?'

'I had a bad dream. I couldn't breathe and was being crushed. Then I opened my eyes and he was on top of me, hurting me. I tried to tell him to stop, to call for help, but his hand was over my mouth.' She twisted the towel even tighter, blanching her knuckles.

'Did you see who this man was?'

Lydia shook her head. 'I could smell his sweat but couldn't see his face. It all happened so fast.'

'It's okay, you're doing really well, Lydia.' Anya felt for this woman who appeared so fragile, physically and emotionally. 'Are you in any pain, does it hurt anywhere?'

'Down below,' she said. 'Doctor Temple says there's nothing there, but it's sore.'

'Would you mind if I had a very gentle look? The nurse might even hold a torch for me.'

Lydia pleaded, 'Please don't hurt me any more.'

'I won't,' Anya promised, and began the examination.

An hour later Anya emerged from the room. Lydia had gone to sleep on the couch, wrapped in a rug, still clutching the towel. The nurse stayed with her.

Hayden had spoken to the staff members and some patients and now waited in the next room, while Doctor Temple had gone to notify Lydia's parents.

'What do you think?' the detective asked after closing the door behind her.

'It looks like intercourse probably took place. There's a superficial abrasion on the vulva, but my guess is he used a condom. Like lots of young women, she's had her pubic hair removed – waxed – recently, but there weren't any odd hairs to sample.' She sat, elbow on the desk, propping up her temple. 'With the amount of medication she's on, sedation included, it's going to be difficult to verify anything.'

Hayden rubbed his forehead. 'It's not the usual level of violence, but Gary Harbourn has to be our prime suspect. If we can get him to admit that he had sex with her, can't you say that she was too doped up to have given consent? Therefore it can't have been consensual.'

'Good try. He's supposedly on medication and sedation, too, remember? His judgement could be said to be impaired.'

A knock on the door interrupted them. Dan Brody stood in the doorway.

'Temple told me where to find you. Just got your message.'

'What are you doing here?' Anya was confused. She hadn't even known about the clinic call when she left her message for Dan.

'That's what I was going to tell you,' Hayden mumbled.

'Judge Pascoe personally "requested" I take on a pro bono client who apparently sacked his lawyer. I didn't really have a choice,' Dan said, 'given his friendship with my senior partners.'

Anya wasn't sure what he was talking about, but pulled him aside for a quick word. 'I got a call today from Jeff Sales at the morgue. You still haven't buried the baby.'

'My father wanted to wait until the brain had been fully studied, which they tell me takes weeks. He won't cremate her without all the body parts.'

'Fair enough, but they do have a diagnosis. The retro-orbital tumour was a retinoblastoma. By the size and extent of it, the baby had no real chance of survival. I'm going to visit your father to tell him, I promised I would.'

'He'd like that. Maybe I can come along. Your son isn't in town, is he?'

Anya smiled. 'No, and I promise not to vomit as well. What's your client being charged with?'

'I gather you already know him. It's Gary Harbourn.'

31

Natasha Ryder hastily pulled on her clothes and carried her shoes to the door, careful not to wake Brian, or was it Baden? On the way out, she stole some cigarettes from the jacket he had worn half an hour before. So much for litigators, she thought. One climax led to an instant coma. Like many lawyers, the concept of afterplay or prolonging the moment was completely foreign.

Damn it. She'd managed twenty-nine days without so much as a craving. It was just a matter of self-control. This time the rush of sex made her covet it more. She could taste it on his lips and in his hair. The sex was average but the anticipation of a cigarette afterwards kept her interested.

Rolling it between her thumb and index finger, she enjoyed the familiar feel of the paper, the smoothness, the sleekness. Just knowing it was bad for her made it so much more tempting.

The last few weeks had been some of the most stressful of her career. If she made the slightest mistake in prosecuting the Harbourns, her job could be on the line.

For God's sake, the whole police force had done a collection for Sophie Goodwin's medical treatment, after already offering to pay for the sister's funeral. The public appeals had received over $50,000 in the last week. Every ghoulish reporter, makeover show and magazine wanted to do a story on Sophie, the miracle survivor. Public demand for justice exceeded anything she'd seen before.

It didn't hurt that Sophie was a stunning-looking teenager in the photos of her before the attack, or that her sister had a smile every parent could be proud of. The girls next door who had tragically lost their mother but pulled together as a family only to have their lives shattered by the most heinous crimes. The grieving father who buried his ex-wife, a beloved daughter and kept a bedside vigil, praying his other child would survive. She couldn't have scripted it better for public sympathy.

Natasha grabbed her briefcase and let herself out the front door of the unit. Outside, she lit the first cigarette with his lighter. The smell of burning tobacco made her salivate.

Instead of a taxi, she decided to savour the cigarette and walk the rest of the way home. Four blocks and a mild night might just make her feel alive again. Not numbed by the politics of prosecuting, or the lame stunts pulled by defence lawyers.

She thought about Anya Crichton and envied her in some small way. Life was simple when you could afford to be self-righteous and principled. She wasn't answerable to the public the next time another victim appeared.

If the doctor had been willing to say she had seen marks on Giverny's face before performing CPR, everything would now be different. She could have laid charges against the Harbourns for conspiracy to murder and kept them in jail. The others could have been rounded up and the Goodwin girls would never have suffered. Sophie would be enjoying being a teenager and her father would be looking forward to the next family Christmas.

How the hell could Anya claim to be ethically superior by sticking to her principles? Those principles had got Rachel Goodwin killed.

The cigarette was burning down too quickly. Natasha sucked every molecule of smoke into her lungs.

The streets were quiet, except for the occasional lovers walking along arm in arm. Restaurants and cafes had closed, business over for the day.

A tall woman, Natasha had never felt physically intimidated. She strutted with confidence and wouldn't hesitate to fight back if anyone tried to hurt her. Besides, she always carried Mace just in case she ran into anyone from a case she'd been involved in.

Anya Crichton, on the other hand, was more maternal, the sort of woman men admired but wanted to look after. Even so, she was more resilient than Natasha had expected. She could hold her own in an argument and, in some way, that deserved respect.

She'd also grown up with the trauma of a missing sister and the subsequent media scrutiny. Maybe that gave Crichton her quiet strength. You never knew exactly what she was thinking, or how she would react.

Natasha stopped before the crossing to light another 'cancer stick'. One more wouldn't hurt. It was calming her down, and she had a few more hours' work on the Harbourn trial tonight.

In her peripheral vision she saw a car slowing, far too early to let her cross. She walked on and saw an elderly man putting out his rubbish. The car still lagged behind.

'Excuse me, could you please tell me the time?'

She put down the briefcase and fiddled with her watch. The old man mentioned the hour and said something about hooligans letting off fireworks nearby. By then the car had passed.

Natasha collected her case and continued on. This trial was beginning to get to her. She was becoming paranoid. At this hour the driver was probably someone who'd drunk too much and didn't want to attract police attention on the way home.

She turned the corner into her street and startled at the sound of a large *crack* followed by fireworks bursting in the air. A few more and then a break. She put the remains of the cigarette in her mouth and opened her front gate, this time juggling the briefcase and handbag to find her keys. The sensor light had blown yet again, which made the simple task more challenging.

Rummaging through her bag, she ignored her ringing phone, scooped out the keys and opened the front door. Whoever wanted her this late would just have to call back.

Just inside, Minty purred at her feet as she bent down to say hello.

'Hey gorgeous, did you miss me?'

She barely glimpsed the dark shoe behind her. Before she could turn or reach inside her bag, her head was shoved forward and her left arm yanked back, forcing her to her knees. A crack exploded behind her.

32

S till angry with Dan Brody for defending Gary Harbourn, Anya prepared some muesli and banana, sat on the lounge and switched on the television to catch the morning headlines.

How could Dan represent a vicious criminal like Harbourn, even if he had been directed to by the presiding judge? She'd thought Brody's behaviour over his mother's affair was appalling, but this topped everything. She couldn't believe William was so conscience-driven and responsible, while his son sought only notoriety and financial gain.

Suddenly Natasha Ryder's face filled the TV screen. With milk spilling on the floor, Anya groped for the remote control to raise the volume.

Footage switched to a terrace home, then to the Supreme Court building.

The voiceover was deep. 'The lawyer was well known for her aggressive style in court, much to the frustration of her opponents. In her spare time, Ryder was a supporter of a literacy campaign for underprivileged children and was known to be a staunch supporter of victims' rights. In fact, this led to a recent complaint to the Law Society about a conversation she had with a journalist about the erosion of victims' rights in favour of the accused. The complaint was not upheld.'

God, what had Natasha done? Who had she managed to offend this time? Or had she been in some kind of accident?

Why wouldn't they say what had happened? Then she realised. The reporter kept referring to Natasha in the past tense.

Anya put down her bowl and grabbed her mobile phone, dialling Kate Farrer. The call went straight to voicemail.

Then the newsreader appeared. 'Just repeating, Crown Prosecutor Natasha Ryder has died overnight from a gunshot wound outside her inner city home. Police are appealing for anyone who saw Ms Ryder, or anything suspicious in the area, to come forward. A $50,000 reward has been posted for information leading to the conviction of her killer. Now we cross live to our reporter at the hospital. Have the police released any information about how the prominent lawyer died?'

'Yes, Kellie.'

Anya slumped in the lounge. Shot and killed. She suddenly felt numb.

The blonde journalist spoke into a hand-held microphone outside the emergency department.

'They're planning a formal statement later this morning, but sources inside the hospital tell us that the lawyer was shot as she arrived home last night, around ten o'clock. A neighbour apparently heard a loud noise he thought was fireworks at that time. He was alerted when Ms Ryder's house alarm went off. He found her lying on her doorstep and we believe that he called paramedics immediately. Ms Ryder was pronounced dead on arrival at Western General at 1.10 am.'

The anchor appeared again. 'It's a sad day when a champion of the people is gunned down outside her home, when she fought so hard for justice. The streets just don't seem safe any more. Let's hope the police find the killer. Ironic that she put so many murderers behind bars and now is a victim herself. Terrible. Now, on to sport.'

Anya felt her face heat up. It was nothing to do with irony. The job *made* her a target. Drug dealers, rapists and murderers were never grateful for being convicted. And they all had contacts outside prison.

As much as Natasha Ryder could rattle her, Anya couldn't help but feel deeply saddened by her loss. Her methods may not always have seemed fair, but she was touched by victims and worked damn hard to do the right thing by them and their families.

It was impossible to believe she was now dead. It didn't seem real. Her mobile phone rang. Kate. She answered after the second ring.

'I just heard about Natasha on the news.'

'We were all pretty shocked when the call came in. Whoever did this made no mistake. It was an execution.'

The detective sounded exhausted.

'Are there any leads? Had anyone threatened her?'

'That's the trouble. Over the last few years she's had a lot of threats. Ryder wasn't exactly popular with defence lawyers and crims alike.'

Natasha had never seemed afraid for her safety and had not discussed death threats. Then again, Anya realised, she really didn't know the woman that well. They had never discussed anything personal. The closest they came was in the restaurant talking about Giverny Hart.

'Could it have been the Harbourns?'

Kate let out a deep sigh. 'We're starting with them, as well as who's recently been released from prison and could harbour a grudge. Then there are ex-boyfriends. Some are pretty high-flyers so we've got to tread carefully.'

'Is there anything I can do?'

'I'm trying to trace her steps in the last few days to see if anyone had been stalking her. If you've seen her, you could help fill in some blanks.'

'Of course. I was with her until about five yesterday afternoon.'

Saying those words made Natasha's death seem unbelievable. Only hours before, they had shared drinks and conversation.

'I'm just headed over to her house to interview an elderly neighbour. Crime scene's still working, so you could meet me there. Zimmer's leading the charge.'

'Give me the address. I'm leaving now.'

Anya hadn't realised that Natasha lived a few short blocks away. They could have run into each other at the delicatessen or fruit shop. Come to think of it, she always had fruit in her office.

It could have been from a shared greengrocer. She wondered what else they had in common.

She parked down Natasha's street, which had been cordoned off. Once considered a working-class area, most of the terraces had been modernised internally while maintaining the original facades.

A tarpaulin had been erected outside number 82, to obscure media and allow privacy for the police officers.

John Zimmer ordered the uniformed constable to let her through.

The hip-height gate was open, and a short path led to a security door with blackened bars. Similar bars adorned the windows. Few other houses in the street had them. Natasha had obviously been safety conscious.

Anya pulled on paper shoe covers and twisted her hair into a knot.

What immediately struck her was the amount of blood between the doorstep and the first few metres of the corridor.

Milo Sharpe was examining the wooden black-wood architrave and doorway frame and didn't seem to notice her. Zimmer seemed to read her mind.

'It looks like she lived long enough to try to move, and lost a lot of blood.' The rings around his eyes suggested he had been there since they got the call. Knowing Zimmer, he would have refused to leave for a break in case he contaminated the scene on his return.

In a mass shooting at a cafe he had stayed inside for thirty-six hours, refusing to let anyone else in or out, for fear of destroying evidence. He hadn't heard whether the shooter had been caught, he'd just got on with the job until it was done.

'Could be that the killer moved her, or whoever found her rolled her over and blood that had pooled without clotting spilled out.' Anya tried to picture the scenario. 'How was she found?'

'The briefcase was on the doorstep. The first witness says

she was face down just inside the door. The security screen was half-closed, blocked by her legs.'

She knew the briefcase. The same one Natasha carried to court each day. 'Handbag?'

'The strap was still around her elbow. It was open but the purse doesn't appear to have been disturbed, it still had cash and credit cards. And get this, she carried a can of Mace with her but it wasn't touched. She was still clutching the house keys. The only footprints inside are of the cat walking through the blood.'

So Natasha had arrived home, opened the screen door outward, then the front door inward. Someone she trusted had to have been with her, or she was ambushed and had no time to defend herself. Anya turned to face the street. A small brick fence would barely have hidden a small child.

'No robbery, what about the actual wound?'

'It looks like she was shot in the back of the head. Emergency doctor said it exited right between the eyes.'

'Got it,' Milo announced.

With a pair of tweezers she carefully removed the remains of a bullet from the lower section of plaster on the right-hand wall.

Anya studied the location. 'If the bullet entered the back of the head, exited the skull and embedded there,' she bent down, 'then the head has to have been reasonably low to the ground when the gun went off.'

'If she were standing up, you'd expect her to have to have her chin tucked right to her chest for the projectile to end up where it did.'

'The killer could have grabbed her and forced her head down.'

'Either way, she didn't have time to react or grab what was in her handbag.'

Anya wondered if Natasha knew she was about to die.

'There is something odd,' Milo chimed in. 'There is no kitchen in this house. There's a bathroom and bedroom, just no kitchen. A coffee machine and a bowl of fruit in the lounge room. No fridge. I'm thinking this woman had a serious calcium deficiency, or maybe an eating disorder.'

Zimmer tried to explain. 'This is a pretty small place and professionals who work in the city aren't home during most mealtimes, so they may decide against a kitchen and have a wide-screen TV instead.' His voice became louder. 'And maybe Ms Ryder liked her coffee black and didn't need a fridge. Can we stick to our job description?'

Either the case, Milo or both were getting to him.

'She walked past a deli and greengrocer on the way to and from work, so she didn't starve if that's what you were worrying about.' Anya could understand Zimmer's frustration.

It was difficult to concentrate, knowing this was where Natasha had been shot. Seeing her colleague's blood where it had haemorrhaged life from her brought a lump to Anya's throat. She could almost smell the floral perfume Natasha wore.

And metres away they were violating her privacy. Suddenly Anya felt claustrophobic and excused herself.

Zimmer followed.

'You okay?' he asked, outside the gate, away from listening ears, but still inside the crime scene tape.

'It's hard to be here,' she said, wiping her nose with a tissue. 'Harder than I thought.'

'I know.' Zimmer bowed his head and spoke softly. 'When it's someone you know, you think this job can't get any worse. But because we knew her, we care. For that reason we should be the ones here.'

She nodded. 'Who's doing the PM?'

'They're flying in a guy from interstate. None of our lot could face it, given how much time they spent with her preparing for trials.'

Anya had a sick feeling. 'Giverny Hart, Savannah Harbourn and Natasha Ryder, all dead within the space of a few weeks. I knew them all.'

Giverny could have been written off as a suicide, if not for the threats made by the Harbourns. And Savannah's death could have been considered an accident, if it hadn't been for the beating at the hands of her brother. And Natasha had been killed while prosecuting the very same, Gary Harbourn.

'It's been rough, but anyone could have murdered Natasha. She upset a lot of people just by doing her job. And as far as I know, your three women died in different ways. Whoever did this one planned it and knew what they were doing. The scene's clean. So far we haven't found so much as a hair.'

'Just like for Giverny. Nothing but my hair was found on her.'

Kate Farrer strolled along and Anya excused herself. The Harbourns had to be behind Natasha's murder. Surely Kate had to understand that.

33

Kate greeted Anya with a worried expression. 'We need to talk.'
'Are you looking at the Harbourns?' Anya removed her
shoe covers and discarded them in a police-issue plastic waste-
bag outside the gate.

'That's what I wanted to see you about.' Kate led her down
the street, beyond the border of the scene.

'We found a property out west they go to a lot. A search of
the place turned up a list in Noelene's handwriting. A number
of addresses and phone numbers.' She shoved her hands in her
trouser pockets. 'Yours was on it.'

She showed Anya a photocopy. Her home address and car
registration were written down, along with an asterisk and the
words *LIVES ALONE*. Suddenly Anya felt light-headed and
leant against the nearest fence.

'Keep reading,' Kate urged.

Anya scanned and saw Natasha Ryder's name and address,
along with the same addendum. *LIVES ALONE*. Further down,
she stopped at the name and felt as if her world was crashing in.

*CRICHTONS YOUNG KID LIVES WITH HER EX. UNFIT
MOTHER???????*

The number, street and suburb were accurate.

'God, Kate, they know where Ben lives.'

The detective moved to her side. 'It's okay, Hayden spoke to
Martin and he's taking Ben to stay at his friend's house for a
few days. Ben will stay in the classroom with his teacher until
Martin gets there.'

'He can't come to stay with me anymore,' she sniffed. 'This
can't be happening.'

'Look, it's not as uncommon as it seems. Noelene's boyfriend works for the motor registry and we suspect he used their database to get most of the info.

'Going by the amount of drugs we found in the family home, these guys are into dealing as well as selling weapons from the armed robberies. That's how they can afford to pay for Gary's medical fees in cash.

'We've treated them pretty much as opportunistic idiots, but they've got more than a few angles going that make money. Noelene obviously wants to protect it all.'

'Why would she collect all our addresses? She can't be planning on wiping out half the police, doctors, prosecutors and their families.'

'We think she got hold of the personal details in case she decides to bribe the boys out of trouble. They've also got Natasha's parents, brother and aunt on the list.'

'That won't mean anything to Martin. He won't understand. Instead, he'll use it to stop me from seeing my son. God, Natasha is already dead.'

Kate put her hand on Anya's shoulder. 'That family holiday had an effect. Hayden tells me Martin was pretty concerned that you were all right.'

Anya coughed and processed what Kate had said.

'Did they have any police names?'

'Hayden and Liz Gould, her husband and kid's name too. Mine wasn't on the list so you're welcome to stay in the spare room for a few days if you want. You know I'm barely there.'

It didn't seem such a bad idea. They could look out for each other. Besides, Anya didn't fancy going home alone, not now.

'Do you think it's necessary?'

Kate kicked the ground. 'I don't want to scare you, but whoever killed Natasha knew what they were doing. It was an assassination: short, quick, no witnesses. It doesn't fit the Harbourn style and, thank God, she wasn't raped. It doesn't add up. But put it this way, misery enjoys company, so they say.'

Anya knew the detective well enough to know that this was the closest she would come to admit being concerned.

'Do you promise to tidy up?'

Kate held her hand over her heart. 'Scout's honour I'll try not to be messy. But only if you agree to water the pot plant.'

As annoying as Kate would be to share a house with, it made sense. 'There's been enough carnage lately. The plant just got a reprieve.'

The detective's phone rang and Kate answered it. 'Just told her now, she's still here . . . We'll be there some time after two.'

34

Later that afternoon they returned to the Homicide office. Anya bought sandwiches from the vending machine, more for something to do than because she was hungry. The mood in the office was flat despite phones buzzing continuously.

'We've just got the photos through from Natasha's PM,' Kate said. 'I'm about to go over them, but understand if you want to give this one a miss.'

Anya wanted to help in any way she could. She sat on a chair next to Kate's messy desk.

'This one's after emergency services were finished.'

Instead of a crumpled body, the image showed Natasha on the outside path. Paramedics had moved her to the nearest flat surface, where there was more room to work. A breathing tube was inserted into her mouth and her shirt was open from attempted cardiopulmonary massage. Two gel plates remained in place along with four adhesive ECG dots. The paramedics had tried to defibrillate life back into her. Just like they had for Giverny Hart.

Blood trickled from Natasha's forehead down to her left ear.

The next image was of the back of the head. A small entry wound near the base of her skull was the only evidence of what had occurred. Anya compared it to the photo of the forehead, which was larger.

'The bullet entered at the back and exited through the forehead, which is why it was found in the wall. It's a small bullet. My guess is a .22 calibre.'

'Easy to get hold of, used by just about every drug dealer in the city.'

The next photos Kate showed were of Natasha's manicured hands. No nailpolish, just perfectly shaped and filed, not long enough to be impractical. Feminine and functional. It pretty much summed up the woman Anya knew.

Above the left wrist on the inside were four one-centimetre wide bruises. One larger, and three adjacent, in a vertical row. It looked as though the killer had grabbed the left arm. What she was looking at were a thumb and three finger marks. There were no grazes or bruises to the wrists themselves.

'Was there any damage to her left shoulder?'

Kate sorted through some papers on her desk. 'She had a bruised, torn pectoralis muscle according to the report. The pathologist is sending his summary later on today. What are you thinking?'

Anya stood up and pushed the chair away. Shaun Wheeler looked up from his desk and put down his phone.

'Can I borrow you for a minute?' Anya asked.

He nodded and stood. 'What do you w-w-want me to do?'

'Kneel down on the floor.'

The young detective forced a laugh and then realised she wasn't kidding. He was quickly on two bended knees. Anya moved behind him while Kate watched. By now they had the attention of most of the Homicide staff.

'She came home, opened the security screen then front door. The briefcase was in her left hand, and the house keys in her right. She put the briefcase down, and that meant that hand was free. Somehow she was either pushed or ordered to her knees. Any bruising or grazes there?'

Kate flicked through some more printed photos. 'There was a hole in one stocking at the knee. And a small bruise over each kneecap, probably from the wooden floor.'

'Okay, she either bent down, maybe to greet the cat, or was pushed down.' She cautiously took hold of Wheeler's left arm and wrapped her thumb and first three fingers above the wrist. Her fingers were in virtually the same position as the bruises on the body.

'The killer has come up behind her, grabbed the arm and, to tear her shoulder muscle, has to have pulled the wrist up behind her back.'

'It's like a half-nelson,' the male detective said, his left hand behind his shoulder blades.

'From there the killer could have easily forced her to her knees,' Kate said, 'which explains where the bullet was found if her head was low when she was shot. There was another bruise on the left side, above the ear.'

Anya deduced, 'She didn't put her hands out to protect herself when she fell forward, or they would have shown marks like the knees did. It looks like someone had control of her and she had no chance to react. There was no time to drop the keys or reach for the Mace.'

The thought of protection being so close made Natasha's murder more difficult to accept. If only she had reached for the pepper spray in time.

Then Anya remembered what they had talked about the night of Giverny's death. No regrets, no what if's or if only's. It was how the prosecutor lived her life.

With Wheeler under her control, Anya shoved her right index finger into the back of his head. At the same time she released his left arm with a forward push and he toppled forward, putting his right arm out to protect himself.

Kate sat forward, hands on her knees. 'So was she hit in the head with the gun at any stage? Could the killer have stunned her first?'

'I don't think so. That bruise above the ear could have happened when she hit the ground. Without her arms out in front, she would have just toppled forward.'

Wheeler stood up and wiped the knees of his trousers. The phone on his desk rang and he moved to answer it.

Kate spun the chair around and straddled the seat, leaning her elbows on the backrest. 'She was executed. No evidence of robbery or sexual interference. The briefcase was untouched as far as we know. This was a targeted killing.'

A minute later Wheeler came back, like a new puppy with a toy he'd retrieved.

'Just had a call from a neighbour. He left for a night shift around 9.45 pm and saw a man with a hat and coat on outside Ryder's house. He f-f-forgot something so drove around the block. He s-s-saw the man a couple of houses down, looking like he was waiting. He did some shopping and met some friends for lunch before c-c-coming back home this morning, which is why he's only just called.'

'Description?' Kate sat straight, ignoring Wheeler's intermittent stutter. It was the worst they had heard it, probably a reflection of his stress levels.

'Average height, overweight, about a hundred and twenty kilos. Big b-belly was what he remembered most.'

Liz Gould entered the office and threw down a satchel.

'Doesn't fit with any of the Harbourns or their known associates. Can you check out the neighbour's movements last night? Make sure he really did go to work.'

'What about the description? It's our first real lead.'

Kate rubbed her eyes. 'Let's put out a public appeal for this person of interest to come forward and assist us with our enquiries, the usual. The killer could have lived close. That might explain why no one else saw him or her.'

Anya hoped that all possibilities were being considered. Police tunnel vision limiting suspects could mean the chances of catching the killer diminished with each hour.

'What about a stalker? She had daily contact with dysfunctional and disturbed people.'

'Her and anyone who works with the public,' Liz added. 'Try working with security company employees, they're a breed all of their own.' She sat, pulled off her shoes and rubbed her feet.

'Find anything useful?' Kate wanted to know.

'Doesn't look like a stalker. I just got back from viewing the court tapes. Ryder's been in court the past couple of days and cameras didn't catch anyone hanging around or following her. Same with the bank footage of the street near where she lives. When she appeared, no one was close or visible, let alone someone with a large belly.'

The detectives were all under pressure to make a quick arrest, pressure from politicians, the police commissioner and the Director of Public Prosecutions, not to mention the public and media.

Liz dug her fingers into the soles of her feet. 'Unless ballistics turn up the gun and it's got the killer's name all over it, we're pushing a waterfall uphill and all we've got is a toothpick.'

35

Anya phoned Martin who sounded relieved that she was all right and even appeared sympathetic about the situation. Whatever Hayden had told Martin was clearly reassuring. Ben was safe and happy. She checked her messages on Kate's computer and downloaded the articles on genetic criminality. Maybe there was something in there that could help the police, or help in the Harbourn trial.

She had to do something or she would feel completely useless. This felt just like one of her times in casualty, when a car accident involved a drunk driver hitting a family with four young kids. Despite working on them all night, none of the family survived. The drunk driver walked away uninjured.

Doctors and nurses stayed in casualty for hours after their shifts had finished, not just to help with the backlog of patients. No one wanted to go home and deal with the emotional fallout of the deaths alone.

Zimmer wandered into Homicide. 'Crime scene's pretty clean. Our killer doesn't want to be found.'

Anya thought that didn't sound like the Harbourns. Getting caught didn't seem to faze them, particularly if avoiding detection meant more work and less impulse. Maybe Noelene was the brains in the organisation after all.

Kate rummaged through her desk for something, ignoring Zimmer.

'McNab is about to go over the casing and the bullet. Thought you'd want to be there.'

Kate found the item she had been searching for – a pack of Lifesaver lollies. 'You need to ask?'

'Hey, I'm a gentleman.' Zimmer turned to Anya. 'Why are you still around? Can't bear to be away from us beautiful people?'

'Something like that.' Truth was, she was waiting for Kate to take her home to get some toiletries and clothes before staying at her place for protection. Knowing Kate, she wouldn't leave until she'd run out of calls to make or leads to chase that day.

Kate headed straight for the stairwell. Anya and Zimmer followed.

As they entered the firearms lab, Zimmer chatted while Anya did her best to disguise how puffed she was.

'How are the drum lessons going?'

'They're not. I've been away and now I'm just too busy.'

'Maybe I'll just have to bring my sax over so we can play some time.'

Kate rolled her eyes. 'Hello? Gagging over here.'

Zimmer looked wounded. 'I'm serious. I play in a jazz band. Anya knows that. We've been trying to get her to jam with us for ages.'

Anya grinned and nodded.

Kate ignored him.

The firearms expert, Nick McNab hung up the phone in his glass office and joined everyone in the lab. He pulled on a white coat and did up the only two buttons that met in the middle.

'Thanks for coming, I know what this case means to everyone here. Guess you'd like to see what we've got.'

They moved around a stereoscopic microscope connected to a television on a mobile stand.

'It's easier if I show you.' Doctor McNab focused the microscope and showed a cartridge case. 'This was found at the scene. The humble case is often overlooked in assisting with identification of a weapon. Most of the markings are found on the closed end, where the primer is located. A crater forms when the firing pin is struck by the hammer and forced into the primer.'

He moved an arrow and pointed to the base. 'As you can see,

this has a few distinct markings. The breech markings occur when the case is pushed back against the breech block by the burning gases. As we have here, in a semiautomatic, extractor markings and ejector markings are left on the rim. We can also look for markings left by the magazine lip on the side of the case.'

Anya watched the screen, unsure of exactly what marks she was seeing. 'The eye of faith' was what her mother called it when a group of experts nodded about seeing something at the same time. Odds were, she wasn't alone in not being able to understand what McNab described.

'Can you point out what exactly we're looking at?'

Kate could always be trusted to get to the point quickly.

'Nick's just saying there are a couple of different impressions made on the head of the case. The firing pin marks on impact, and through recoil when the base is forced back against the breech block. By the way, this is a rim fire.'

McNab looked up from the microscope. 'That's what I said, except for the rim fire bit at the end.'

Zimmer put his hands up, 'Sorry, just making sure we're all on the same page.'

Kate stood, hands in pockets. 'Can you identify the make and model from these markings?'

'This is from a .22 calibre semiautomatic. From what John says, it was a hand gun.'

'What about the bullet in the wall?'

McNab sighed and swivelled on his chair. 'Not much left of it, I'm afraid it's only a fragment. I can tell you it was a hollow point, but there was something odd we found. It had wheel-bearing grease on its nose.'

Kate glanced up at Zimmer. 'When I was a kid, my father used to use hollow points to cull rabbits.'

'The structure facilitates expansion on contact,' McNab explained, 'thereby killing the animal more quickly.'

'What's the wheel grease for?' Anya asked, having not encountered it before.

'It's new to me too,' said Zimmer. 'I don't know the significance.'

Kate rubbed her temple. 'It may or may not be relevant, but my dad used to put a smear of vaseline on the tips of his bullets. I remember because I used to help. Reason was, he said it made the bullets pass faster through the barrel.'

'Grease has a higher melting point than water, so it would accentuate the concept of the bullet expanding, like a ramming device, you could say.'

'Isn't that what I said?' Kate whispered to Anya.

'So, whoever shot Natasha had knowledge of guns and was probably a hunter?'

'Or just grew up on a farm like I did,' Kate added. 'If that's the case, the choice of weapon doesn't sit right.'

'Go on, Detective,' McNab folded his arms in anticipation.

'We all know the .22 is fairly easy to come by. Sporting shooters, armed robbers, security men and every wannabe crook has one. Hell, before we heard of corruption, police used them as fit-up guns.'

'Those were the days,' Zimmer put his thumbs over his belt and rocked on his heels, 'when you could shoot some bastard then fire the fit-up gun and whack it into his dead hand. No doubt about it, any judge would rule self-defence every time. Yep, those were the good old days.'

Kate smacked his arm with the back of her hand. 'This is serious. A .22 isn't exactly sniper material. It's a huge risk, having to get so close to be accurate, especially if the target's mobile. I wouldn't even use one for self-defence.'

McNab suggested, 'Maybe the shooter wanted Natasha Ryder to know who killed her. Maybe he deliberately went that close. I mean, if it was personal.'

Zimmer became sombre again. 'Or could be our shooter doesn't care if he gets caught.'

With that, discussion halted. Anya and Kate seemed to have the same thought. The Harbourns not only had reason to dislike the prosecutor, but were not afraid of the legal consequences.

They acted as if they were above the law. Even so, it still wasn't their style. Unless they had hired a professional this time to remove Natasha from the trial.

Noelene had plenty of seedy connections and Natasha had been involved in prosecutions against the family before. This time the stakes were higher than ever. They had a lot to lose.

If the killer were someone else, the Harbourns had definitely benefited. Luck didn't seem to be something that followed the family around.

'Nick, everything okay?' Zimmer appeared concerned.

McNab uncrossed his arms. 'Something just doesn't sit right. There's something familiar about these cartridge markings that's bothering me. Let's run it through our database. If it matches anything, we'll know in a couple of hours.'

Kate headed towards the door. 'Thanks, and call me any time. No such thing as too late.'

The trio exited the laboratory and walked the two flights back to Homicide.

'Wheeler found out that Noelene Harbourn's brother has a farm west of here – the one where we found the list. Apparently the boys would go up and shoot foxes and rabbits on weekends. Maybe we should go up there with a metal detector and check it out.'

'Did they keep weapons out there?' It was a long shot but if they had killed Natasha maybe the murder weapon was hidden there.

'No such luck. They wised up. Those guns we found in the wall of their house were from a robbery. They probably sold the rest on the black market or have another stash somewhere.'

Back at her desk Kate threw her jacket over her chair. 'Still bothers me, though. We think these guys have access to firepower better than a .22. This just doesn't fit their pattern of using a truck of dynamite to blow away a cockroach. Natasha got one shot in the head. Quick and clean. No signs of overkill or any other violence.'

She sat down and put her feet up on the desk. 'It doesn't fit their usual lust for blood and suffering. I mean, look at what they did to Rachel Goodwin.'

Zimmer sat on Wheeler's desk. 'Got to admit that car accident wasn't their style either. Far too subtle. If they wanted to send a message to the rest of the clan about sticking together, they could have made more of a show of Savannah's death.'

As a mother, it was possible that Noelene had more control over her sons than they realised. 'What if the mother hadn't agreed to the killings? What if they were out on their own, knowing the police were sniffing around. Wouldn't that make anyone more cautious?'

'Not necessarily, we had one serial killer know he was under surveillance. Didn't stop him walking into a house and killing a victim with the police outside. A ferret still kills for pleasure, whether it's hungry or not.'

Anya and Kate looked at him, then laughed.

'God you're corny,' Kate said.

'What? I used to keep ferrets as a kid. They kill for fun, it's what they're bred for.'

Kate laughed until she snorted, then the other two joined in.

It was enough to break the tension. The truth was, they were all intimidated by possible threats to their own safety and this was one place they could feel relaxed despite the late hour.

Minutes later, Anya was headed to her home to pick up a toiletries bag and change of clothes, so she could stay the night in Kate's spare room – for protection from the Harbourns. All humour was quickly forgotten.

36

The detective had changed into exercise pants and hooded top. She had set up an office on her living room floor, sitting barefoot with one leg tucked under and the other outstretched, papers spread around her and a large bag of potato chips at her side. Anya found patches of carpet to step between.

'I've been thinking. Zimmer might have had a point about ferrets being bred to kill. It's in their make-up, just like dogs are naturally carnivores.'

'Okay, you lost me.' Kate crunched on some more chips.

'The nature or nurture concept. I used to think that the environment we're brought up in makes us what we are, but studies are starting to challenge that.'

'Monkey see, monkey do. Does it matter when the end result's the same?'

Anya appreciated Kate had little patience for theories that didn't alter outcomes. And she had a point. She was task oriented and focused on end results, not necessarily on the process. It was one of the things she liked about Kate. Not one for sitting around contemplating the meaning of life, her friend was the most practical person she knew. The bookshelf that still sat in pieces at Anya's house would have been assembled as soon as it arrived if Kate had her way.

'Beats me how you separate genes from environment anyway.' Kate continued to munch away while Anya sat on the arm of the lounge.

'It's interesting, looking at studies of adopted children. They've found that children born to a criminal parent but adopted into a law-abiding family still have a much higher chance of committing crimes than their adopted siblings. Whereas kids born to noncriminal parents but adopted into criminal environments are more likely to stay within the law.'

Kate grinned. 'Those studies are like statistics. You find one to justify anything. Remember all that work on identical twins separated at birth?'

Anya did. 'Like the two women who met by chance in a cafe, appeared identical, were dressed in the same clothes and had the same job. Then discovered they were sisters.'

Kate laughed. 'You intellectuals have selective memories. There were identical twin boys. One was racist and became a Nazi, but the other ended up working with natives on some island. Pretty much blows your theory about genetics.'

'No one's saying it's absolute, but both of those men you mention were arrogant, saw themselves as leaders and were pretty unpleasant to be around. They couldn't even get on with each other when they met.'

'Sounds like most of the people I work with. God, they must all be related.'

Anya picked up a couple of cushions and pelted Kate, who toppled backwards then lay on papers singing, 'We – are – fa-mi-ly'. She suddenly sat upright. 'Hey, we can play charades. Who am I?' and pretended to vomit, multiple times.

Anya couldn't believe how childish Kate was being, but thinking about Ben and Brody's car still made her laugh until her stomach cramped.

Kate's phone interrupted them. Anya retreated to make drinks.

When she returned, Kate punched the air. 'That was McNab. The marks on the casing match one found at the site of a killing in Chinatown three years ago.'

The firearms expert had been right. After all the bullets and casings he and his team had examined, his memory of markings he had seen once before, years ago, was accurate.

'Were there any suspects?'

'Apparently.' She kept reading her notes from the call, placing the pen between her teeth.

Anya handed her the coffee. 'Thanks,' she mumbled through the pen, before removing it from her mouth to drink.

'Before that, it was used in a drive-by where no one was injured, and an armed robbery. Chinatown victim was Andrew Li, who owned a restaurant. No one was ever charged, although the major crime squad thought Li was killed for refusing to pay protection money, as an example to anyone else in the community who thought they could stand up to the gangs.'

She searched around for a specific piece of paper and then cross-checked something while Anya made sure all the curtains were drawn without a gap. She then rechecked the back-door lock.

'You need to find out if Natasha worked on that case, or any others involving those gangs.'

Anya knew that getting anyone to help with information would be even tougher, if it involved a closed, frightened community. Organised crime being behind her murder could explain the execution style.

It always surprised her how prosecutors made numerous enemies just for doing their job, but the same people loved their defence lawyers, even if the client ended up in jail. The list of potential suspects in Natasha's killing was enormous.

'I'm thinking the elders in charge wouldn't tolerate a renegade killing. They act through discipline and a hierarchy. As far as I know, killings are usually for revenge, and that's the end of the violence.'

Kate had a valid point and sanctioning the murder of a prosecutor would be extremely risky. The last thing any criminal group wanted was even more police scrutiny into their illegal activities.

'It was found during a raid on a massage parlour, along with a cache of weapons.' She scanned further. 'After that, it's listed here as having being destroyed.' She reached into the bag and filled her mouth with more chips. A couple of crunches later she looked up.

'Shit. It's a phantom.'

Anya climbed onto the lounge, legs folded beneath her, sipping no-name tea. 'Which means?'

'Remember the national buy-back scheme after Port Arthur?' Kate arched her back and moved her neck to the side, cracking the vertebrae.

Anya nodded. Over a decade before, a lone gunman killed thirty-five people and injured another twenty or more in the popular tourist spot in Tasmania. Public outrage against the pro-gun lobby led the government to legislate another gun buy-back scheme, to promote better gun control. There had been rumours about some of those guns going missing, ranging from hundreds to thousands flooding the black market and making it into the hands of criminal networks.

Pro-gun groups hailed the scheme a dismal failure, and those in favour of gun control labelled it a success, citing a reduction in the number of mass shootings since.

'Well, those guns were combined with confiscated and recovered weapons. They went to warehouses run by contractors the public thought were impenetrable. Only thing is, hundreds of these guns have turned up since. Some of the contractors had contacts with pawnshops.'

'So the foxes were in charge of the chicken house, which was full of, let me guess, .22 guns.'

'Exactly.' Kate sipped her coffee. 'The firearms squad think it's the largest illegal gun distribution network to date. Got to give it to incompetent agencies. So people think the streets are safer, politicians pat themselves on the back and criminals have a bigger monopoly on guns. It's a populist policy that has only made our job tougher. The licensed people with registered weapons were the ones who handed them in.'

Even so, Anya was relieved that she had seen fewer women threatened with guns in situations of domestic violence since the buy-back scheme. Even if one woman was spared being murdered on impulse by a man with easy access to a gun, the policy was, in her view, already a success. She wasn't about to start a philosophical debate with Kate on the subject.

'Some of these demolition guys were paid by the government for incinerating the guns. The more honest ones found a loophole and officially rendered them inoperable. That way they could be sold to their pawn dealer mates as replicas, which could of course be made functional without too much effort.'

Anya enjoyed the warmth of the mug in her hands. 'One casing led McNab to all that?'

'He had seen another casing that has very close markings. They retrieved the gun in a Chinatown raid, and the serial number had been ground down, but McNab's boys managed to rescue it.'

Anya had seen it done. Hydrochloric acid, copper chloride and water was used to temporarily differentiate between the stamped metal numbers and the surrounding metal.

'So there's no way of tracing the gun or how it got into our killer's hands after it hit the black market?'

'We'd need the gun to prove it had the same serial number, but it's like DNA. You need the killer to give it to you for comparison.'

Anya rested her mug on the floor. 'Okay, what are we looking for?'

Kate handed her a box of old files. 'Anyone from these cases who could have had a grudge against Natasha. Apart from that, I'm not even sure at the moment.

'We've got an assassin. Someone who apparently didn't want anything from Natasha Ryder, just killed her. My informants have got nothing.

'It has to be someone who isn't smart enough to understand how much heat they'd bring down on themselves, or someone who just doesn't care.'

Like the Harbourns. Kate's expression suggested they both had the thought at the same time.

Anya put the box down beside the lounge and asked to see the autopsy report again.

'The gun was a .22 calibre. Right?'

'A .22 rim fire with a hollow point bullet.'

And the grease, she thought. Something had bothered her about the entry wound. If the muzzle of the gun had been held against Natasha's head as the gun was fired, there should have been specific signs present. The wound was not indented, suggesting the muzzle had not been pushed into the skin, and there was no soot or searing of the wound edges. Usually, soot was so embedded in the wound, even enthusiastic washing of the skin wouldn't remove it. The absence of findings could not be explained by examining the wound after the body had been cleaned.

There was also no mention of visible grease in the entry wound. That suggested a silencer hadn't been used. So how did the killer prevent anyone from hearing the shot?

'Do you have the neighbour's statement about the man loitering around Natasha's house?'

Kate handed it across. 'You have that clever look in your eye. What is it?'

Anya looked at the witness statement of a man with a hat, coat and large frame.

'This killer knew Natasha personally. I don't think it was a hired assassin. Something was held between the gun barrel and Natasha's head, my guess is to dull the sound. The witness said the man he saw had a big belly, like a fully pregnant woman.'

Kate pulled a cushion from the lounge. 'And how do you make yourself look pregnant?' She shoved it under her hooded top to emulate a protruding belly.

'Damnit. We've all wasted critical time looking for someone with the wrong description.'

37

Anya returned Ned Goodwin's call. As if Natasha's murder hadn't been disturbing enough, Sophie was back in theatre with a bowel obstruction, secondary to scarring from the hysterectomy and the abdominal surgery she endured after the stabbing. Her suffering was nowhere near over. Ned promised to call when she was safely out of surgery.

Anya would visit as soon as it was safe to.

Kate had Michael Bublé playing softly in the background, which was surprisingly calming. Then again, that could have been the effect of a glass of wine and fatigue.

After their makeshift dinner of bread rolls and protein bars, Hayden Richards arrived, having called to say he was on his way.

'Have something you may be interested in,' he said to Anya, looking around the mess, presumably, for somewhere to sit.

Anya cleared off one side of the lounge. She got the impression that Kate would have left him standing indefinitely while she continued working. She either didn't encourage visitors or wasn't interested in being a good hostess.

'Coffee? Wine? Beer?' Anya offered.

'No thanks.'

'Everything's fresh. I bought milk and the coffee's just brewed.'

'In that case, white, no sugar, thanks.'

Kate seemed indifferent to the conversation, or chose to ignore it while she read and occasionally sipped beer from a bottle.

When Anya returned with the coffee, Hayden had some photos to show her.

'It's taken a while, but those fragments of plastic you found on the road near the fatal crash site came from the front left indicator light and the headlamp from a silver Jeep Cherokee. We've narrowed it down to a model between 1993 and 1998. The damage to Savannah's car on the right side rear matches, from the height where the two cars impacted, to the flecks of silver paint on her vehicle.'

Kate looked up. She had been listening.

'Good call. You were right.'

Anya felt satisfied, and hopeful that Savannah's killer would be found. 'So do the Harbourns own a car like that?'

'Not officially, but there are a few cars that come and go from their place; some are probably stolen or belong to dead-beat friends. Neighbours said a silver Jeep Cherokee was parked outside the house around the time of the accident but haven't seen it since. Not that it would help us, the tribal mentality means they leave the keys in the sun visor so they can borrow whichever they want.'

'Or get away in a hurry. What are the chances of finding it?'

'We've put out a notice to all the spare parts suppliers in the city, to see if anyone has ordered replacements, but there is a long list for silver Jeep Cherokees. If someone's hiding it in a garage or at an illegal smash-repair business, it could take longer.'

At least Hayden had confirmed that about a kilometre from where she had died Savannah Harbourn's Colt had been hit from behind by another car.

'What about the speed cameras and the red-light camera at the intersection we looked at?'

Hayden pulled a photo from his file. It showed Savannah's car in the intersection with the light red according to the camera behind and to the left.

'My guess is, whoever rammed her deliberately pushed her into traffic. That road has good visibility, it's not as if the lights are round a blind bend. It's a straight approach. According to calculations on the skid marks, when she crashed Savannah was doing at least ninety kilometres an hour. Either someone wanted to scare her, or chased her down with the purpose of running her off the road.'

'Or,' Kate offered, 'she was scared and panicked after a minor bingle.'

Anya and Hayden stared at her.

'That's just what your smarmy friend Brody would say. You know we need more than that.'

That reminded Anya. She hadn't spoken to Dan since seeing him briefly at Saint Stephen's. Somehow she'd almost taken personally his decision to defend Gary Harbourn, even though he had said it was initiated by Judge Pascoe through the other senior partners at his firm. And the work was to be pro bono. Officially, Gary Harbourn was unemployed.

She had decided to visit William again at the nursing home, to find out what exactly he knew about the baby's father. For now, though, discussions with Dan had to wait.

'How's Lydia Winter doing?' she asked Hayden.

'Forensics came back from the rape kit you did. Nothing helpful, I'm afraid. Lydia seems to have mysteriously forgotten the events of the other night.'

Anya couldn't blame her if she recanted the story, or even blocked it from her memory. Besides that, medication could have interfered with her short-term memory, particularly if she'd been given certain benzodiazepines.

'I spoke to Natasha Ryder's replacement. He doesn't think we have a case. If Gary did rape Lydia Winter, he's just committed the perfect crime.'

38

Anya left Dan a message telling him she was visiting his father that afternoon. She arrived at the nursing home with a bunch of flowers and a tin of store-bought shortbread. If she knew how, she would have baked them for the older gentleman.

William Brody sat in a wheelchair next to his bed, facing side-on to the door. He appeared to be listening to 'The Conversation Show', in which authors were interviewed about their fascinating lives and books.

Anya had just been listening in her car and was enthralled by the story of a doctor who had dedicated her life to operating on victims of militia rape in Africa. The Australian-born surgeon spent ten hours a day repairing extensive gynaecological injuries. She described systematic sexual attacks that intentionally mutilated whole villages of women. Those who survived suffered shocking long-term injuries, which often rendered them incontinent of urine and faeces and no longer able to have children.

She thought again about Giverny Hart's attack and the support she had been given by the unit, counsellors and her loving parents. That was more than any of these African victims received. Sophie had no womb, and was now suffering bowel complications, all due to the initial rape and attack.

Sexual violence against women seemed, sadly, to be universal.

In the villages, the rape victims' own families refused to have the women back home. Not only had they been defiled, but they were no longer socially acceptable due to the incontinence. The surgeon had bought a special van to take these women to receive medical care. No bus company or taxi driver would even carry them.

The announcer was declaring, 'You don't just perform surgical miracles, you restore lives with no local financial, political or social support. And all the while you risk being attacked yourself for the work you do.'

Judging by the intensity on Mr Brody's face, he felt the same admiration as Anya did for that doctor.

As a phone number was given for donations, he turned his head and noticed his visitor. His eyes brightened when he recognised her.

'I was just listening to that too. What an incredible woman.'

William Brody nodded. He still radiated dignity, despite being in a dressing-gown and slippers. His good hand flattened what little hair he had on his head.

She placed the flowers next to her. Anya hoped they could have a conversation this time, so pulled out an A4 sized whiteboard with marker and eraser attached. Just like the ones Ben's class used at school.

The show was finishing and Anya sat on the made bed before she spoke.

'It's hard to imagine how people can be so depraved,' she said.

He gestured for the whiteboard and began to write.

MONEY + POWER.

'True. Together they often incite corruption. But the sort of depravity that leads to groups of men raping and maiming women for economics . . .' She shook her head.

'Would you like a biscuit?' she asked, and opened the lid of the tin, offering the scribe a piece of shortbread. He didn't need encouragement. The pen dropped to his lap and he held the piece of shortbread to his nose, closing his eyes as if smelling an expensive cigar. Instead of chewing it, he seemed to roll it around in his mouth, making it last as long as possible.

She realised that even the simple pleasure of eating what he wanted when he wanted it was no longer in his control.

'I know the key to your heart.'

His cheeks glowed and he reached over to squeeze Anya's hand. He then collected the pen from his lap and wrote again.

HOW IS DAN?

'Assume he's working hard, haven't seen him much.'

The conversation stalled when a nurse entered the room and fussed over the flowers. She scurried off to find a vase and disappeared as quickly as she had appeared.

Anya noticed a chess set on his bedside cabinet. 'Do you play?'

As with the shortbread, his eyes told her he didn't have to be asked twice.

She wheeled over the bedside table and began to set up the pieces. The senior Brody might be more comfortable with the distraction of a game. She knew she would be.

YOU BELIEVE ABOUT ECONOMICS?

Anya looked across the table. This man's physical disabilities belied his brain function. The whiteboard was already a hit.

'Women are the ones who tend the fields, bring back food and water. By attacking or killing them, there's no one left to do the job, so the militia cuts off the villagers' food and source of income – they starve them out.'

INDEFENSIBLE.

'That's not what a defence lawyer is supposed to say.' Dan Brody had mentioned that his father had chosen a career in legal aid. His son had opted for the prestige and remuneration of private practice.

RETIRED. NO MORE MITIGATION.

William rested the pen on the board and began the game by moving a pawn. Anya responded and they settled down to a series of safe moves.

'Do you mind if I ask you about what happened when Therese's first baby was born? We need to know whether or not she took a breath.'

The elderly gentleman moved another chess piece before writing, *STILLBORN. MIDWIFE TRIED. I TRIED. NO BREATH OR HEARTBEAT.*

'You were there with Therese. That must have been awful to go through. Were her parents in any way supportive?'

He shook his head.

DISOWNED HER.

'That must have been so difficult. Did Therese suffer in the labour?'

SO MUCH PAIN. SO QUICK. NO TIME FOR HOSPITAL. DID WHAT WE COULD. 1 BRAVE LADY.

Anya captured one of William's knights.

'I'm assuming that nobody else but the midwife knew about the baby, or there would have been questions.'

FEW KNEW. WE TOLD THEM WE LOST THE BABY. STILLBORNS NEVER REGISTERED.

Now the story made sense. Therese had become pregnant and hidden herself away, after being disowned by her family. It was a different time, with no acknowledgement of loss from miscarriage or stillbirth. People carried on as if nothing had happened.

GOOD WOMAN. NOT HER FAULT. FATHER MADE HER GO OUT WITH HIM. 1 TIME.

They played chess for a few more minutes before Anya spoke again.

'You said before that the father was still alive but he didn't know about the baby.'

THERESE MADE ME PROMISE.

Dan had mentioned that his maternal grandfather had been a judge. So the baby's father had known the family, and presumably had social status on par with theirs.

It couldn't have been easy. 'You must have really loved her to stand by a pregnancy to another man and take any flak for a shotgun wedding.' She wondered if William had been her choice or her only option.

I ALWAYS LOVED HER. NO REGRETS.

241

'Did you know the man responsible?'

MONEY + POWER.

'Okay, anything you didn't like about him?' she joked, moving a castle. 'Check.'

ONE-EYED.

'There are a lot of people who are biased and opinionated.' She studied his face and then realised what he meant.

Instead of counterattacking on the board, her opponent took a while to write.

INDEFENSIBLE.

Anya stared into the man's face, trying to read him. He lowered his head, avoiding her gaze, and scrawled over the word, obliterating it with black pen.

Anya remembered him scribbling over another word when she'd visited him before. Slowly, things were falling into place. She grabbed his hand to make him stop and felt the spasm in his fist.

Suddenly it made sense. The secrecy, the protective husband.

She locked eyes with the old man. 'Did this man rape Therese that night?'

The silence answered her question. Her mother always said that the words people refused to speak said more about them than the ones they actually spoke.

Therese Brody had not been responsible for the pregnancy. The man her father had forced her to go out with had raped her on their one outing. As a result, she had been ostracised and left without support. Apart from a young man who loved her unconditionally.

William Brody was one of the most honourable men she had ever met.

The man who raped his wife had got away with it and continued to live without prosecution. Anya knew they could confirm his identity from the foetal DNA, but only if they knew who they were looking for.

'Why did you place the baby in the box, in your home?'

He hesitated, then turned back to the whiteboard.

CHARLOTTE ANNE BRODY.

OURS.

THERESE WOULD NOT LET HER BE BURIED IN GARDEN.

Anya understood. If they'd gone to the hospital, a stillborn child would have been put into either a mass unmarked grave, or thrown out with hospital waste. It was as if the system wanted mothers to forget these children. And there wouldn't have been counselling for the mother either.

NO CATHOLIC BURIAL THOSE DAYS.

She nodded. If Charlotte had not been baptised, the Church would have refused to bury her. So much for compassion and valuing life. It must have been so painful for Therese – having been raped, she was rejected by her family for shaming them with a premarital pregnancy, then delivered her daughter, whom she'd grown to love, stillborn. No wonder she kept the baby's remains close by.

It was the only way for her to grieve and gain closure.

The man who loved her had kept the secret, until now.

William handed back the pen. The game and the discussion were finished.

But not for Anya. She had to know. Therese's parents' ambitious marriage plans for their daughter, the baby's tumour behind the eye, William striking out the word 'Judge' before. 'Was the man who raped Therese Judge Philip Pascoe?'

William's hand began to spasm, and he arched his neck in distress.

'I'm sorry. I guessed. Charlotte had a retinoblastoma and was so unlucky to have died that early. It's a rare form of tumour, often inherited and associated with unusual cancers if sufferers are lucky enough to survive into adulthood.

'Pascoe lost an eye as a child and has had a rare form of bone cancer recently. It all adds up. His age fits, the ruthless ambition for the bench, his attitudes to women. Dan said you disliked each other from years ago.'

Anya wondered how she would explain it to Dan. Not only

had his mother been raped, she had delivered a stillborn child conceived as a result. The man who raped Therese was still alive and had yet to answer for it. Money and power, William said.

Suddenly she realised she had nothing to explain. Dan had been standing in the doorway all along.

39

Anya chased Dan to his car, refusing to be left behind. She had to make him see reason before he did something foolish so she climbed in the passenger seat. Despite all her efforts he didn't speak on the way. There could only be one place they were headed.

Outside the white 1920s art-deco home, Anya grabbed Dan by the arm. 'Think what you're doing. If you launch in there and do something stupid, you'll lose everything. He'll make sure you never practise law again. You'll be arrested. And for what?'

Dan pulled his arm free, left the car and strode up the pathway to the front door.

'Hurting him isn't going to bring your mother back, or change what he did to her. Instead, it'll just destroy your father.'

The lawyer stopped but didn't turn around. 'I need to face him and tell him that I know he raped Mum.'

Two more steps and he was on the doorstep, ringing the bell.

Anya caught up, short of breath, as a woman wearing dark glasses opened the door. 'Can I help you?' she said.

'Mrs Pascoe, my name is Brody. I work with your husband.'

'He's in the study, please come in.'

She was dressed in a matching blue knit top and pencil skirt, and camel heels, but didn't appear to be blind, despite the glasses. 'I'll get Philip, please make yourself comfortable.'

Dan paced the room, which overlooked the harbour. Glass from ceiling to floor highlighted one of the most expensive views in the city. Anya moved between him and the foyer, from where she assumed the judge would enter.

He appeared a few minutes later, wearing a business shirt and cardigan with suit pants.

'I don't need to tell you, Brody, that this visit is totally inappropriate. I could report you to the Law Society and Bar Association for this. And your little doctor friend will be in trouble as well.'

'It has nothing to do with the trial, this is personal,' Dan announced. 'It's about you and my mother.'

Pascoe scoffed. 'I barely knew the girl.'

'Then you wouldn't object to a DNA test.'

The judge smiled. 'You're deluded if you think I'm your father. That's just wishful thinking. For a while I thought you were different, but you're a lot like your old man. He never had the guts to make it on his own. So he spent his life sheltering behind legal aid.'

Mrs Pascoe returned with a tray of canapés and wineglasses and placed them on a side table. 'There's red and white wine or, if you prefer, spirits are in the cabinet.'

Dan seemed unperturbed by the comment about his father. 'She had a baby, a little girl, in 1962. The child had a tumour behind the eye.'

'Philip, what's he talking about?' The woman's voice rose in pitch.

The judge remained standing, but by the way he swayed it was as though the bones in his one good leg were beginning to melt.

Anya explained, hoping to keep Brody calm in the process. 'The child had a rare type of inherited tumour called a retinoblastoma.'

Mrs Pascoe lowered herself into a chair.

'Philip had one as a child, it was a miracle he survived.' She leant over and touched a faded colour photo of a baby propped up against pillows. 'Our Erin wasn't so lucky. The first tumour was diagnosed at three months. Within two weeks there was one in her other eye. The day she turned four months we lost her.' She tugged on her skirt and smoothed it over her lap. 'You don't need to tell me how rare retinoblastomas are. Erin inherited the gene,' her tone turned from sad to bitter, 'from her father.'

Pascoe responded, matter-of-fact. 'Woman, stop carrying on. I was unaware of the inheritance until after you had the child.' Up close and without his glasses on, the artificial eye was more obvious. When he spoke, it lagged behind, out of sync with the left eye.

Anya turned to his wife. The dark glasses obviously didn't obscure her vision, and her foundation was thicker than she'd expect, even though the judge's wife was clearly used to entertaining at a moment's notice, judging by the way she automatically presented canapés and drinks.

'We didn't have any more children. I couldn't go through that again, or put another poor baby through the suffering.'

Dan seemed almost deflated, as if his anger had dissolved into compassion for Pascoe's wife. He moved to the lounge chair beside her.

'We believe that your husband fathered a baby with my mother. She was stillborn, from the same tumour.'

'That is pure nonsense,' the judge declared, as if he were in control of everyone present. 'This is a malignant effort to extort me during a trial. I'll have your balls on a platter before this night ends.' He pulled a mobile phone from his pocket and dialled.

'Then just agree to the DNA test and it'll be settled,' his wife snipped.

He abruptly ended the call.

Mrs Pascoe turned to Dan. 'Who was your mother?'

'Therese Brody, well, she was Therese Robilliard back then.'

'We used to play tennis when we were in our teens. Then she went away and when she came back she was married to William, her mixed doubles partner. There were rumours, of course, about her being "in trouble", as we used to say, but they didn't have a child for a few more years. I remember because she was lovely. Unlike the others in the Catholic club, Therese never had a bad word about anyone.'

'What do you want, Brody? Let's lay it on the table then you can get out.'

Anya couldn't believe he could be so dismissive of a child he had just found out was his. He assumed Dan wanted money and that would make him go away, and he could pretend that none of this had happened.

She couldn't hold her tongue. 'Judge, we came here to—'

'Anya, wait. Let's see what he has to say.'

The judge hobbled over to a desk bureau and removed a chequebook. 'How much do you want?'

'How much are you offering?' Dan asked.

Anya felt nauseated. How could Dan accept money from a man who had raped his mother? At this moment she realised how little she knew him. She stood to leave.

'Sit, Anya.' He sounded like the judge. 'We're not finished yet.'

'You may not be—'

'So your little man-hating friend wants to be paid off as well.'

'Before you sign anything,' Dan said, 'how did you come to get my mother pregnant?'

'How the hell do you think? It was years ago, and before contraception. We were young. I barely even remember. In our day we all sowed our oats. From what I hear, you're rather an expert at that yourself. Do you remember every detail of every woman you've ever slept with? At least I recall your mother's name.'

It sounded as if Therese was privileged to have him remember that much. The arrogance of the man was overwhelming.

'Plenty of girls back then would have given their all to catch someone with money from a good family. And many did.'

The man spoke with no deference to his wife, whom he seemed to forget was in the room. She kept unnervingly silent.

'Did you go out often? I gather your family knew my grandfather, Judge Eugene Robilliard.'

'That's right. My parents thought it could help my career if I got in with the judge, so I agreed to take your mother out. She used to have your no-hoper father salivating after her, and your grandfather wanted me to break them up.'

'Seems you failed.'

Anya tried to read Dan. One minute she thought he would take a bribe, now she wasn't so sure.

'You claim I got her pregnant, but we only went out once. The odds aren't too convincing. And retinoblastoma can occur sporadically.'

'With respect, Mr Pascoe, may I ask what my mother was like? I always thought she was shy and reserved.'

Pascoe scoffed. 'The quiet Catholic ones were always the biggest surprise.'

Dan sat still. Anya suspected he would launch at the judge at any second.

'Go on, I mean, did she make the first move?' Dan smirked. 'I must have got my roving eye from somewhere.'

Mrs Pascoe shifted in her seat, clearly uncomfortable.

Pascoe's glass eye wandered as he seemed to be remembering. 'If you want to know, we had sex in the car and she wanted to go straight home afterwards.'

The judge's wife closed her eyes and covered her face with one hand. 'Oh my God, Philip, what did you do?'

The veins in Dan's neck and forehead were bulging.

Seemingly oblivious, the self-absorbed judge shrugged. 'She was dull so I didn't bother calling her again. The first I've heard since is you turning up alleging I fathered her bastard child.'

'You son of a bitch, you raped my mother.' Before Anya could stop him, Dan crossed the floor and punched Pascoe to the floor.

The older man lay moaning, holding his jaw. 'That's assault with intent to commit grievous bodily harm. And you were fool enough to do it in front of a witness.'

Anya bent down to help the judge up, who pushed her hand away. What she saw on his face was sheer hatred. She couldn't help Brody now, he'd gone too far. God, why did he have to hit the judge?

Anya looked up to see Dan panting, as though he were waiting for Pascoe to get up so he could hit him again.

'Get off the floor, Philip, you're making a fool of yourself.'

'Penny? You saw him come at me. Unprovoked. A man with one eye, he could have blinded me with one hit. Call the police. Right now!'

'Philip, I don't know what you're talking about. All I saw was you topple over. That prosthesis can be tricky to balance on.'

'Don't do this, Penny. You'll regret it.'

The mouse-like woman stood over her husband. 'No more than I regret marrying you. You are a bully, no more, no less. Be man enough to admit that you raped Therese.'

Anya stared at Dan in disbelief.

'I'm not admitting anything. His mother didn't complain at the time.'

Mrs Pascoe held Dan's wrist.

'This is the final straw. I'm leaving you.'

'I forbid you to go anywhere!' he bellowed. 'They can't prove anything. It's a bluff. Get back here now and help me get up.'

She walked, with a new air of confidence, over to the bureau drawer and removed a notepad. 'This is my number, Mr Brody, should you need me to give a statement. I'm sorry about your mother, I really am.'

Anya moved over and had to know. 'Why are you doing this?'

'I can't live like this any more.' Mrs Pascoe removed the sunglasses and the reason became obvious. She had a blackened eye.

'It's no consolation, but your mother wasn't the only one he's hurt over the years.'

The judge struggled to his feet and Anya stood between him and his wife in case he lashed out. From the way Mrs Pascoe positioned herself next to Dan, she feared the same.

'You are all going to regret this,' he yelled.

Without warning, a barrage of explosions shattered the large window and sent glass and bodies flying.

40

Anya's head hit the floor and it took her a moment to realise that the weight on top of her was Dan Brody. She checked on Mrs Pascoe, who still remained upright, and then a second set of blasts went off. Her reflexes took over and she pulled the woman to the floor. Dan moved quickly to the judge, who lay crooked on the lounge, bleeding.

With the next series of volleys, Anya knew they were under gunfire. Lights still on, they were like giant targets in a gallery.

She commando crawled on her elbows to the light switch and slid her hand up the wall. With that, the overhead lights were off, but a lamp still gave off enough of a glow to highlight every movement and shadow.

'Dan,' she called, 'the lamp.'

Brody dived for the cord and yanked it from the wall. In the process, the art-deco antique crashed to the floor.

In the dark, she fumbled for the phone in the judge's pocket and called emergency with the phone braced by her shoulder. She could feel warm moist fluid on her hands. The judge was bleeding from the top of his thigh, just above the amputation. She peeled off her cardigan and tied it as a tourniquet and felt the shard of glass protruding from the skin. In the dark, she was careful not to move or push it in further.

'We're being shot at. I'm with Judge Philip Pascoe who's been wounded. We need an ambulance. There are four of us trapped in his home.' She left the line open so the police could hear what happened next.

'Are you all right?' Dan whispered loudly from the side of the room where the window had been smashed.

'Pascoe's been hit by glass and he's bleeding. His wife's in shock. I'm okay.'

'I can't see anyone. Stay down until the police get here.'

'If it's the Harbourns, it's me they're after.'

The seconds seemed like hours as Anya tried to decide what to do. Adrenalin pumped through her arteries as she crawled to Mrs Pascoe. 'I need you to put pressure on Philip's leg, but not on the piece of glass. Don't touch it. Do you think you can do that for me?'

There was just enough moonlight to see her nod.

'Where's the back door?'

'There is one at the laundry at the side, through the kitchen, and another through the patio at the back.' She held Anya's hand and pointed in the direction with it. 'There's a torch under the sink in the laundry.'

'Anya,' she heard Brody call but she had already headed for the kitchen.

She moved quickly, staying low, sliding her hand up to turn off lights as she went. She assumed whoever was shooting was out front. Even so, she doubled back and headed out the laundry exit. In the darkness of trees, she silently lifted an outdoor chair and scaled the neighbouring fence. Working her way through that backyard, she looked into the street from two doors up.

She couldn't see anyone in the street. No signs of the police. The area had become deathly quiet. If the shooter had been in a car, he was long gone.

Pascoe needed medical care, and quickly. She headed back to the house, careful to stay away from the front doors, behind cover of trees and bushes, just in case the shooter was watching.

The front door was locked, but the inside light was on. No one was visible through the window.

She worked her way around to the back, and entered slowly through the laundry door. No other rooms, apart from the lounge room, had lights on.

The hairs on her arms and neck stood up. Something wasn't

right. There had been no more gunshots. As quietly as possible, she found the cupboard under the sink and put her hands on a torch. The heavy, maglite kind, just in case.

Then she felt the barrel in the back of her head.

'Get up slowly and put down whatever you're holding. And don't think of trying to be heroic. I have nothing to lose.'

She implored for decency. 'A man is bleeding, can I help him before you kill me?'

'No. Not this time.'

Anya's mind raced. She'd heard the voice before. Who was it? Why did he say 'not this time', as though she'd helped someone he knew before?

And if he were going to execute her, why didn't he do it near the sink from behind, quickly, without witnesses? The way he did with Natasha.

'The police will be here any second. You can still get away,' she tried.

'I'm in no hurry. Everything I need is here.'

He pushed her forward from behind, along a corridor then down a spiral staircase. Her eyes darted sideways for a weapon or means to escape, but her captor made sure he had the advantage at all times.

What was here, and what did he need?

She still couldn't recognise the voice, which sounded muffled. He had something covering his mouth. Most frightening was his complete control and calmness about what he was doing. This was calculated, but she still had to try to talk him out of hurting her.

They stopped at a wooden door with a temperature gauge on the front. It read ten degrees Celsius. Too warm for a fridge room, it had to be a cellar.

'Open it, please. We're going to join the others.'

Anya's heart drilled in her chest, but she dared not make a move with the gun still in the back of her head. Images of Natasha on the ground flashed through her mind, and she thought of Ben losing his mother. If there was a chance to survive, she had to take it. The only way out of here was the open spiral staircase, which made her too easy a target, even if she could overpower him. Now wasn't the moment.

Inside, Dan was standing straight and alert. Mrs Pascoe was sitting with her husband on the ground, but without making contact. He put pressure on his own wound.

'God, Anya, why did you come back?'

'I thought the judge needed help,' she said and moved forward. Behind her, the door closed. She turned around and saw her captor pull off a balaclava.

She gasped and knew she was about to die.

41

Bevan Hart stood in front of them, eyes hollow.

Anya knew he was in pain, but he had seemed so in control in court. She should have seen something was wrong. He was a grieving father, and he had every right to be angry. Because of her, the Harbourns couldn't be charged with murder.

'I am so sorry about Giverny. I tried to save her, but it was just too late. I am so sorry.'

'What the hell is this about?' Dan took a step towards Anya.

'SIT DOWN!' the gunman ordered. Dan complied. Mrs Pascoe began to weep.

'Doctor, this doesn't involve you. Sit down.'

Anya lowered herself to the floor alongside Dan and shivered. The room suddenly felt much colder.

'I know all about your little boy, Doctor Crichton, and I don't want to hurt you, but if you get in my way, I'll do whatever has to be done – for Giverny.'

Anya felt light-headed. She didn't understand what was going on. She, like the police, had suspected the Harbourns were behind Natasha's death. But if Bevan Hart wanted to punish someone, it made sense to punish her.

'This is about justice. It's something my family used to believe in.' He gestured to Judge Pascoe with the gun. 'You and your friend are going to answer for what you have done to so many people. It can't be allowed to go on.'

Anya spoke, struggling to stay calm. 'You killed Natasha, didn't you? Why? She worked hard to convict the Harbourns responsible for your daughter's attack.'

'That's a laugh,' he said without any emotion. 'She didn't hesitate to drop the charges against them for what they did to Giverny. It was as if she – we – never existed. My little girl went through a living hell and the people responsible think it's all one great joke. Those bastards were never going to face charges for what they did to her. And Ryder was considering a plea bargain, dropping the charges of sexual assault, as if that never happened, in return for admitting they killed Rachel Goodwin. Victims are just bargaining chips in some sort of game, only some lives are worth a lot less than others. People like Ryder, all you lawyers and judges, ruin more lives than the Harbourns ever could.'

Anya turned to Judge Pascoe. Hart had been in court and heard him arguing against mentioning rape in front of a jury. Now she knew why. If anyone found out what he did to Dan's mother, Pascoe would be slaughtered.

Mrs Pascoe wiped her eyes with the back of her hand and looked up. 'I know what it's like to lose a daughter. Mine died from cancer.'

Bevan seemed to freeze, as if he felt for the woman in front of him. 'How did you hurt your eye?' he asked.

Judge Pascoe blustered, 'We can't take back what happened to your child, but there are processes. We all have to follow them. Society will destroy itself if vigilantes take over. It's the only civilised way.'

Dan Brody clenched his fists and his shoulders tightened. 'That's bullshit, there's nothing civilised about what we do and you know it. It's all just one big game. The only goal is to win, and the best tricks and theatricals beat the truth every time. You personally know of instances in which a rapist has walked free.'

Anya held her breath, hoping Brody knew enough to stop talking.

Pascoe, visibly shaken, said nothing.

'Doesn't take much for the cannibals to turn on each other,' Bevan said. 'If you did this to the Harbourns, my daughter would still be alive.'

Penny Pascoe cleared her throat. 'Can you tell me about her? What happened?'

Footsteps pounded upstairs. 'Judge, you phone the police and tell them to get out of the house or I'll kill us all.' He looked around the cellar. 'There's enough drink in here to keep us for weeks.'

He turned to Dan. 'You look like you'd know how to spend someone else's money. Open something but don't smash the glass, I have enough ammunition to shoot all of us in less than three seconds.'

Penny Pascoe didn't seem the least bit intimidated. 'Tell me about your daughter. Giverny is such a pretty name. Is it French?'

'She was seventeen. We named her after Claude Monet's home in France.'

'I've been there. It's beautiful.'

Dan had chosen a wine and extracted the cork with a cork-screw lever attached to the wall. Before sitting down again, he offered it to Bevan, who took a sip and handed it back.

'They want to talk to you.' Pascoe held up the phone.

Hart shook his head. 'No.' He reached over, took the phone and smashed it against the wall. The four on the ground recoiled at the sudden and loud noise.

Still, Hart remained unflustered. Even with the police above him, he was beyond panic. Anya knew he was prepared to die in the next few minutes.

She thought about Savannah's death, wondering if he was behind that as well. 'What about Savannah?' she asked. 'Savannah was not like the brothers. She was different.'

'No. She was just as responsible for what they did to my daughter. She knew about other attacks and kept quiet to protect them. If she'd spoken up, those animals would have been locked up, not out on the streets the night they abducted Giverny.'

'How did you know about that?' Anya needed to know. She had sworn secrecy to Violet and Savannah.

'I have a police contact who kept me informed when no one else would.'

'Did he tell you that Savannah was regularly beaten by Gary Harbourn, had bones broken and lived in constant fear of what they'd do if she ever told a soul? If she ever even saw a doctor? The mother didn't do a thing to stop it.'

'I didn't know that, but she could have received help. She had choices. The other victims didn't. Judge, and Mr Defence Lawyer, do you have any idea what Sophie Goodwin suffered while her sister was being murdered? The fourteen-year-old listened while her sister was repeatedly raped and stabbed to death. She heard her sister's final scream. Knowing her sister was dead, she was then raped and left for dead, but not before she had her head pulled back and her throat cut. A fourteen-year-old girl, for godsake. She spent the night crawling to the road to get help. You tell me she'll ever get justice when you argue over painful sex being normal or nonconsensual. Doctor Crichton told you they were the worst injuries she had ever seen and you just played word games about rough sex being what some women want.'

'God, Philip, surely not?'

'You tell me those two innocent young girls would agree to have sex, be beaten up and stabbed by the Harbourn brothers. Strangers who barged into their home wielding a baseball bat?'

Mrs Pascoe began to cry again.

'And another thing. Who do you think cleans the blood all over the floors and walls of the Goodwin family home once the police have come and gone? Imagine facing your dead child's blood-soaked mattress and trying to scrub away her bloodstains off the ceiling, walls, floor. Even her favourite stuffed toys. That's what Goodwin faces while you play word games about consent. Can you hear yourselves? You're destroying lives that are hanging by a thread already.'

Dan put down the bottle and moved to stand. 'You're right. I've never thought about that and I should have,' he said. 'I want to be shot standing up, not cowering on the floor.'

Anya rose, both hands out in front of her, to buy even a few seconds. 'I understand, I've been a victim as well. In my own home. A rapist broke in and I was lucky not to be killed. But I still trust the people who really are trying hard to help victims.' She needed desperately to get through to him.

'Savannah could have helped Giverny's case. But did you kill her, too?'

He shook his head and aimed his gun at Dan. 'That was an accident. All I wanted was to talk to her. I stole the Jeep thinking she'd stop if she knew the car, but she didn't. I wanted answers. I nudged her rear tail-light at the traffic lights to get her out of the car. But instead of stopping she drove off like a maniac. I didn't know about her arm. I didn't imagine she'd have an accident.'

Hart suddenly changed aim. 'It's over, there's nothing I can do to bring anyone back.' He pointed the gun at Philip Pascoe. 'But you deserve this more than anyone.'

Brody grabbed and threw the bottle at Bevan's hand, making contact as the gun went off. The shot missed, but Hart held onto the weapon. Anya moved in front of the Pascoes as the door smashed open. An armed police officer burst in.

Bevan Hart swung around, gun in his hand and moved towards Anya.

'NO!'

She stood and saw the flame as the crack rang out.

She reeled backwards with Bevan, and felt pain in her stomach, warm liquid oozing across her abdomen.

42

Bevan Hart was on top of her, and would not move. She felt pain around her stomach. Brody and a police officer rushed to pull him off her, and he didn't resist. They laid him to the side while two others pointed weapons, ready to fire.

Anya's pain eased as she clutched Bevan's gun against herself, relieved it was no longer digging into her from the owner's weight. She slowly sat up. Out of the corner of her eye she noticed Dan peeling off his tie to use as a tourniquet for the judge's leg.

To her side Bevan Hart struggled to breathe.

'Get the paramedics,' she yelled, desperate to help.

Blood poured from a gaping wound in the middle of his abdomen. Penny Pascoe knelt on his other side. 'I was a nurse. What can I do to help?'

Anya glanced across. From the degree of blood loss, there was little anyone could do without fluids and intravenous access. 'Do you have any towels, something to put pressure on with?'

The judge's wife immediately pulled off her skirt, exposing a half-slip. 'Will this help?'

'Thanks,' Anya pushed hard into the wound. 'An ambulance is coming. Just hang on, Bevan.'

He was agitated and tried to push her hands away.

'This will help stop the bleeding,' she said.

'Please,' he managed. 'Let me go.'

Anya heard him but refused to believe he meant what he was saying. She had failed to save his daughter but wouldn't fail him.

She pressed harder and he winced, moving his head from side to side.

'No, no more. I want to die,' he whispered. 'Giverny is here.'

She continued to apply pressure but Mrs Pascoe bent over the man's face.

'Bevan, do you see her?'

He nodded.

'Is she happy?'

He smiled broadly.

'He's about to pass,' she said, one hand stroking his cheek. The other hand rested over Anya's.

Bevan gasped and expelled his last breath. Still with a smile.

Two ambulance officers pushed past the police and bent down to examine their patient.

'It's too late,' Mrs Pascoe said, 'he's gone.'

One checked for a pulse and the other tore open the shirt and attached ECG dots to a portable machine.

The line on the monitor was flat. 'No pulse, no spontaneous breathing, he's lost a lot of blood.'

Anya and Mrs Pascoe stepped back as they worked through their protocol, pushing fluids into a vein, still trying to find a heartbeat, even trying to shock it into motion.

Anya was unaware of anything or anybody else in the room. Just the tragedy of Bevan Hart. First Giverny, then Natasha and Savannah, all dead, all unnecessarily.

Mrs Pascoe placed an arm around her shoulder. 'He's at peace now, I felt him go.'

Anya excused herself and moved between two rows of bottles for some space. One of the officers removed an envelope from Bevan's jacket.

'Looks like a suicide note,' he said, gloved hands unfolding the lower half.

I am sorry for everything that has happened. But I can't trust in justice any more. It doesn't exist. Judges, lawyers are just playing a game. They don't care about the victims of crime or their families. We're just pawns to move around, no matter how much it hurts us.'

Judge Pascoe was being tended to by one of the ambulance officers. 'Do we need to hear the ravings of a vigilante?'

'Wait,' Anya said. 'I think we should all hear it.'

The officer continued reading aloud.

'I've already been through the trial process. After all the pain the judge decided to call a mistrial because of some stupid petty reason.

Did he care what that did to me or my family? Did he ask how hard it was to stand up and face the men who raped me? Then it felt like their lawyer raped me again, with the things he said about me and how he made out I was nothing but a liar. It was like being humiliated and violated all over again.

I thought I was strong enough to do this a second time, but I'm not. I am so sorry, Mum and Dad, for everything I put you through. I wish I hadn't walked home that night and could take everything back. But no one can.

I hope you find it in your hearts to forgive me.

Your loving daughter,

Giverny'

The room fell quiet. Bevan Hart was no longer a maniac who broke into a judge's house with a gun. This was a grieving father with a genuine reason to be distraught. It was never going to end well. His daughter's final words would haunt them all.

Anya now understood why she hadn't remembered petechial haemorrhages on Giverny's face. They weren't there. Giverny had killed herself, without anyone else present. She flashed back to that morning. Bevan Hart had been to the bedroom before finding his daughter. He could have picked up the note and hidden it from them. From his point of view, the Harbourns had driven her to suicide, helped along by judges, lawyers, and Savannah's forced silence.

No one involved had won a thing, so far. Except the ones who were responsible for the entire chain of events.

The Harbourn brothers.

43

The following morning Anya stood with Dan Brody in Judge Pascoe's private chambers.

They expected him to excuse himself from the trial, even though the damage to his leg was superficial.

He sat in a brown leather chair, behind a walnut desk. He did not invite either of them to sit.

'I will not discuss the events at my home last evening. I believe they are irrelevant to this trial.'

Dan stood in a relaxed position, although from the way he was wringing his hands he was anything but comfortable. Anya wasn't sure whether she was here to chaperone or act as a witness.

'In reference to the issue of your accusations, if you repeat your ridiculous claims I'll sue you for defamation. You have no proof of nonconsensual activity, and DNA merely confirms relations took place, which I do not deny. This will be the end of the matter.'

'Well then, Your Honour, I formally request to be excused from this trial on the grounds of personal conflict.'

The judge placed his hands downward on the edge of the desk.

'I believe I just explained the situation. What possible grounds do you think you have?'

'Well, Your Honour, I believe you are the father of my late sister and that could be viewed as a form of nepotism. I therefore feel it's unethical for me to continue.'

Pascoe slammed a book down on the desk.

'Nepotism? My boy, I could charge you with contempt of court. Your client has pleaded insanity at the time of the crime for which he is accused. If you lose, and the insanity plea is rejected, your client is entitled to appeal. Your duty is to comply with your client's wishes, and defend him to the best of your ability. Anything less and I'll have your arse in a sling. You will not be excused from this trial.'

Dan tensed and Anya thought he was about to strike the judge again. Thankfully, he seemed to have more control this morning and resisted the urge.

'Your Honour, I have advised my client against the insanity defence. I don't believe it's in his best interests; however, he insists that's what he wants. My client is refusing my instructions, which are based on the best of my experience and knowledge.'

'In that case, you will represent your client by complying with all of his wishes. Do I make myself clear?'

Dan didn't answer.

'Doctor Crichton.'

'Yes, Your Honour.' Her mouth was dry. This was worse than being in the principal's office, not that she'd ever been in trouble at school. But a hostile judge could make her testimony in any trial detrimental to a case. Lawyers might then consider her too high a risk as an expert witness and her work would quickly dry up. Her pulse raced and she felt a rash develop on the back of her neck. She despised this man, for what he did to Therese Brody, to his wife, and for the way he dismissed Bevan Hart's reasons for what he did. Right now wasn't the time to show it, though.

'You will remain a witness and I'll permit Mr Brody to call on you if you have an expert opinion that is relevant to the case. Again, if you repeat the ridiculous allegations against me, by the time I'm finished with you, you won't have either an ounce of credibility or a cent to your name.'

Anya felt the rash heat as her anger rose. This man was abusing his power to threaten her, even after she'd tried to save him last night. She felt even angrier that Bevan Hart had died in front of him, and he wouldn't even make reference to it.

'Do we all understand each other?'

Dan and Anya exchanged glances and muttered through near closed teeth, 'Yes, Your Honour.'

Outside the chambers and courtrooms, Dan remained remarkably calm, while Anya began to seethe.

'He's a rapist and a wife-beater, and he threatens us on ethics and credibility. Can he do that?'

Dan rubbed his chin. 'If you don't want to be charged with going around to his home, threatening him and assaulting him, yep, he can.'

'But you hit him! I tried to stop you.'

Dan tried to place his hands on her shoulders, but she pushed him away. 'He's going to make damn sure the Harbourns get acquitted and it's because of us. What's that going to do to Sophie Goodwin and her family? God, it's just like Bevan Hart said. This is criminal.'

'Let's think for a minute. He's making me defend Gary Harbourn, who wants to plead insanity. Why?'

'Because then his sentence is dependent on some psychiatrist saying he's on medication and is no longer insane. Easy, soft option. He'll get the sexual assault charges dropped, because he thinks every girl consents to sex with any group of strange men. Water down the charges and insanity quickly becomes a soft option.'

'Or does it?'

Anya stopped pacing and looked up at the lawyer. 'What do you mean? You have that sinister look you get just before you go in for the kill.'

'Trust me. I'm going to do exactly what Pascoe ordered. Are you with me?'

44

B enito Fiorelli stood in court.

'I wish to recall Doctor Anya Crichton to the stand.'

Anya entered the courtroom and saw Gary Harbourn sitting alongside Dan Brody at the defence table.

On the other, sat Benito and his assistant, Sheree Elliott.

A jug of water and plastic cups sat on each table.

Noelene and her remaining children sat watching from the gallery.

Taking her place on the stand, Anya took a breath and glanced at Philip Pascoe. He glared back with contempt.

Instead of Benito questioning her, Sheree Elliott stood and buttoned her jacket.

'Your Honour, the jury has already been informed of Doctor Crichton's qualifications, and I believe the defence has accepted her as an expert witness.'

'Correct, carry on.'

'Doctor, on 24 November have you ever had cause to treat a family member of the accused?'

'I did. Gary Harbourn's sister, Savannah, presented at the sexual assault clinic.'

'Objection, Your Honour, the place of examination is irrelevant.'

'Jurors, you will disregard the doctor's comment about the sexual assault aspect of the clinic.'

Anya had deliberately mentioned it. Juries prickled when they heard the phrase, and Pascoe had inadvertently helped it remain in their mind by repeating and drawing attention to the name.

'In what capacity did Savannah attend your specialty facility?'

'She had been brutally assaulted and needed urgent medical attention.'

'Can you describe her injuries?'

Brody's chair scraped the floor as he stood, which, due to his size, had a dramatic effect.

'Objection, Your Honour, relevance?'

Fiorelli argued, 'The injuries suffered by Savannah were relevant to her discussion with the doctor regarding the accused.'

'You may continue,' Pascoe said, his false eye lagging behind the other as he watched someone stand, nod and leave the courtroom.

'She had injuries consistent with having been hit multiple times on the face, possibly with a solid object. Her left eye, cheek and both lips were swollen and bruised. The left forearm was fractured and displaced, with obvious deformity when she presented.' Anya turned to the jury to demonstrate the swelling, using her own arm as the example. 'This occurs when the bones are broken and pulled out of alignment. Savannah also had multiple contusions, or large bruises, on her back and ribs, consistent with the story she gave of having been kicked once she was beaten to the ground.'

Two female jurors squinted, as if trying to avoid the image.

Noelene coughed loudly from the gallery.

'Did you take photos of the injuries?'

'No, Savannah requested confidentiality about her visit and what she told me that night.'

'Did she intend to press charges against the person who inflicted her injuries?'

'No. She expressly wanted no one to know she had even been to the clinic.'

'Did she say why?'

'She said she was afraid that if her attacker found out she had gone to the hospital, he might think she had spoken to the police as well.'

Sheree looked at the jury. 'Afraid? Of what?'

'She said she was afraid that she, or the person who brought her in, could be in serious danger of being killed. At one stage, she was concerned for her friend's safety and mine as well.'

'Doctor, this sounds a little far-fetched. Did you doubt Savannah Harbourn's reason for being so frightened?'

'No, I did not. Her fear appeared to be real and justified, given the severity of her injuries, because she knew her attacker and had regular contact with him. He also knew where she lived.'

'Objection,' Brody's chair scraped backwards, 'this is an alleged attack. No one has been charged, and the doctor's comments are only hearsay.'

'Which brings me to the next question, Your Honour. Is it possible to call Savannah Harbourn to the stand?'

'No,' Anya answered. 'She died in a hit and run accident shortly after I saw her.'

'Objection, Your Honour!' Brody called.

The gallery murmured and the press took copious notes. Judge Pascoe ordered quiet and turned to Anya. 'The cause of Miss Harbourn's death is irrelevant to these proceedings. The jury will disregard the comments last made by the witness.'

But the damage had already been done.

Sheree went in for her version of the kill. 'One more question, Doctor, did Savannah Harbourn tell you the name of the man she accused of violently beating her and causing her to fear for her life?'

'Yes. She said that the man who attacked her was her brother, Gary Harbourn.'

Gary jiggled his legs as he sat.

Sheree moved back to the prosecutor's table and flicked through a file of pages, leaving the words to linger for maximum impact before she changed the line of questioning.

'Now, Doctor Crichton, did you examine the accused prior to interview regarding the homicide of Rachel Goodwin?'

'I did.'

'And what was your professional opinion regarding acute mental state?'

Again Brody objected. 'This witness is not an expert in psychiatric diagnoses.'

The judge overruled. 'As a forensic physician, one of her roles is to assess an individual's acute mental state prior to police interview. Please answer the question.'

'I found that he was mentally fit to be interviewed regarding the homicide of Rachel Goodwin.'

'Not insane?'

'No, he was coherent and lucid when I saw him.' She didn't mention the psychiatric hospital by name or description.

'How long did you spend with the accused?'

'About an hour, which was sufficient to establish that he was not under the influence of medication, alcohol or illicit substances or suffering substance withdrawal. He was oriented in time and place and answered questions appropriately.'

Dan Brody rose and stared at Anya with raised eyebrows, presumably for drama.

'You described Savannah Harbourn as a frightened, secretive young woman. Is it possible that she was less than honest with you?'

'It's possible. Any patient could lie to a doctor, either outright or by omission, but the story given by Savannah was consistent with the injuries and mechanism of trauma she suffered.'

'I see. Did you do a mental health assessment on this woman?'

'Not specifically, but she was lucid and orientated. There was no reason to suspect—'

'Thank you, Doctor, please just stick to answering the questions.'

Anya's palms began to perspire. What the hell was Brody doing?

'Now, Doctor, did you perform a toxicology screen on Savannah Harbourn that night, looking for evidence of excess of alcohol or illicit drugs?'

She felt her fists tighten, out of view of the jury.

'No, I did not, as she had no alcohol on her breath, and her friend informed me that Savannah did not take drugs or consume alcohol.'

Anya knew how bad it sounded as soon as the words came out.

'However, one was conducted at post-mortem—'

'I am asking about the specific night Ms Harbourn attended your clinic.'

He had not allowed Anya to explain that the results of the toxicology report at Savannah's post-mortem were negative for all medication and alcohol. The liver results showed she had not taken regular intravenous or oral narcotics, and so confirmed that she was not a drug addict as Brody was trying to suggest.

'So a *friend* of your patient told you and you took that as gospel. It didn't occur to you that drug addicts present, often with injuries, just to be prescribed pain relief in the form of narcotics like pethidine?'

'Initially, yes. I told her over the phone before we met that I never carry narcotics and would not give them.'

'I see.' Brody began to pace, slowly, as if trying to make sense of Savannah Harbourn. 'Did she at any stage ask you for painkillers?'

Anya thought back. She had asked for something to have by mouth, but hadn't asked for an injection. 'Yes but—'

'Thank you. So she did request analgesia from you, a doctor who had no knowledge of her prior history. And by her story about the need for confidentiality, you were bound not to request verifying medical information from her usual doctor. Or did you?'

'No, I did not.'

'I see. Is it possible that Gary Harbourn had tried to stage an intervention at the family home and Savannah had become violent herself, suffering the injuries when Gary and his brothers tried to calm her down?'

Anya knew exactly what Brody was doing. He wanted to

completely discredit Savannah now that she was no longer able to defend herself. Anya thought last night had changed him, but apparently not. What he was doing here in court sickened her. The worst part was that he was using her to do it.

'The injuries to Savannah were inflicted with significant force and with a solid object, possibly a boot.'

'I heard that, but in your experience as a forensic physician, have people been injured resisting arrest, even though the police did everything in their powers to prevent that occurring?'

Damn him! Brody was telling half-truths and causing her to lie by omitting the true details. The jury weren't getting the real story.

'Yes, but—'

'Thank you—'

Dan was distracted by Gary Harbourn knocking over a glass of water. He was twitching and shaking. Dan leaned over to speak to him.

'Your Honour, may I request a recess? My client is becoming agitated and requests to see his psychiatrist at this point.'

'I'll grant a half-hour recess, court will resume at 10.30 am.'

Everyone stood as Pascoe left via a side door.

Anya had not been dismissed, she had been put on hold. Fiorelli chose not to interject or ask anything about Savannah and her injuries. He obviously considered her irrelevant to this trial after Brody's short performance. And now that it was clear Bevan Hart was responsible for Savannah's killing, Gary would get away with that assault as well.

As she left the court, Anya saw Violet Yardley sitting in the back row. The young woman had tears in her eyes and gave Anya a look of despondency.

Anya couldn't help but feel she had just done Gary Harbourn a favour. Dan Brody was doing exactly what Judge Pascoe had demanded, even if it meant committing a terrible injustice in the process.

She had never been more disappointed in herself, or in the man she had considered her friend.

45

Outside the courtroom Fiorelli tried to calm Anya down.

'This is about Harbourn's insanity plea. Savannah was never going to help us prove he was competent the night of Rachel Goodwin's murder.'

'Not now she's dead.'

Kate Farrer approached. 'Brody's just doing everything he can to goad you. Don't get suckered. He's a slimeball and that's what he does for a living. Either that, or you've pissed him off big time.'

Anya looked at her friend, never the epitome of tact. Even so, she had said exactly what Anya had been thinking. Maybe he was doing what Pascoe ordered and making sure there was no reason for Harbourn to appeal at a future date. Or he wanted to discredit her, in order to show Pascoe his dirty secret was safe and there was no nexus between him and Anya.

Either way, she didn't want to go back on the stand.

'Here,' Kate said, offering her a black coffee. 'Take a few minutes. You've got that rash on your neck again.'

Anya took the coffee and walked outside for some fresh air.

Brody crossed the road outside the courts and ignored her. How could he be doing this? Surely he couldn't be trying to impress the man who had raped his mother? Bevan Hart's pleas about the victims and their families obviously made no difference. He didn't care about anyone but himself and his moneymaking career.

Her phone rang and she checked the number. Martin. She quickly answered.

'Everything okay?' she asked.

'Yeah, just letting you know that Ben came third in his first race in the athletics carnival. Not bad, given he's half the size of some of the kids in his class.'

For a moment nothing else mattered. 'That's so great, but winning isn't everything.'

'Can you just be happy for him – he did his best and ran his little heart out. Even if he did look like he was stirring a pudding the way his legs go all over the place.'

She knew exactly what her ex-husband was describing. Ben wasn't blessed with the athletics genes, but she adored watching the joy on his face as he ran.

'Sorry, I'm about to go back into court. Please tell Ben I'm really proud, and thanks for letting me know. I wish I could be there to have seen him.'

'So do we.' There was slight hesitation before he said, 'Anyway, you can talk to him later, but just act like you didn't hear it from me first.'

'Hear what? Gotta go, but thanks, Martin. I mean it.'

She sipped the coffee and felt the heat dissipate from her neck and upper chest. A few minutes later, she was back on the stand.

Gary's shaking seemed more evident than before the break.

'Doctor Crichton,' Brody began, 'in your experience, which I concede is not in the specialty of psychiatry, is insanity, or what I'll describe as psychosis, a constant state?'

'Not necessarily. People who describe hearing voices often say they come and go.'

'Is this dependent on the type and dose of medication?'

'No.'

'You say that the defendant appeared lucid during your time with him. Does that mean he cannot possibly have been in a state of psychosis the night of the assaults on Sophie and Rachel Goodwin?'

'No.'

'So is it still possible that he was in psychosis that night, and that you saw him on one of his better days?'

274

'Yes.'

'And is it possible the medication at the psychiatric hospital and care he was receiving was beginning to improve his condition?'

'That is possible, *if* he were actually psychotic that night and not faking. He was quite capable of using a computer keyboard just before debilitating tremors became apparent, coincidentally, when I was present. Then he regained complete coordination when he smashed a picture when I angered him with a question about his sister's suspicious death.'

Gary grunted and glared at Anya.

Brody did a double-take but didn't refute the comments.

He half turned, as if deliberating.

In that instant Gary Harbourn grabbed the carafe of water, smashed it and leapt over the table towards the stand, jagged weapon raised.

Someone screamed 'Look out!', and Anya saw the crazed look in his eye as he came.

For her.

Dan Brody dropped his shoulder into Harbourn's chest and deflected his path. Harbourn bounced off the railing in front of the jury as they scattered towards the back of their box.

Dan grabbed Harbourn's arm, holding the glass away from himself, and a court officer and Fiorelli wrestled Harbourn to the ground. Brody kept his knee in Harbourn's back until the man could be handcuffed and restrained.

Harbourn ranted, 'I'll kill you. You and that Ryder bitch have been after me for years,' in full view of the jury while bucking to free himself.

Noelene Harbourn shouted, 'Don't hurt him, he's ill.'

Anya looked up for the judge, who had retreated to the door near his chambers. Once it was clear that Harbourn was no longer a threat, he returned to the bench.

'Silence!' he ordered. 'Everyone return to your seat. Mr Brody, is your client under control?'

Dan was puffing and sweating, but he nodded.

With that, two uniformed police officers relieved Dan of his quarry. They lifted Harbourn from the ground and stood him upright, one with a leg between his from behind. He had no way of moving again.

Pascoe addressed them. 'Take him to the cells until he sees his psychiatrist and cools off. Jurors, please take your seats.'

'That bitch is out to get me!' he could be heard yelling as he left the court.

Anya took a staccato breath and looked at Dan to make sure he was all right; she noticed some blood on his right hand.

'We will take a short recess. I must say to you, jurors, that the event you just witnessed should be disregarded in terms of this trial. We will return in one hour.'

The journalists were the first to leave after Pascoe exited the courtroom, eager to file the story of the crazed defendant's attack.

With the press out of sight, Noelene Harbourn stood proud.

Anya stepped down and approached Dan, who was sitting, stunned.

Fiorelli and his assistant hadn't moved either. It was as if no one could believe what had just taken place.

Anya asked to look at Dan's hand, which he raised. There was a superficial cut to his palm, but it wouldn't need stitches. 'You'll need to clean that and put a sterile bandage on it.'

The lawyer nodded.

'Are you okay?' he asked. 'He really was after you.'

'I know. Thanks for stopping him, and you, too, Benito.'

The prosecutor shrugged. 'After what just happened, it'll be tough to convince the jury that Gary Harbourn is anything but insane. He can't be responsible for murder if he has diminished responsibility. Hell, even I could believe it after that.'

Noelene Harbourn approached them. 'You little slut, you think you were clever just then, but the joke's on you.'

Dan and Benito moved closer to Anya, despite Noelene being alone and out of arm's reach. Anya appreciated the gesture.

'I know your type, you act like the Virgin Mary, all sweet

and brainy, but you'd root anything if it helped your career. That little stunt you pulled, all innocent-like on the stand? Well you've just done us a bloody great favour.'

She turned to Dan, and her voice took on a softer tone. 'Well done, Danny Boy. You've just scored yourself a bonus.'

The woman pulled on oversized sunglasses as if bracing to meet her fans, and turned on her heel to leave.

Dan Brody suddenly looked very pleased with himself.

46

That night Anya went home. Following Bevan Hart's death and confession to the killing of Natasha Ryder, Kate and Hayden thought it safe for her to return home.

She opened the front door and nearly tripped on the pile of papers and mail on the floor. She disarmed the alarm and switched on the lights. Everything was as she had left it.

Nevertheless, the fact that the Harbourns had her name and address still had her spooked. Especially after Gary's outburst in court.

She kicked off her shoes in the hallway and bent down to retrieve her mail. With Elaine still away, a pile of junk mail had accumulated inside the door. Sorting through the papers, something caught her attention. A letter from Ben.

She grabbed a letter opener from her office and sat on the calico lounge opposite Elaine's desk. The answering machine could wait.

Ripping the envelope open revealed a brightly coloured painting of a rainbow. Ben had drawn what looked like a man, woman and boy in the picture. On the back was his name and class name.

This has to go on the fridge, she thought, and stood up. A number of bills fell to the floor. Among them was a book-sized envelope with immature handwriting.

There was no post mark. It had been hand-delivered.

She opened it tentatively in case it was from the Harbourns.

Inside was a diary, the kind to be found in any newsagent. On the inside flap was a name, Savannah Harbourn, and the words:

If I die or get killed I want this to go to my friend, Violet Yardley. I love my family, but can't go on hoping things will change. When I saw that girl in the hospital, I knew who done it. So many bad things happened. If there is a God, maybe he'll forgive me for keeping quiet so long.

Anya sat and flicked through various entries about lonely days, isolation and how much fun her sisters could be.

Today Mum was laughing again about how stupid the cops are. It's only the dumber crims who ever get caught, she reckons. You just have to stick to your story, stick together and nothing bad'll happen to you. Jail doesn't scare them either. They'd all do time for each other. It's what family does. You stick together. That's what the police don't get.

I am sorry for all the bad things my family done. Someone has to stop them hurting more people. I wish I was strong enough to do it.

The diary contained a list of dates, names and attacks. Some of them were unfamiliar to Anya, like Choko, Lizard, Rastis.

It also included a crumbled piece of note in a different hand. It said, *111 Rosemont Place.*

Anya moved to her desk and looked up the Goodwins' address. 111 Rosemount Place.

She switched on her laptop and Googled a map of the locality. Within minutes she had discovered that Rosemount Place was a suburb away from Rosemont Place.

Had the Harbourns gone to the wrong house that night looking for drug money? The notion made the tragedy of what had happened to the girls so much worse.

She slipped Savannah's diary into her bag, slid into her shoes and armed the alarm before heading out.

Kate searched the database. 'Got it. It's been reported by neighbours as being suspicious. Darkened windows, unmowed lawns, same car always parked there. No one comes or goes in the day time. Uniforms went around but no one answered.'

'Did they follow it up?'

'Without a warrant, there wasn't much they could do. Don't you love the way the system protects the innocent?'

Kate made a couple of calls to the drug squad. 'Now we wait,' she said. 'And I still can't figure out where Bevan Hart got the gun from. The serial number matched the one that was supposed to be destroyed. No barrel changes, same gun exactly. Where that came from there'll be others and that's a real concern. If men like Hart can get hold of one, who the hell else can and already has?'

Benito Fiorelli entered the Homicide office at about 9 pm, in a dinner suit with black bow tie. He kept a busier social schedule than Dan Brody, it seemed.

'This better be good. It's opening night of *La Bohème* at the Opera House,' he said as Kate handed him photocopied excerpts from the diary.

Sitting on Shaun Wheeler's empty desk, Fiorelli read Savannah's confession then listened while Anya explained why the Goodwin address might have been a mistake.

'God, how can we tell Mr Goodwin that his daughter's murder was the result of a mistaken spelling?'

Kate argued, 'But it gives us motive for why the Harbourns were at the house in the first place. If it was a planned revenge attack for a drug deal gone bad, then Gary's claims of temporary insanity are out the window.'

Benito rubbed the dark circles under his eyes. It occurred to Anya that he had come into the trial midway, after the murder of his colleague and friend. It can't have been easy for him and it looked like the pressure was wearing him down.

'After today's performance, it may be too late. The looks on the jury's faces pretty much said it all. While they listened to the gruesome details of Rachel's murder, a few metres away Harbourn was demure and controlled, no sign of the earlier outburst. I could see some of them were thinking that anyone who did that would have to be mad. Today just reinforced the Jekyll and Hyde insanity impression.'

47

Anya saw Violet Yardley outside the food co-op. Dressed in dark purple that could have passed for black, she hugged herself with one arm while smoking with the other.

'Thanks for agreeing to see me,' Violet said. 'I can't believe that bloke killed Savannah. Jesus, she hated her brothers as much as he must of.'

She drew back and blew out through her nose.

Anya watched a woman with a shopping cart down the road dig through rubbish bins. 'Hatred can blind you to a lot of things.'

'Tell me about it.' Violet stubbed out the remains of the cigarette and lit another.

'Would you like to go somewhere comfortable to talk?'

'This is where I'm most comfortable. Out here, with people who never want anything from you. They're grateful for just a smile, and they have less than anyone else I know.' She gestured with the cigarette hand. 'You know, most people are scared of Esther, because she's dirty and rifles through garbage. Truth is, it's the bastards they know and live with who are far more likely to hurt them.'

Esther meandered along towards them, singing to herself, in perfect pitch.

'You know, she used to be a concert pianist. Sometimes she sneaks into the music shop and plays the keyboard. If anyone asks her to play something, she just leaves. Guess she can't stand the pressure.'

Anya leant against the wall and reached into her purse, pulling out a five dollar note.

Violet covered it. 'She doesn't take money, but you can buy her a sandwich. Call it a donation to the co-op. That way she won't piss it up against a wall.' She called to the homeless woman. 'Hey, Esther, you hungry?'

The woman looked up, removed her hands from the rubbish and pulled the trolley along. Anya followed them inside the shelter as a half-smoked cigarette was extinguished again.

Violet handed Esther some antibacterial hand-wipes. 'Here, my lady, these are from Persia. Notice the exotic essence?'

The pack said aloe vera.

'Did the Maharaja leave it?'

'Just for you.' Violet led them into a small kitchen and pulled down a breadboard.

'We get leftovers from the restaurants on a good night,' she said. 'The Maharaja asked that you try a salad and pork sandwich this morning.'

Esther was busy scrubbing every inch of her hands with the scented wipe, then she started on her neck and face, as though this was luxurious and had to be relished.

'Don't worry, she's not mad, are you, Ez, it's just a game we play. And you can say anything in front of our Ez, she's very good at keeping secrets.'

Anya sat at a stool near the bench. 'I wanted to talk to you about Savannah. Last night I opened my mail. Her diary had been pushed through my letterbox.'

Violet buttered a third slice of white bread and put the knife down.

'What'd it say?'

'That she was sorry for everything her brothers had done and wanted to tell the police everything she knew.'

She pulled out some lettuce leaves from a plastic container and added some slices of roast pork from another. A slice of cheese, then a piece of bread. 'I knew that.'

'Violet,' Anya tried to break the news gently, 'she mentioned your attack, your name and when it happened. The police are going to be asking you questions.'

The double-decker sandwich completed, Esther dropped the wipe and took it from Violet's shaking hands. The ravenous visitor retreated to a bench as if protecting a precious find.

Violet headed outside again, lighting a cigarette as she went. 'You told me no one had to find out. What's in her diary is just ramblings to help make sense of stuff. I'll just deny it.'

'If the police have copies of the diary contents, then the Harbourns' lawyers will see it before too long.'

Violet shook her head. 'Shit. I didn't think of that.'

Anya knew then who had delivered the diary.

'I already got a call from Ricky on my mobile but I just let it go to voicemail. No bloody prizes for guessing why he wants to meet up.'

Anya thought for a moment. 'If there was a way to make them pay for what they did to you without you having to go through a rape trial, would you help?'

Violet thought for a moment. 'Savannah wasn't afraid of them except when Gary was around. He's the violent one of the lot.'

'He's under police guard in a psychiatric hospital. It looks as if he won't be going anywhere for a long time.'

Esther wandered out, crumbs clinging to her tattered waistcoat. 'Give my compliments to the Maharaja. I wonder what the poor people are eating today.' She chortled through a toothless mouth and continued on her way.

'I'll see Rick,' Violet said nervously, 'but only on my terms. You don't know him like I do. He wouldn't hurt anyone – ever. If he could have stopped them that night with me, he would have. Gary is the evil one who controlled the others. And I'll prove it.'

Anya immediately regretted making the suggestion.

48

At the end of the trial, the packed gallery rose for the verdict. Pascoe eyed the crowd before asking the jury foreperson whether they had reached a verdict. 'We have, Your Honour.'

Gary Harbourn grinned and looked towards his family. His mother waved. Fiorelli stood, hands by his side.

'On the charges of murder of Rachel Goodwin, how find you?'

'We find the defendant not guilty.'

Fiorelli's shoulders rounded and Anya felt as if she'd been punched.

Noelene squealed and Gary waved to his supporters.

'Quiet!' Pascoe bellowed, then waited for silence. 'On the charges of manslaughter due to diminished responsibility, commonly known as insanity, how find you?'

'We find the defendant guilty.'

'Thank you for your time and effort in this, a truly difficult trial and verdict. You are discharged.'

The Harbourn family cheered and Gary placed his hands up to have his cuffs removed.

'Silence!'

'In light of the verdict, I have already considered sentencing. I find Gary Harbourn to be a deeply disturbed, dangerous man. I hereby order he be sent to the psychiatric facility at a high security prison, until such time as he is assessed as no longer a risk to himself or the community.'

Gary punched the air but Dan Brody stayed remarkably stone-faced.

Court was dismissed and Gary shook Dan's hand before being led away by the court officer, still handcuffed.

'Love you, Mum, see you soon!'

Anya felt a combination of nausea and revulsion. She'd helped Brody provoke Gary Harbourn into a crazed rage in front of the jury.

That image had been far more powerful in the jury's mind than Savannah's diary and any suggestion that Gary had led his brothers on a revenge mission, killing Rachel only because she had been at the wrong house.

She turned to leave, but Dan was quickly by her side.

'There's nothing we have to say to each other. If you're expecting some kind of congratulations, forget it.' She walked outside, past the media and Noelene's soapbox.

At the set of lights on Oxford Street, she raised her hand to hail a cab.

Brody was by her side, with his briefcase. 'Anya, wait. Listen. I didn't just win. We won. Do you understand? *We* won.'

He grabbed her by the arm. 'God, you are a stubborn woman. Pascoe knew exactly what he was doing when he told me I had to follow Harbourn's instructions.'

She felt the heat rising in her neck again.

'You're unbelievable. You have no idea what you've just done. When some psychiatrist is taken in by Gary Harbourn's sob story, he'll be out, free, never to serve prison time for what he did to Rachel.'

'I don't think so.' He grinned. 'There's a tiny detail you appear to be missing. The discretion to free him is still up to the governor of the state, at least until new laws take effect, and there's no retrospective clause. Do you know how many people have been freed in this state once they've been sent to the psych prison? Take a guess. Go on.'

Anya was in no mood for games but knew the number was small.

'Okay, I'll give you the answer. Zero. None. Not a one. Gary's chances of ever being released are slimmer than Paris Hilton becoming US president. No Governor will risk letting him out, especially given Sophie's trauma and the added publicity Noelene has brought to the case.'

Anya struggled to accept what he was saying. 'Is that really true?'

'My client is completely deluded if he believes he's beaten the system. He thinks insanity is a soft option, but the truth is, even if he'd been found guilty of murder, he could have been out in seven to ten years. Pascoe knew what he was doing when he told me to follow Harbourn's instructions to the letter.'

The judge had been adamant, but Anya had thought it was punishment for the confrontation at his house. Bevan Hart might have made a difference after all with his comments about victims and Giverny's final letter.

'And,' Brody moved closer, 'Pascoe has made sure he will suffer. Psych prisons are far worse than any jail in the state. No access to females, which means he won't be raping a woman again.'

On impulse, Anya reached up and hugged Dan. She wished Giverny and Bevan Hart – and Natasha Ryder – were here to see the result.

'Aren't we lucky I'm such a damn good lawyer?'

Anya pushed him away, but this time she was laughing. 'Thanks. I really have to go, but we'll talk soon.'

'What about celebrating? You haven't told me how Sophie Goodwin's doing, either.'

A taxi pulled up and she got in. 'She should go home next week. Her father's planning a party. Maybe we can celebrate at that.'

*

Violet Yardley knocked on the front door, with a six-pack of beer in her hand.

'Congratulations,' she said.

'What do you want, you little slut?' Noelene Harbourn had answered the door. She was wearing a kaftan and holding a glass of champagne.

'I want to see Ricky.'

'Well he's free for now, no thanks to you.'

'What did I do? I didn't tell the police anything. Savannah tried to dob them in but I wouldn't go along with it.'

Rick appeared from inside.

'Mum, I want to see her.'

Noelene stared at Violet, before slinking back to her boyfriend. 'I'm telling you, she's trouble. She'll come between you boys.'

Rick stepped outside and closed the door behind him.

'I'm glad you came.' He reached forward and kissed her cheek, pausing to see her reaction. When she didn't pull away, he nuzzled her face with his nose. She felt the same rush he always used to give her. God, he was good-looking. And he smelt the same as always. When his lips moved towards hers, she had no control. She parted her lips and let his tongue wander inside her mouth, gently at first, then far more urgently. He tasted of beer. She kissed him back with all the excitement she remembered from when they were together.

Things could be different now Gary was gone.

'Hey, wanna go for a walk?' he asked.

He held her hand and she wanted to be closer, sidling up until he put his arm around her. Instead of pulling her closer around the waist, he draped his hand over her shoulder.

'Something's different about you,' she said.

'I've changed. Good thing you still look the same, though.'

He stopped to kiss her again, and she felt a wave of excitement through her back and stomach. God, she had missed him. He hadn't meant to hurt her; it had been Gary's idea. Without his big brother leading the pack, Rick was gentle and kind.

They headed for a park a block away and sat together on a bench. 'Must have been rough, what you went through,' Violet tried. She wanted him to tell her everything about himself. Everything she'd missed since the night at his house.

He stroked her hair and she felt her scalp tingle.

'I knew you wouldn't rat us out. Gary said you would, but I knew you better,' he said.

She thought about Savannah. 'Why did Gary have to hurt your sister so bad?'

Rick sat back, arms extended across the back of the bench. 'She didn't get it. The family honour code. We all have to respect it. It's what keeps us together. If we keep it, no one can touch us. But she was still one of us and that prick shouldn't have done what he did to her.'

They sat watching two young children playing on the swings with a mother standing behind, pushing them.

'Do you think we'll ever be like that?' She nestled into his shoulder.

'Are you trying to tell me something?' he laughed and carried her onto the grass, while she squealed with delight. He placed her on the ground, lay on top and kissed her again. 'God, I've missed you.'

She couldn't have been happier. He rolled her over onto her stomach.

'Want to do it prison style?'

'There are kids here,' she laughed.

He was already unzipping his fly.

'I'm not kidding, Rick, cut it out. We're in public.'

Rick moved his face to the back of her neck and yanked her head back by the hair.

'You're hurting me,' she cried.

'Do you know how easy it would be to cut your throat?'

Violet froze, she couldn't see anyone left in the park. 'You wouldn't do it.'

He twisted some hair around his hand. 'I will if I have to. It's easier than you imagine. Slicing that bitch's neck was like cutting roast chicken off a bone, only faster.'

Violet didn't believe what he was saying. 'You said Gary did it.'

'We all said that. It was his idea. We knew he'd get off lightly if he acted nutso.' Violet struggled, but his weight was too great. 'But I can't tell you how good it felt to pull her head off the floor and just . . . slice. Made a hell of a mess, but it was worth it.'

Violet began to cry. 'Why are you telling me this?'

'Because the bitch could have identified us. For Christ's sake, she did. I'm only sorry I didn't kill her. Next time, I won't make that mistake.'

Violet stifled back tears. 'I don't believe you. The papers said you didn't hurt anyone, that you tried to stop him and save the sister. It had to be Gary. He's the one that bashed all those people. I saw what he did to Savannah.'

'You stupid fucker. Who do you think got the idea for passing you around? We share in our house, even the slops, like when we picked up that Giverny slut with her up-herself ballet clothes. It's the family code.'

His free hand groped under her skirt. 'Stabbing the one in the bedroom felt just like shoving a knife into a tender piece of pork. We all took turns, but I got three stabs in. You should have seen her face when I shoved her top down her throat.' He reached up for her panties. 'That shut the whimpering bitch up.'

In that instant, he moved some weight onto his side, off her. Violet rolled and freed a hand, gouging him in the eyes with all her strength.

He screamed and grabbed his eyes. It was enough time for her to get up and run as fast as she could.

'Help me!' she screamed. 'Somebody help me!'

She sprinted through the park, too scared to look back. As she swung around the fence, two hands grabbed her.

'It's okay, you're safe now.' Violet crumpled into Anya's arms, crying.

'You were brilliant,' Liz Gould said, rubbing the distraught girl's back.

'Kate, Wheeler and Hayden have got him. It's over. He won't hurt you again.'

Violet sobbed. 'I didn't believe he did it, not until he tried to rape me. I'm so sorry.'

Anya knew Violet had nothing to be sorry about. She had trusted Rick, even after being raped by his brothers. She thought she was in love with him, and had been taken in by his charm. Again. Now she might be able to accept that the gang rape had never been her fault, and could move on with her life.

Not only that, but Violet had got him to confess to killing Rachel and slashing Sophie's throat with the intention of leaving no witness alive. And the third brother would go to prison with him or have to turn on Rick to negotiate a better deal for himself. Savannah's diary, despite being hearsay, only confirmed their guilt.

Sadly, Bevan Hart wouldn't be around to see them be punished for what they had done to his daughter. At least Fiorelli could finally take Giverny's case to trial. The tragic irony was that without Bevan's actions the Harbourns could have got away with all of their crimes. He had sacrificed himself for the sake of his daughter.

Ambulance officers on standby took Violet to their vehicle to ensure she was all right. With Rick Harbourn handcuffed in the car with Hayden and Shaun Wheeler, Kate pulled Anya aside.

Instead of elation at the arrest, she frowned.

'I have to ask you something and it's important. Did you see any police you recognised the night Bevan Hart was shot? Either inside or outside Pascoe's home?'

Anya tried to think. The acute response team had burst into the cellar, but none had been a familiar face. 'You came later, with Hayden.'

'I mean, anyone else you've seen before.'

Anya looked over towards the rear of the ambulance to check Violet. The officers were taking her blood pressure.

'No. I've given a statement. You were there. You know who I saw.'

Kate tugged the back of her hair. 'The reason I ask is, I don't think Bevan Hart was working alone. There was another set of fingerprints on the gun magazine in his pocket that night.'

They were interrupted by Shaun Wheeler who barrelled over. 'We're going to take him to the station. Do you want to meet us back there?'

'No, Liz and Hayden can take him. You can ride back with

290

Anya and me in the surveillance van. Those guys can handle any media.'

'Sure.' Wheeler breathed out, seemingly deflated. This was probably his biggest arrest to date, and he had been pumped with adrenalin as Hayden had wired Violet with the listening device.

He turned towards the ambulance. 'What about our star witness?'

'She's going to casualty so the doctors can give her the once-over. We need to make sure she's okay – officially.'

The trio headed back to the van where the driver was waiting. Kate opened the sliding door to the back and gestured for the other two to get in. Once she was strapped in, she started to loosen up.

'Feels good to finally get that bastard. Can you imagine the expression on Noelene's face when she finds out?'

That was one thing they would all like to have seen.

'Chalk one up to the good guys,' Wheeler proclaimed.

'Not bad for your record, given you've been in the force for what, three years?'

'Four. I spent a year in a small country station, near where I grew up, before moving to the city.'

'A country boy,' Kate smiled. 'I'm from the country too. Hey, didn't you transfer from the dog squad?'

Anya glanced at Kate. It was the most small talk she'd ever heard her initiate. Her conversations always had a point to them. She suspected Wheeler was heading for a reprimand over something he'd done, or failed to do.

'Uh-huh.'

The van hit a pothole and Anya grabbed the armrest on her seat. The surveillance equipment didn't shift, with everything locked into place. Kate didn't seem to notice the lurch.

'Did you ever work with a guy called Bomber? He was a bit of a rogue and liked to bend the rules a bit, but he always got a good result, if I remember.'

With no windows or other distractions, maybe Kate was in the mood to talk.

'Yeah, he believed in the Scouts' motto of always being prepared. He saved my skin once.'

'Just wish we could have saved Giverny Hart. When I think how cut-up her father was, it was a good thing he had someone to talk to.'

'He worked on a farm before he joined the army, so we kind of clicked, I guess.' Wheeler broke eye contact with his superior officer. 'Poor bastard. When he saw what the Harbourns did to Sophie . . .'

Anya flashed back to the night at Pascoe's house. Hart had mentioned the blood on the walls in Rachel's room when he described the father having to clean it off. Someone had shown him the crime scene photos or told him the intimate details.

'Is there anything you want to tell us about that?' Kate asked.

Wheeler was hiding something. His eyes darted around the van.

'No.'

'Shaun, how do you explain the fact your fingerprints were on the magazine he carried?'

Anya's heart raced. Wheeler sat, frozen, then rubbed his hand vigorously across his closed eyelids before meeting Kate's piercing gaze.

'He said he j-j-just wanted to confront the Harbourns. I told him it was suicide to approach them himself, unarmed, so I g-gave him the .22 for his own protection. It was a fit-up that Bomber gave me last year. His idea of being p-p-p-prepared.'

'Where did it come from?'

'Don't know for sure, but it was found along with a shitload of weapons on a raid of some d-d-drug den. Officially, they were destroyed, but some were kept – f-f-f-for emergencies.'

'Meaning for fit-ups.' Kate swallowed hard. 'Shaun, I'm going to have to arrest you. You understand that.'

'I swear to God that I didn't know he'd kill that prosecutor with it or go after the judge or—' He looked at Anya. 'I'm s-sorry. You saw what the Harbourns did. We're supposed to be the good guys, and we couldn't stop them.'

Kate unstrapped herself and moved across. 'I need your weapon.'

Wheeler reached into his holster and removed it, handing it to Kate. 'He said he just wanted to make them face him. I swear to God, I thought they killed his daughter too.'

'You don't have to say anything else,' Kate said. 'This conversation's being recorded, and in the presence of an independent witness. You're going to need a lawyer – a really good one.'

49

Anya stood outside the crematorium, having come from Bevan Hart's memorial service. Despite being a long-term Rotary member and popular mechanic, few people turned out. It was difficult to know what to say to Val Hart, for her incomprehensible losses, but Mary Singer had made it easier, if that was possible.

Anya watched Dan Brody lift his father from the car and into the wheelchair. What should have taken five minutes took a lot longer, with the fussing Dan was employing. Even so, Anya resisted the temptation to walk over and help.

This was something Dan needed to do and it was the only way he would get better at it. Besides, she enjoyed watching the two men interact.

The minister wandered out and shook her hand, then waited for the Brodys. William looked immaculate in a grey suit, white shirt and tastefully patterned tie. His wispy hair had been trimmed and combed. Shiny black shoes befitted the occasion. Dan wore a dark suit and white open-necked shirt. The family resemblance was even more startling today.

The hearse pulled up, with two men accompanying the glossy white coffin, adorned in lilies, with a bright yellow sunflower in the centre.

The sight of the miniature casket brought home the sadness of the death of any child. As a mother, Anya felt it very deeply. Her eyes welled up and she could imagine the pain Therese Brody had experienced at the delivery, compounding all she had already been through. And yet, this woman had enough love to care so much about her stillborn child that she did not want to be too far from her. The way the box had been lovingly kept for so many years showed that.

Now Dan and his father had decided to place the baby's ashes alongside those of her mother.

Dan kissed Anya on the cheek and thanked her for coming. William held out his good hand, and Anya bent over to kiss his forehead. He even smelt different. 'Is that Passion?' she asked.

The old man gave his best half-smile.

The whiteboard was now in a small bag attached to the wheelchair, for easy access.

The minister asked if they were expecting anyone else, and Dan checked his watch.

'I'm not sure, but we might give it another couple of minutes,' he said, glancing around.

A large, circular drive surrounded a stunning display of petunias, violets and lavender. In the centre of the oasis was a bench. To the left of the building a car park contained a handful of vehicles.

Anya wondered if anyone else had been invited to the ceremony. A metallic-blue Mercedes swung into the car park and Dan turned around. A woman with a scarf and dark glasses climbed out of the driver's seat.

Mrs Pascoe, dressed in a navy skirt-suit, approached them, carrying a small yellow bear.

She nodded at Anya and Dan, and introduced herself to William.

'I'm Penelope Pascoe, well I used to be Shechan. Therese and I were friends a long time ago. I wanted to pay my respects.'

William shook her left hand.

She turned to Dan, 'I hope you don't mind, but this was something I had for my little Erin. I want you to have it.' She glanced over at the coffin and her voice wavered. 'After all, she was this little one's half-sister.'

Dan took the little toy and glanced at his father. 'Mum named my sister Charlotte.' He bent over to hug Mrs Pascoe. 'We'll be putting the ashes with hers.'

The minister asked if they all would like to begin.

Anya pushed the wheelchair into the crematorium hall, following Dan and Mrs Pascoe.

Therese Brody hadn't wanted to forget Charlotte. Decades later, the baby had managed to bring together Therese's son and the man she had always loved, Dan's father.

Both mother and daughter had earnt the right to rest in peace. Finally they were together as a family.

KATHRYN FOX

MALICIOUS INTENT

At a crime scene, blink and you'll miss the truth. Move over Kay Scarpetta – a new forensic pathologist is on the case . . .

When Dr Anya Crichton is asked to look into the seemingly innocent suicide of a teenager, she notices similarities between the girl's death and several other cases she is working on with her friend and colleague, Detective Sergeant Kate Farrer.

All the victims went missing for a period of time, only to be found dead of apparent suicide in most unusual circumstances.

As Anya delves deeper, the pathological findings point to the frightening possibility that the deaths are not only linked, but part of a sinister plot. Nothing can prepare her for the terrifying truth . . .

> '*Malicious Intent* will keep you gripped from start
> to finish . . . What a compelling new talent!'
> Jeffery Deaver

HODDER